The Empty Lot Next Door

The Empty Lot Next Door

Arthur M. Mills, Jr.

Editor: Shirley Kennedy
Artist: Seshadri Roy
Cover photo: Dave Bonta

Library of Congress Control Number: 2010904422
ISBN: Hardcover   978-1-4500-7222-9
               Softcover   978-1-4500-7221-2
               Ebook   978-1-4500-7223-6

To order additional copies of this book, contact:
Xlibris Corporation
1-888-795-4274
www.Xlibris.com
Orders@Xlibris.com
72091

The Empty Lot Next Door

"To the dream undreamt
To the tune unheard
To the mystery unsolved
To my kaleidoscopic past"

Dedication

This book is dedicated to my wife and to our two children. Many people have told me that my past would make a great book but it was my wife Yonsun (name changed to Jean in the book) who finally convinced me to start typing. For over a year I spent every waking hour either at work or in front of my computer typing away. My wife never complained and neither did my sons, Arthur and Allen. Without their support, this book would not have been possible.

ACKNOWLEDGEMENTS

I originally believed I could write *The Empty Lot Next Door* from cover to cover completely on my own. Boy was I wrong. I needed a lot of assistance. I have told the story to many people throughout the years. Countless people told me I should write a book about my ordeal. I attempted to write it down many times but I gave up after just a few pages. I just didn't know how to write. But in April 2009, while stationed in Korea, I finally started to write my story. I completed my first draft completely on my own just by reminiscing in the past. But I still needed some help putting my story into a novel format. After a simple Amazon.com search, I found the answer. *How to Write A Damn Good Novel I* and its sequel, *How to Write A Damn Good Novel II*, by James N. Frey. After studying his books for several months, I finally had the basic acknowledge to start my second draft. Thank you Mr. Frey for not just giving me the instruction but the motivation too! After months of rewriting, I gave my manuscript to a co-worker of mine, Brandon Baila. I asked him to read my manuscript and search out areas that could be improved. At first, I didn't think a co-worker was the best person to ask to read my manuscript and provide feedback. However, Brandon took my manuscript and completely dissected and afforded many suggestions. Thanks, Brandon, for your immeasurable help. Next, I needed an editor to help me find the right words. Who did I find to help me with my ghost story? Shirley Kennedy (www. shirleykennedy.com), a professional romance writer. That's right-a romance writer was going to edit my ghost story. I was skeptical too. I quickly felt at ease when she provided me with a rock solid manuscript. Thank you, Mrs. Kennedy, for helping me find the right words and for

9

your coaching. You helped me immensely. I also needed an artist to draw sketches for the book. After surfing the internet, I came across Seshadri Roy (www.portraitnpainting.com). I took a gamble and hired him to draw one sketch. He hit a home run and I hired him to draw all the sketches for 4extremely accurate sketches. If I didn't know better, I would believe Seshadri jumped in a time machine and travelled to 1984 in Austin, Texas, and drew the sketches. Thanks, Seshadri, for bringing my story to life. I would like to thank Robert Ferguson for providing me valuable research assistance as I wrote my story. Robert really brought truth to the story. Thanks, Robert, for all your help. Lastly, I would like to thank my third grade teacher, Mrs. Haddock, from Mollie Dawson Elementary School. It must have been 1983 when she read the class a book and had us students write a one-page sequel to the book. As we wrote our stories, Mrs. Haddock walked from student to student and read over their shoulders. One by one, she praised each student for a job well done. She approached me and read over my shoulder. I just knew she would grab my paper, crumble it, and toss it in the trash. Instead, she took it and read it aloud to the whole class. She made me feel like a million bucks. I knew I would be a writer some day. Thank you, Mrs. Haddock, and all past, present, and future teachers at Mollie Dawson Elementary School.

FOREWORD

"Are ghosts real?" Many people ask that question. Some want to hear, "Yes, they are," to assure themselves that they're not crazy. Others want to hear, "No, they're not," to calm their own fears or concerns.

However, as this book reveals, the question, "Are ghosts real?" is far too simple. The greater adventure is finding the truth behind the ghost stories.

Like many children, anything eerie fascinated me, especially ghosts. I think Arthur Mills' novel will ring true for most readers. We can recall the chills of discovering a ghost story next door or a few blocks from home. As children, many of us crossed the street as we walked home from school, avoiding the sidewalk in front of the town's "haunted" house.

As we grow up, people often put away those stories along with nursery rhymes and tricycles. We're more comfortable thinking that ghosts and "things that go bump in the night" are just make-believe.

Then, something happens to remind us of a particularly chilling tale or encounter from childhood.

As this book demonstrates, the truth behind that experience can be as rich and exciting as the original encounter.

"The Empty Lot Next Door" is both engrossing and entertaining. However, I hope readers will be inspired by it as well.

"Are ghosts real?" Every person will answer that question differently.

Finding the truth behind your own childhood questions about your neighborhood's "ghost stories" or something odd that happened to you . . . that can be an unforgettable adventure, and one that changes your life for the better.

Fiona Broome
HollowHill.com

CHAPTER 1

I have made many mistakes in my life but will never forget two of the biggest. I committed one just hours prior to leaving my family in Hanau, Germany, as I left for a six month deployment to war-torn Kosovo. That's when I told my wife about my ghostly past, revealing a deeply repressed memory about a family of four, including a little girl, that was killed in a house fire next to my childhood home.

The neighborhood kids believed the family turned into ghosts and haunted the neighborhood at night. At first I didn't believe in ghosts but soon became a believer when I made another mistake, perhaps the biggest of my life: I challenged the ghosts to appear if they were real. Candle Face, the name I gave the little girl who died in the fire, took me up on my challenge. To make matters even worse, I told my wife the truth about the circumstances of my brother's suicide and the dreams of torment (if they were dreams) he and Candle Face bestowed upon me.

A few hours prior to my shocking revelation to my wife, my unit's First Sergeant had a shocking revelation of his own. He informed me I would not be deploying to Kosovo with the unit in two weeks. Instead, I would be deploying at the crack of dawn the next morning.

I finally managed to get home from work well after darkness fell. I wasn't looking forward to telling my wife I was leaving in a few hours instead of a few weeks. After all, this would be our first major separation in our short five year marriage. My wife, Jean, and my two young sons greeted me at the door as they had always done when I came home from work.

"Welcome home, honey," Jean said cheerfully as she kissed me on the cheek.

Words stuck in my throat. I could not look into her eyes. She knew instinctively something was amiss and her demeanor quickly changed from cheerful to gloomy as she asked me what was wrong.

Not having time to beat around the bush, I chose the words my First Sergeant had used. "I've been chosen to leave for Kosovo two weeks early."

"Two weeks early! But you leave in two weeks," she said. She hadn't understood what I was trying to tell her.

My blue eyes gazed down into her brown ones. "You were always good at math," I said in a bad attempt at comic relief. When she didn't answer, I blurted, "My First Sergeant has just informed me I'm leaving for Kosovo early tomorrow morning."

Jean examined my face carefully. She did not blink. I knew she was hoping this was some kind of a sick joke.

I reached out and took her right hand. "I'm serious. I need to hurry and pack my gear."

A silent cry escaped her lips. I could see her eyes were watering. I let go of her hand and turned towards my five-year-old son, Arthur. I picked him up and placed him on the floor next to Allen. "You two go play now. Mommy and I have to talk."

I turned around to face my wife and instinctively raised my arms to catch her as she began to go limp. I held her up and guided her to the couch. We sat there with our arms around each other for what seemed like ages. I had told Arthur that Jean and I were going to talk, but we just sat there without speaking. Arthur looked over at us questioningly, but he somehow knew not to say anything. Now that the crunch had come, I settled my dilemma by telling myself we didn't need to speak. We understood each other perfectly, including what had remained unsaid.

What could a soldier say to his wife hours before his deployment to a war zone, knowing he would not be back for six months, or worse, not at all?

I eventually told my wife I needed to start packing my gear. I went to our bedroom, selected all that I would need over six months, and piled everything on the living room floor. Playing around the living room, my children were keenly interested. Arthur searched through

Arthur M. Mills, Jr.

everything till he came across my Kevlar helmet. It seemed as big as he was. Fascinated, he put it on his head.

"Look Mommy, I'm a soldier," he said.

I hope not, I thought to myself. I would be proud of my son if he were to follow me into my profession, but I hoped he would never have to be in the same predicament I was in right now.

When Arthur finished playing with my helmet, he set it aside and got up to play with his younger brother. I sat down in the middle of all the scattered gear and began to sort and pack it into several large duffel bags. My wife sat by my side, quiet and contemplative, but not for long. "If I break my leg, would you have to go?" she asked.

I laughed and replied, "Yes, I would still have to go. You really want to break your leg?"

She nodded emphatically, her long, silky black hair falling around her pretty face. "If I knew that would stop you from going."

I believed her, knowing she'd do just about anything to prevent me from going to Kosovo. Like most military wives, she didn't want her husband going into harm's way.

Meanwhile, Arthur and Allen were unaware of the emotional drama going on between their father and mother. They began to play their favorite game, which I had christened 'the windowsill challenge.' Our living room windowsill was about five inches wide and about 18 inches off the floor. It spanned the entire length of the room. Its height was just right for two active boys to want to clamber on. Their sole objective was to hang onto the window frame while they scooted along the windowsill to the other end. They clung to the window but often fell off. When that happened, they would get up, dust themselves off, and climb back onto the windowsill all over again.

I had seen them scoot along this windowsill many a time. But this evening something on the panes caught my attention. I was looking at the handprints my boys had left on the window pane when all of a sudden a strange feeling came over me. My eyes widened. My heart began to thump against my chest so hard that I could actually hear it. Something in my memory was stirring, slowly.

I was about the same age as Arthur when I moved with my family into a house in Austin, Texas. My time there was blessed with good friends, but at the same time it was filled with immeasurable fear.

Fear of a little girl and her little handprints.

My wife looked at me curiously. "What are you looking at?"

I could not answer. Feeling my face flush, I stood, hoping my odd feeling would pass. It didn't, and I began to feel faint and sway on my feet. This time it was my petite wife who instinctively raised her arms to embrace me. She's only five feet three compared to my five feet eleven, so she had to use all her strength to hold me upright.

"Hello, are you there?" she asked as she struggled to keep her balance.

I still couldn't answer. If I could have, my answer would have been no. The feeling lingered. Other images streamed through my mind from a place far away. I felt as if I were not really there, that I was elsewhere in a dreamlike state revisiting a time long past, a time when I was a prisoner of fear and torment. My eyes remained fixed on those fresh handprints on the window panes. And then, coming back to me out of the mists of time: a horribly familiar burning smell.

I found my voice. "This can't be happening," I said faintly, but loud enough for my wife to hear.

She asked, "What can't be happening?"

I had to come up with something. The burning smell was stronger now. It took both of us the next few seconds to identify that the strong

Arthur M. Mills, Jr.

burning smell in our apartment was from something Jean had left in the oven and totally forgotten.

She darted into the kitchen yelling, "With all the excitement, I forgot your dinner." She yanked open the oven door and the smoke alarm took off. Arthur and Allen ran to their bedrooms to escape the loud buzz of the smoke alarm. Jean took care of the crisis and came back to the living room. She knelt next to me, wanting to be near. Despite the kitchen crisis, I was mentally far away and contemplating those long ago terrors I thought I had buried.

"Can't you tell me what's wrong?" she asked. She stared at the window trying to understand why I had looked at it the way I did. She tilted her head in all directions trying to see what I saw.

"Those handprints on the windows remind me of a story," I said.

She went to the window and pointed at the handprints. "Everything reminds you of a story."

I asked, "You remember the story about my brother Richard and how he died?"

"Yes," she responded but didn't seem too happy about me bringing up the topic just now.

"One thing I never told you about is the story of me and Candle Face."

She laughed and asked, "Candle Face? Who or what is Candle Face?"

"Candle Face is the name I gave to a little girl who haunted my dreams when I was a child."

Her amused expression faded, replaced by concern. "You never told me."

"It's not something I've ever wanted to talk about."

"Well, you had better tell me now."

For the first time I let it all come out. I told Jean about the house in the South Austin neighborhood where I'd moved as a little boy. About the vacant lot next door where a house once stood, and how I discovered the house had burned down years before and a little girl had died in the fire. "Don't laugh, but I came to call her Candle Face. She would visit me after everyone else had gone to sleep. I would have nightmares about her torturing me. Or were they nightmares? I still don't know if those were dreams or whether they actually happened. Candle Face seemed real to me."

Jean was listening patiently. When I collected my thoughts I continued, "I didn't tell anyone, but I saw signs of her everywhere. I saw her childish handprints on my windows at home in Austin on several occasions. I could see her charred face and I could even feel her touch me with her skeleton-like fingers. I even smelled her nauseating burnt flesh odor, she was that real."

"Stop," my wife interrupted. She was looking at me, but now it was a look of new discovery, of wanting to share any dark unknown facts from that part of my life, from my past. "Why didn't you ever tell me about this?"

"I think I just wanted to forget about that time and those memories. I haven't thought about them in years."

A small voice interrupted us. "Mommy, I'm tired." Allen spoke in his usual soft voice.

"Hold that thought, honey," My wife said to me as she picked up Allen and took him to his room. Arthur toddled behind her. She put both of them to bed. It was quite late now and way past our children's bedtime. I thought about the nightmares I'd had in my own childhood and how lucky I was that my kids didn't have the same fate. They slept the sleep of the innocent.

Jean came back to sit on the couch next to me. She still didn't know what to think of my dark secret. "I can't believe you never mentioned anything about Candle Face to me before."

We were so much part of each other's lives that she was amazed she had no inkling of this part of my childhood. "I never said anything about it before because I haven't thought about it for years. The last time I saw Candle Face was soon after Richard died. The last time I thought about it was on the night of my high school prom seven years ago when I was taking my prom date home. The prom was some time before you and I met."

"So what happened?" she asked.

"You really want to know?"

"I want to know everything about your life." She sat expectantly, her knees pulled up to her chest, her chin pressing down on her knees as in a sitting fetal position.

I had more or less finished packing by now. I piled my gear near the entrance and looked at my watch. I had a few hours left before I would have to leave. I wanted to tell her that particular story about my childhood. I needed to unburden myself. She was ready for a story and so was I.

Arthur M. Mills, Jr.

CHAPTER 2

My first memory of the ordeal was back in June, 1979, when I was barely six-and-a-half-years old. I was riding with my family in our old rusty AMC Rebel Station Wagon. We turned into the rocky driveway of our new house on Ben Howell Drive in South Austin. The house wasn't really new, but it was new to us. We didn't care that the house was built in the 1950's and in bad need of some love and tender care. All we cared about was that we no longer lived in the city projects. As we drove into the driveway, my mother couldn't contain herself any longer and called out, "Here it is. Home sweet home."

My three older brothers stiffened their backs so they could get a better look out the dirt-covered windows. I tried to take a peek but my brothers blocked my view.

Once the car came to a stop, we all jumped out and ran across the front lawn, the grass tickling the bottom of my bare feet. I remember declaring the days of stepping on the jagged rocks and glass that lay around the projects were over. Finally Dan and Felix, my two oldest brothers, lost interest in the grass and ran onto the front porch. "Look at this porch, it's huge," thirteen-year-old Dan said excitedly.

"Hey, which is the front door?" eleven-year-old Felix asked. "There are two doors. Is this a duplex?"

"No," my father said. "It's one house but there are two front doors making it look like a duplex. The door on the left leads to the living room. Go ahead inside, the door's unlocked." Back then people rarely locked their doors. My parents even kept the car keys in the ignition.

My two oldest brothers were so excited they nearly broke the door down as they opened it. I walked onto the porch and began to fantasize about all the games I could play on it. I visualized playing cars with the new friends I was going to have. We could even sleep on that big front porch. There must have been enough room for ten kids to sleep over. I couldn't wait to meet the kids in the neighborhood.

Richard, my eight-year-old brother, was still standing in the grass. He appeared to be talking to himself or he may have been talking to the grass. I didn't think much of it at the time because he may have been fantasizing about the grass just like I was doing with the front porch. I turned around to head into the house when I saw my mother and father embracing in the front yard. I stopped and watched. This was the first time I ever saw them embrace. I could hear my father telling my mother that everything would be better from now on. She looked happy and ready to start a new life outside the projects.

This was my mother's third husband. She met Dan and Felix's father way before I was born. Their marriage didn't last. Neither did Richard and my real father's marriage to my mother. Sometime after that divorce, she met her current husband, Raymond, twenty-one years her elder. Raymond, a second generation Mexican-American, vowed to rescue us from poverty, and he was well on his way with that promise by removing us from the projects. Raymond was the only father figure I ever had. Because of that, I never introduced him as my stepfather. He was always and will always be my father.

I stood there for several minutes watching my father and mother holding each other and dreaming of a new beginning. *How I wish now I could go back in time and warn them of the nightmare that was soon to follow.*

I stepped inside the house into the small living room, which was quite dark and bland. I didn't much like it, but anything—well almost anything—beat the small apartment we just came from. I could hear my two older brothers claiming the shed that was attached to the large back porch as their bedroom.

My parents walked into the house. "Ray!" my mother called. Ray is the name my father gave me shortly after he met my mother. I suppose he named me Ray after his own name, Raymond.

"Ray!" she repeated. I ran to her thinking I was in trouble. Instead, she showed me the bedroom Richard and I would share. It was huge. Well, it appeared huge to two six—and eight-year-old boys. It already had two new twin-size beds against opposite walls. Before I could pick my bed, Richard claimed the bed next to the window. I was stuck with the bed next to the boring wall, but I really didn't care because at least Richard and I didn't have to share a bed any longer. Back in the projects, we shared a couch that folded out into a bed. Richard was notorious for stealing the sheets. He loved to wrap his body with the sheets as if he were in a body bag. I would try to unwrap the sheets from around him, but it was no use. One day I got tired of sleeping without a sheet so I used my mother's toenail clippers to shape my toenails into a jagged saw. That night Richard pulled the sheet off my body and wrapped it around his own. I kicked his upper right thigh with my saw-shaped toenails and ripped his skin wide open. My father spanked me until my butt was as red as Richard's blood. But it was worth it. Richard never stole the sheets ever again. I was victorious. *That didn't last long.*

I walked to the closet door located on my side of the bedroom and took a peek inside. Our clothes were already there. Actually we didn't have our own separate clothes; we shared them. Since Richard was older and stronger, he always got the first pick. Maybe I should have used my saws to enforce my will on him.

Many new toys lay on the bottom of the closet. Among them were several large bags of new Army Men, several tall wooden dolls, and cheap imitation Hot Wheels. I knew they were meant for me because Richard thought he was too old to play with such childish toys. After all, he was eight! I didn't care because I was six-and-a-half-years old and I loved toys, even those wooden dolls.

As I was scavenging in the closet, Richard discovered we had our own outer door to the front porch. This was the extra door Felix inquired about. So we had our own entrance to the porch! I thought about the exciting possibilities—how I could sneak out in the middle of the night and play in the grass or run around the neighborhood without my parents ever knowing. Maybe I could sneak to a friend's house.

All my thoughts focused on leaving though that door. I never once thought about the possibility that someone or something might try to enter the same way.

Our front yard pretty much resembled the other front yards of the houses on our street, but the backyard was much larger and had an old garage in the corner. The huge pecan trees in the back provided plenty of shade. I now recall it was a dark place, even in the middle of the afternoon. It was a good place to play hide and seek.

With a couple of exceptions, Ben Howell was a typical street in South Austin. One exception was a large boxy building up the street. When I asked, I was told it was part of the phone company. The other exception was the very noticeable empty lot next door to our house. At first I considered it the neighborhood playground, although it had no swings or a sandpit. It was just an empty lot about the same size as our front and back yards. No one bothered about it except us children and people who wanted to park their junk. The front of the lot had obviously not been tended for some time because tall grass grew there. However, there were plenty of clovers, and later on, my best friend, Mark, and I made up something called a clover picnic. We would get down on all fours and graze the clovers like cattle. Our edible charms had to be four-leafed and growing wild out in front. Mark and I loved the pickle taste, but the people across the street thought we were crazy. They would shout this fact to us from their side of the street. Mark and I would look up, puzzled at first, and they would laugh at our clover-smudged lips and bulging cheeks. We would then do our best to ignore them and go back to the search for four-leafed clovers. *Four-leafed clovers are suppose to bring luck, I guess those four-leafed clovers were defective.*

The back of this otherwise empty lot was a grassless, fire-ant-filled mess. It was called an empty lot because there was no house on the lot. It did, however, have stuff strewn all over it, like dirty mattresses with springs sticking out and other medium and large household junk items which the original owners had simply thrown out.

Then there was the most unusual part of this strange empty lot: the huge wide hole in the back. It must have measured five feet all around and went three feet straight down underground. At first, I could find no explanation for its existence. In fact, none of us kids ever mentioned it. I just accepted that it was somehow a part of our play area, though I didn't like the looks of it and did my best to avoid it. So did the others in our group. From the first day I noticed it, I couldn't look at it without a small pinprick of fear.

Within no time after moving into our home, Dan and Felix searched out and found other kids their age. Their best friend was Edwin, who was Dan's age. They quickly hit it off because all three shared a love of music. Soon they started their own band in Edwin's garage. The band demanded a lot of Dan's time. Edwin's younger sister, Silvia, soon demanded even more of Dan's time and they became quite inseparable. Felix, not to be out beaten, found his own girlfriend, Lorry. She lived right across the street from Edwin. They were very young but they sure seemed to be way older, based on the things I saw them do.

Just like we shared the same clothes, Richard and I shared the same friends. We met six-year-old Evan who lived in the much larger house located right next door on the left. Evan seemed to have it all: clothes, toys, and parental attention. He, his sister, and parents were very close. Out of all the neighborhood families, their family seemed to be the closest and also the weirdest. Evan and his sister didn't walk to school like all the other kids did. Their parents drove them to school. The whole way to school was spent singing songs together as they clapped hands. Sometimes on rainy days they offered Richard and me a ride. Richard would usually opt to walk but I always accepted. I was glad Mollie Dawson Elementary School was only a few minutes' drive away because I couldn't stand all that whole family singing together nonsense for long. Their close family ties made me sick.

Thinking back, this country needs more families like theirs. They were the all American family.

But what made this family really weird was how they loved to chase sirens. Whenever I heard a police, ambulance, or fire truck siren, I would run to the front porch to watch them dash to their car. Off they went to chase the siren to the accident or fire. I liked going to Evan's house but I didn't seem to fit in. I was from the house next door where those crazy kids lived.

Randy, who wore glasses and braces, was another kid who seemed to have it all, like GI Joes, Dungeon and Dragon figurines, and real Hot Wheels, not the cheap imitation ones I had. Randy had it all except one thing: freedom. His parents kept a very short leash on him. My brothers and I didn't have a leash.

Again, thinking back, maybe we should have had a leash. Better yet, we should have never been allowed outside of the house.

Randy had to ask for permission to do everything. He was not even allowed to have company, especially Richard and me because we were from the crazy house from across the street. Randy snuck me into the house once and I found it had more fish aquariums than a pet store.

Randy and Richard were better friends than the two of us because they were the same age. However, Randy and I were good friends, too, when Richard was not around.

Then there was Andre, a little older, and mean. He hardly ever played with us because he was a bully and we didn't really want to be bullied by him.

Lastly there was six-year-old Mark, who became my best friend. I could talk to Mark and share with him my deepest darkest thoughts. *Well, not all of them.* It seemed I spent more time at Mark's house than my own. I walked to school with him nearly every day, but it was more than his friendship I cherished, it was his whole family. His mother was the neighborhood Cub Scout leader and disciplinarian. If one of us kids acted up while we were in her house, she would threaten us with the paddle she kept in the pantry. I never saw that paddle, though. To this day, I doubt the paddle ever really existed.

Mark's mother never went with us on our summer scouting trips. That job was left to Mark's father. During those trips, Mark's father would tell us stories about when he was a young native American-Indian. We did not believe the stories but loved to hear them anyway. In fact, we suspected little to no Indian blood ran in his Mexican-American veins.

There were so many stories and rumors running around in those days, I didn't know what to believe. One thing I did believe, though, was that my father had a special liking for me. It seemed he preferred my company more than that of my brothers. *Or was it that I preferred his company more than that of my brothers?* My father and I would often watch the TV show, *All in the Family* together. We watched every single episode together.

My relationship with Richard was not as warm. We could not stand each other. *But what young brothers don't feel that way?* I can see now that I loved Richard in many ways, despite his offhand manner towards me and despite the beatings he sometimes inflicted upon me. But whatever he did, I kept my mouth shut. It was understood I had to keep this unpleasant fact of Richard's behavior from our parents.

Even so, Richard must have felt some sort of exasperated love for me as I did for him, or at least I hope so. He would often get into a jealous rage and tell me that our father favored me. I realized his accusation may have been true. Even at the time, I was aware our

Arthur M. Mills, Jr.

father did single me out for attention. What I couldn't figure out was why our father had never tried to draw Richard in as he had me. *Or was it that Richard never tried to draw himself in?*

Richard was brilliant in many ways. Our friends thought so. His teachers in school and peers in church considered him the perfect child. There were some who thought of Richard as a softy. I had seen him when our older brothers and bullies set on him. I would have thought this true because of those incidents, but there was a side to Richard that only I knew about. He and I were supposed to share a couple of things besides our bedroom, but knowing my vulnerabilities inside out, Richard got to choose the better part of the bedroom as his and got to wear the better clothes, even though Mom had told us we should share our clothes and toys. And he got me to do his share of the housework. Otherwise, he threatened to say the fault lay with me, that I was the shirker. He claimed Mom might ground both of us, but I would suffer more.

Richard was troubled. Our elder brothers could turn on him any minute when our parents weren't around. This was quite often. He couldn't get away from what they did to him. In turn, he vented his frustrations on me by doing similar stuff to me when no one in the family was looking. Of course our friends knew, but they left us alone.

The boys our own age probably thought the fights between Richard and me (*which Richard always won*) were family matters, best dealt with if overlooked. Their mothers and fathers probably thought of us, Dan and Felix in particular, as a troublesome lot. They were right. We were trouble.

My friends, Richard and I all went to Mollie Dawson Elementary School. That's where I met another friend, Nolan. We hit it off our very first day of kindergarten. He didn't live nearby like all my other friends, but since we had grown up together from age six, a couple of blocks didn't make a great deal of difference. Nolan lived with his grandparents who gave him a great deal of love and attention.

And so, those first years on Ben Howell Drive were grand despite the occasional sibling rivalry. We, mostly me, played hard and had plenty of sleep to recover. Eventually that all changed.

CHAPTER 3

For as long as I lived in that house, I was scared of that large hole in the back part of the empty lot next door. When I wasn't quite eight years old, I asked Evan and Randy about it but got no answer. Why was it there? Why did I feel the way I felt about it? Why did the empty lot next door even exist?

A couple of days later when we were on the lot, I asked my friends again. Randy, older by two years, must have decided it was time for an explanation. But he had to step closer and talk in a whisper. Was it a secret? Who else could want to listen?

"In the early '70s a house used to stand on the lot but a fire burned it down," Randy explained.

This was news to me. I could have asked a lot of questions then, but something stopped me.

"A whole family died in the fire," Evan added.

I was taken aback. Evan's words ran around inside my head. A family? How many in the family? When did Evan find out? He had not ever breathed a word to me.

"Yeah, the father, mother, young boy, and a young girl. All of them died in the fire. It was no ordinary fire. It came from there." Randy pointed skywards. "It was started by lightning in the middle of the night. The people who lived here didn't know their house was on fire. They died in their sleep because of all that smoke from the fire billowing around inside the house at night. It's called something like smoke ass-pickion, I think."

Richard chimed in, "It's called smoke asphyxiation. Their lungs must have filled up with smoke."

Annoyed, Randy glanced at Richard. Was Richard going to rob him of this chance to be the center of attention? He decided to carry on quickly without giving my brother another chance. "They had no other family, no relatives, and no money. The City didn't want to pay for their funeral and four places in a cemetery. Nobody wanted to pick up the costs for the whole family, so their bodies were buried right here." Randy pointed straight to the hole. Mark was nodding his head as if he knew the whole story.

"Mark, you knew about this?" I asked.

"Of course."

Why was it everyone there had known about the fire but me? This was more dramatic than I could have ever imagined! But I couldn't afford serious doubts because now Mark had backed up what Randy and Evan had just told us, and so had my brother Richard. I had been the only 'baby' who hadn't been told. As far as Richard was concerned, I had tried hard not to bother him so as not to draw any unwanted attention. But I believed that Richard and I shared everything, not only our bedroom, toys and clothes. As it turned out, I discovered he had known a great deal more about the empty lot next door than I did. And he probably knew about that hole and why it was there.

I was stung. "How do you know, Richard? You didn't live here when it happened. You may have not even been born."

Meantime, Randy was growing more eloquent. Perhaps it was his only chance at being center stage. "See, the City buried the bodies here and at night they come back alive. They leave you alone most of the time but all of them will hunt you down and kill you if you ever jump in the hole."

I wondered if I should believe Randy's shocking words. I would have to test him. "You're just trying to scare us because you're bigger and you know more," I said, trying to mask the knot in my throat.

"Yeah, maybe." Randy looked a little shamefaced, and then perked up. "But the part about the City burying the bodies here is true, Ray. Why do you think I stay away from that hole? Why do you think I've made sure you guys stay away too?"

But I knew why I had stayed away from that hole in the ground. I just didn't like it. It had been slightly scary long before Randy, Evan and Richard finally spoke up. Now it was going to be more so. Mark and I exchanged a glance and I knew he was thinking the same thing. I kept wishing the story wasn't true, but there had to be *some* explanation for the empty lot next door with its huge, ugly hole in the ground. I decided I had to get to the bottom of this strange story I had just been told by my friends and brother. Maybe there was a more reasonable, less scary explanation.

We might have steered clear of our adopted playground for a few days but soon went back to playing in the empty lot. Now my friends and I did even more to avoid the area around the great big hole at the back. Richard, who loved to tell ghost stories, began to focus on the lost family who lived in the house on the empty lot. They were macabre tales of their skeletons coming out at night and roaming the streets of South Austin as they sought their skins. The ghosts wanted to regain their original looks, he explained. Luckily (according to Richard), they had failed till now in this mission and would re-enter their resting place by the time the first rays of the early morning sun arrived. Richard had a way with words. We shivered as we listened to the same story over and over again, with small changes in the storyline.

Arthur M. Mills, Jr.

CHAPTER 4

By early spring, 1984, I was eleven years old and in fourth grade while Richard was almost thirteen years old and in sixth grade. Mark, Randy, Evan, Nolan, and Andre all still lived in the neighborhood. Our neighborhood was like a roach motel: You can enter but you can't leave. *I soon realized that death was the only way out.*

I also realized that all the neighborhood kids liked me, that they let me decide what games we would play and where and when to get together. I sometimes felt I was the leader of our little group. They often asked Richard and me to come over, but usually Richard didn't go.

By this time, Dan was seventeen and Felix fifteen. Dan was no longer in school and Felix probably didn't go either. All four of us siblings had our own interests. Dan was busy working at Hut's Hamburgers on 6th Street and only the Lord knows what Felix was doing. Richard was busy writing poetry and practicing for church and school plays while I was always running around—literally. I loved to run and would run like the wind. Sometimes I would run around the block or run around the track at Saint Edwards University which was about a mile and a half away. My father would take me there and watch me run and encourage me to push myself. It was the best thing he had ever done for me. Some day, I told myself, I was going to run world marathons and run in track meets.

My mother complained that my running was keeping me horribly thin. But she did not say this often. There was possibly another reason why I was thin. What food there was in the house would usually get eaten by Dan and Felix when they were there. My mother had a hard-working job at an engraving shop at Sears. She worked all day and got home at six in the evening. She would then cook our dinner, though that would usually get polished off by my brothers before I had a chance to smell the food.

My mother didn't talk much. She struggled to control my two oldest brothers but seemed distracted a lot of the time. All her life she'd had difficulty relating to people, whether family or acquaintances. She didn't remember matters small and major. She didn't know, or didn't remember, which grades my brothers and I were in at school. At the beginning of school each year, she would ask which grade I was in. I would tell her, but she soon forgot.

There were a couple of things I wasn't good at. For one thing, I couldn't get my words out as I would have liked. My mother frowned at my stutter, though my father and friends ignored it. My brothers would tease me and mimic me incessantly. I constantly worried that my stutter wouldn't go away when I most wanted it to, like in class and with my teachers. I actually had to attend after-school speech therapy several days a week for many years.

Also, I wasn't good at schoolwork, nor could I deal very well with the authority at school. My friends and I would rather play the fool than follow what was going on in class. I got failing grades but somehow always made it to the next grade at the end of the year. At the time I suspected this was because my teachers couldn't bear the thought of putting up with me all over again.

Back then, I was awfully scared of the dark and anything that was responsible for making it dark. Most of all, I was scared of the huge hole in the ground in the empty lot next door.

On the other hand, Richard wasn't scared of anything, maybe with the exception of our two older brothers. He was a good student and his teachers loved him. I was known as "Richard's little brother," as if I didn't have my own identity.

Richard was undoubtedly talented and was sure of a captive audience, whether in the empty lot or when he played the lead in church and school plays. Near home, he performed magic tricks and narrated ghost stories. We sat on the ground and watched and listened enraptured. It didn't matter that we knew how those tricks worked, or that we had some stories of our own to tell. Some of the kids tried, but

Arthur M. Mills, Jr.

no one came anywhere near Richard's talent. We knew we preferred him. He simply was the best.

For Richard's performances we had at first built a small and rudimentary tree house in the massive oak tree located at the back of the empty lot next door. We balanced a four foot by four foot square board across the two largest branches high above the wide tree trunk. The many branches were huge, much larger than the other trees around us. I thought of it as the largest tree for miles. It was our own trophy tree. We thought we just had to build that house up on that tree, never mind the mysterious hole not so far away. Our efforts to build a tree house eventually gathered momentum. At first it was just a board, then a tree house with a roof. Ultimately that tree house became a massive tree house.

Later, I would regret starting with the board.

I can still picture all of us on the bare ground looking up at Richard as he went about being the star, the magician and storyteller all rolled into one. He was going to try and get a special girl to come and watch him do magic, but the rest of us didn't allow girls near that tree and the tree house, so it never happened.

We had the perfect tree house in the back of the empty lot, but we had to do something with the front part. I seem to remember it was my idea to cut the tall grass. Mark was concerned that the clovers would never grow back, but they did and we continued to secretly participate in our clover picnics when the rest of our friends were not around. Meanwhile, we all took part in cutting the grass and picking up the trash from the front of the lot.

We now had something closer to a proper playground, even if it was missing the swings and slides. My friends and I decided it had to be utilized well. I devised a cycling game which started farther up the street, from the other end of Ben Howell Drive. This was the end where it joined with Edison Drive next to the phone company building. We had to pedal furiously down the street then turn sharply at the empty lot and point the front wheel of our bicycles up in the air before we came down right side up and wheels balanced on the ramp that we built from old discarded wood. I called it, "let's-cycle-furiously-down-the-street, steer in and jump onto the ramp and down on our butts." It was dangerous, but the adults didn't know and we didn't care.

The neighbors in the house located on the other side of the empty lot were not as fascinated as we were with our self-devised games and entertainment. They called the cops if our playful noises rose above the softest roar. In fact, they routinely called the cops on us. We would run when the law arrived, and then come back again when they had left. The neighbors would call again. It was hard work, leaving and coming back, but we were drawn to our empty lot play area and knew the cops would eventually tire of coming.

Virgie, the woman of the house, would sometimes march onto the lot and threaten us with the police, but we would just yell out, "Virgie is a virgin, Virgie is a virgin." That always did the trick to drive her away. In the back of my mind, I always worried we would someday lose our playground and, more importantly, Richard's tree house.

Despite bloody noses and sprained ankles from riding our bicycles on the ramp, we were content with our lives, and that included eating clovers, playing hide and seek, and watching Richard do his magic tricks. We admired our star performer and insisted we didn't need to go anywhere else for our entertainment and games. We decided the empty lot would be our only play area. Even with the strange hole, the empty lot was our world. It was our oyster.

Sure, I kept dark secrets from my parents and friends. I knew a great deal about what Dan and Felix were up to. I berated myself because I seemed powerless to stop them from tormenting Richard. By now I felt I should be trying harder at school even if my mother had little idea what I did there, the failing grades I was getting, and the grade any of us were in.

We still walked to school by the usual route. I managed to scrape by every grade and thought I knew a lot more than I actually did. *Looking back, I didn't know anything.* At home, things hadn't changed a lot. Both my parents still had the same jobs and worked long hours. My father left early in the morning before Richard and I woke up. Mom would put our breakfast on the table and leave for work. If Dan and Felix were around, Richard and I ate as quickly as we could, or sometimes not at all if our older brothers had other ideas about who should get the cereal and who shouldn't.

My friends and I had a great time just being together. As time went by we indulged ourselves less with the bicycle game and the clover picnic. By now we preferred ball games which were better played in school. Mark was the best football player, Nolan the best soccer player, Randy the best baseball player, and I the best runner.

Of course, Richard was the best entertainer. He had greatly improved and by now was confident in his ability to entertain. The neighborhood kids and I still went to the empty lot a couple of days a week. He now excelled in magic shows and occasionally called on me to be his assistant. I loved that. We still tried to keep the empty lot as tidy as possible. Virgie the Virgin still lived in the house on the other side of the lot. By now she realized we weren't little kids anymore, but she still raged at us and called the police now and then. The police, though, had got used to us and our ways. They gave us a wink and a smile on the occasions when they turned up.

Even though a lot of time had passed, I was more wary than ever of the hole in the ground. I still didn't know what to believe. Had a family really died there when their house caught on fire? Richard's story-telling talents had made the incident seem real, yet I still had doubts and wondered how I could best unravel the story. What I needed was for someone to fill in the facts for me. I didn't need any more speculation from my friends or Richard. Finally, at long last, I decided to ask my parents.

I had given some thought to how and when to ask either my mom or dad whose lives had been based on hard work and solid facts. I didn't want my stutter to come in the way of my query. I rehearsed what and how to ask and finally got enough courage to ask my father during dinner what he knew about the empty lot next door.

"P-p-a, why is there an e-empty l-lot n-next d-door?"

Forks fell onto the plates beneath. I could feel all eyes on me. Dan and Felix looked incredulous and faintly amused. Richard looked at me steadily, as if to say he didn't know I had it in me to ask outright, not when I was our father's favorite in his opinion, and could have asked for anything, anyhow. Our mother looked wary.

Our father looked around and cleared his throat. Five pairs of eyes switched to him while I stared at my empty plate. "There used to be a house there but it was destroyed by a fire," he said, slowly and clearly.

It was true then, the story that Randy, Evan, Mark, and even Richard had come up with all those years ago! My mind whirled. So the grown-ups had known as well, but what exactly was true and what not?

It appeared I was the only one who didn't know whether to believe the story. But at least my father had just confirmed the part about the house burning down. Beyond that, I couldn't ask him if there was any truth in the stories about what happened to the family after they died. I could not very well give away what was said when Richard and my friends spent time together!

Or could I? I found my nerve and decided to give it a try. If I didn't at least ask, I would never know so I took the plunge. "How about the f-family? Did they die, and d-d-did the city bury them p-properly? Did they h-have any relatives or f-f-f-friends? I heard one of the other c-children say in s-school that if that happens, the city is f-free to bury people anywhere. They would not have b-buried the bodies in the b-back, w-w-w-would they?"

My father laughed at the scenario I presented. "Bodies in the back yard?" He laughed again.

It was rare to see my father laugh, but then, I had given him something to go on. I was annoyed my stutter had given me away, especially since my father guessed my fear and found it funny. I was beginning to wonder why I had asked at all. I was eleven years old

Arthur M. Mills, Jr.

now. Why could I not just accept those tragic events and get on with whatever I had to do? I wondered if I could quietly slip away to our bedroom after dinner, away from this fun at my cost. But the problem was, it was Richard's room, too. He spent a lot of time there writing and studying. If I went there now, he would soon come in to do his homework, but he was sure to take time out to tease me, which he loved to do. No, going to my room wouldn't work. What else could I do?

I had the answer, run. But before I could actually get up to run, my mother blurted out, "Where did you ever hear that story?"

My father was still laughing. My brothers joined in the laughter. "No, they did not bury any bodies in the back. I believe only one person died in that fire" my father said.

"Stop. You're going to scare the children," my mother retorted.

Our normally quiet dinner was getting animated, and it was all my doing. Dan threw me a grimace and said, "It's okay, all of us on this street know the story, give or take a couple of details. The fire was started by lightning. The people in the house were caught unaware because it was night time and they were asleep. The parents managed to save their young son and themselves but were unable to save their young daughter. I think he was around eight and she was around eleven years old. They found her burned body lying under her bed as if she attempted to hide from the flames instead of escaping. We are quite sure she's buried in the hole at the back."

I was amazed all over again. Everyone knew about the house fire. My brothers knew what had happened to the people who lived there. That boy might just be still living in Austin.

I tried to pull myself back from such thoughts. I was just being silly. My counselor in school told me eleven was a tough age, never mind the teens. But my thoughts carried on yo-yoing. A boy and girl living next door? She would still not be allowed in the tree house. And then I remembered if that family still lived next door, we wouldn't have had the empty lot to play in, or built a tree house in the branches of that great oak tree. All of it would have been theirs.

By now my mother was really annoyed with Dan. "That's enough. Stop," she exclaimed. "We will say a prayer when we leave this table tonight, just like Richard did when he said grace in Spanish. This time we will include that child who died in our prayers."

I noticed that my mother and I had been the only ones not laughing. Everyone stopped when Mother said her bit. I rose from the table with Dan's voice still ringing in my ears. Randy had added some extra detail to his version. Dan sounded more convincing. He knew, all of my family knew, the gory details all this time! My mother might have known too. Knowing her, it would be only natural she had kept it to herself. It was too much for me to deal with at this instant at the dinner table. I thought I might have a heart attack.

I had a great deal more to figure out but didn't dare ask. If I did, I knew my stutter would be at its worst. I would just have to find the answers for myself.

Arthur M. Mills, Jr.

CHAPTER 5

Later that night I was in the bathtub thinking about those people who had lived next door. Again I wondered what they could have been like. A mother and father, a girl maybe my age and a young boy. Would they have been like our family or like Evan's or anyone else from school?

I caught myself and wondered what was the matter with me. I had thought my obsession was behind me, but instead here I was, still obsessed with the family, the lot next door and the hole at the back. I thought about the bodies in the hole. Could there really be a body in there? Perhaps more? I determined to try and get to the bottom of the mystery. If I didn't, the empty lot next door would haunt me forever.

Some months before, my older brothers had tried to scare Richard and me with a ghost story about an English Queen called Bloody Mary. We tried to tell them we weren't really scared, even if she really existed. Dan and Felix insisted that not only had Queen Mary been real but she was infamous. Mary's religion had forced her into a huge argument with a great many people from her own country. She thought they should have their heads chopped off because they didn't go to the same church she did. Dan and Felix looked straight at Richard and me when they said this, probably because in our family we were the only regular church-goers.

We asked Dan and Felix if the Queen had turned into a ghost. They said she had when she died but only because she hadn't managed to kill all the people she didn't like. Queen Mary had gone down in history for chopping off the heads of nearly three hundred people. They said there was a way of proving that in her ghostly guise she still roamed the earth, but whoever proved this theory would die. The way to prove this was to go into the bathroom, turn off the lights, face the mirror and say out loud, "Bloody Mary, Bloody Mary, Bloody Mary." According to my brothers, Bloody Mary would appear and kill the one that summoned her.

My eleven-year-old reasoning power told me that if I tried this and Bloody Mary really appeared in the bathroom mirror, it would only prove that other ghosts could arise from improperly buried bodies.

I jumped out of the tub, tried to gather my wits and stood in front of the small mirror. My heart began to beat faster, but I brushed aside all thoughts of a heart attack. I had never wound myself up this much. The teasing and laughter I got from my family made me even more determined. I told myself I needed to know any truth. First about Bloody Mary, even if it meant death. The next proof could be derived from this.

I had to walk a few steps to the light switch near the door. Would I be able to force myself to turn it off? I planned my steps back to the mirror and counted to three in front of the light switch.

"One . . . two . . . three." I turned off the lights and carefully walked in the direction of the mirror trying to keep my mind blank, since stray thoughts would be likely to make me change my mind. I felt a little stupid mostly because I was still naked, but managed to get into position and say out loud, "Bloody Mary, Bloody Mary, Bloody Mary."

Bang! Bang! Bang! The thumping seemed to come from outside. I jumped, slipped, and landed butt-first on the hard floor. I thought I was dead, but instead of nothingness, my thoughts rushed back. Was Bloody Mary coming to kill me?

"Hey, what are you doing in there?" It was my father on the other side of the bathroom door. "Why do you have the lights off?"

I hesitated, knowing I would not be able to explain myself. "Huh, n-nothing," There had not been enough time for me to come up with any excuse.

"You weren't having a bath on the floor in the bathroom with the lights off, were you? Come on, get out." My father was not amused like he'd been during dinner. He sounded annoyed.

"I'm all right," I called. " "I'll be out in a minute." I must have sounded convincing because he left. Relieved, I sat on the floor

Arthur M. Mills, Jr.

thankful he was gone. I was also relieved Bloody Mary hadn't shown up. Now I knew the story wasn't true.

When I got back to my room, I sat on my bed and thought about what had just happened. Richard had said I was an idiot for bringing up all that stuff about the people next door. He worried that he might not be allowed to carry on with his shows in the tree house and had even threatened to discontinue my services as the magician's assistant. But I wasn't in a mood to be threatened just now. I was elated. What I had just proved in the bathroom had sunk in. I thought if Bloody Mary was fake, then the story about the bodies buried in the hole was also fake. Like I had told Randy some years ago, these stories were made up just to scare kids.

I felt like a million dollars. I *had* got to the truth, cracked the case about the empty lot next door with its huge ugly hole. I had proved to myself that the ghost of Bloody Mary did not exist. That meant people did not turn into ghosts just like that, whether they had been good or bad. Of course, this meant there wasn't a body in the hole next door which could turn into a ghost.

But wait. Just like I tested the Bloody Mary story, I had to confirm the story about the people who used to live in the house next door. Like my father and Dan said, they were still alive except for the girl. Then again, they might have all died in the fire, like the kids in our group had insisted on.

Did I believe in ghosts? I wasn't sure. Either way, I wanted to know if there was just one child ghost or the whole family.

I would show Richard ultimately, I decided. It would help if I proved something, anything about the people who lived in the house next door. The common consensus was that whether it was just the little girl who had died in that fire or the whole family, they very well could have been buried in that fearful hole in their back yard. I had to think carefully about how to prove this story right or wrong.

There was no one I could ask. I would have to rely on myself. As with Bloody Mary, I would have to test for this ghost (or ghosts). I was sure about this now. *But later, I would wonder if I could not have just left it alone.*

Meanwhile, Richard was noisily airing his opinion of me. I was an idiot for bringing up all that stuff about the people next door. He might not be allowed to carry on with his shows in the tree house, and all because of me. Again he threatened to discontinue my services as the magician's assistant.

I only half listened. I had a plan and was preparing carefully for what I had in mind. I wanted to go and inspect that hole in the empty lot next door. It would be best done at night when I could do a thorough job without being disturbed. The only problem was that it was awfully dark and I was scared of the dark. I told myself I couldn't have it both ways. I had to appreciate the convenience of a dark night, and if I tried, I could break that taboo I had about the dark. What better than a real live experience?

Arthur M. Mills, Jr.

CHAPTER 6

Later that night, with stealthy steps, I left my bedroom and went outside. I stood on the porch for a long while, steeling myself and looking up at the sky. I saw no stars so it must have been cloudy. I walked to the edge of our lot and shimmied up a tree. It was not *that* tree, but it had bark that I could get a good grip on. Among its many branches, there was a long, thick low hanging branch which stretched across to the empty lot next door. I sat on this branch, and then edged along it carefully to stare deep into the darkness of the lot. I told myself it didn't scare me because I had overcome my fear of the darkness.

Next, I willed myself to think about that forbidding hole. I thought about how silly it would be to actually find bones in that stupid hole and human bones at that. I thought about how stupid I was for being half persuaded by such a story. I was determined to find out, telling myself I needed the truth.

That the truth could be different than that dictated by my new-found confidence scared me. The next instant, I wasn't so sure. My loss of confidence was soon compounded when the tree branches began to ruffle. I looked up through the darkness and thought I saw a hanging body twitch somewhere deep, near the top of the tree. My pulse raced. I'd had enough of this adventure, but before I changed my mind and turned around, I tried to convince myself my long-standing fear of the dark was making me see things, fuelling my imagination. Shapes appeared different when there was not enough light to reflect off them. This observation may have been a small nugget of information I had retained from a science class, but I was glad for my rational line of thought.

In the course of the past years, I had played here often enough with my friends. I had run around the larger area to improve my skill at running marathons. This was just an empty lot, no matter the ghoulish stories. I hopped off the low branch, picked up a large stick, and headed into the lot.

It was not easy. I managed to reach the edge of the hole with my heart racing a mile a minute. I peeked in, but now, in the darkness, there was no way I could fathom the bottom of that five foot wide hole in the ground. My eyes started to adjust to the darkness. I turned round to look back at the tree I had used as a bridge. The hanging body was gone. *I did not know it then, but what I had seen was to be an omen.*

Right now, in the dark on the edge of the hole, I thought there was no way the city would just bury the body or bodies here. We have rules and a constitution. Something like this just didn't happen in America in the 1980's.

I pumped up my courage and walked around the rim of the hole. I had never come this close. Then I closed my eyes, held my breath, and jumped into the hole. It came to somewhere above my knees. The earth didn't stop. Ghosts didn't jump out. No one complained about being disturbed. My heart wasn't doing a flip-flop as it had at dinnertime.

I found my voice. "This story has to be fake, too," I said aloud. Then I listened, and heard nothing!

I felt liberated from fears of my own making. I didn't have to be afraid anymore. My friends may have accepted me as their leader, but now I would also get my family to look up to me. I would be known as Ray Mills instead of Richard's little brother. I had lessons to teach everyone from life, tell them how I had bravely disproved a nasty rumor. *Hadn't I?*

I was elated. I could tell everyone the truth, just as Dan had expanded on what he knew. Now they would know the whole thing was just a nasty rumor. I would no longer be nervous and have to stutter when I asked my friends and even my family about any incident I needed to find out more about. I would not be compelled to creep around in the dark to keep my investigation private, as I was doing now. Everybody would assume that I was methodical in my investigations. That I had disproved the lie for what it was.

Arthur M. Mills, Jr.

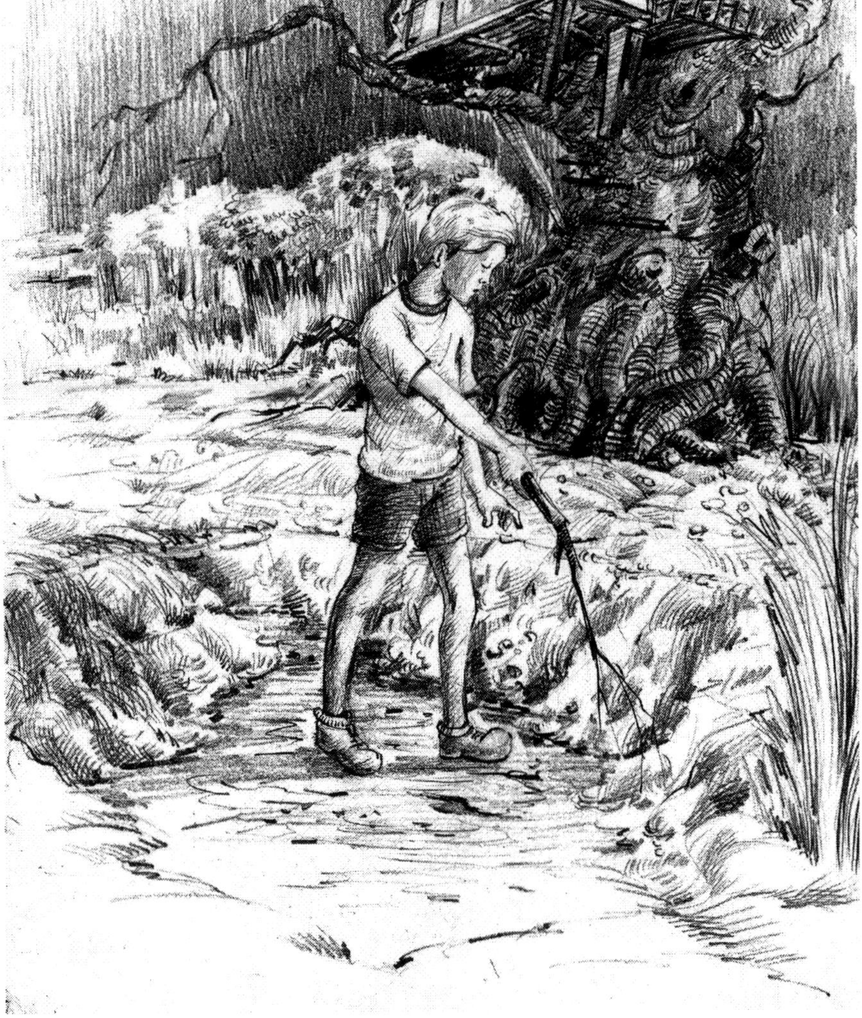

My mind raced on. Richard would not be the only one from my family to hold friends spellbound in the tree house, or on the school stage or in our church. I knew I could never do what Richard did, but I could impress them with my singular achievement. They would then hold me in some esteem. I could take on the world. I started to poke at the bottom of the hole with the stick. Nope, no ghosts.

I continued standing in that hole, my behavior towards any spirits became even more exaggerated. I called out to them. I dared them. "Show yourself! Where are you, burnt-out ghosts?" I asked without stuttering. I listened carefully for a response but none came. *I had made a huge mistake, but didn't know that at the time.*

I carried on, railing, "The story about you is bullshit!" Leaving the stick behind, I clambered out of the hole and walked straight back to the house, never once looking back.

By the time I walked into our bedroom, Richard had gone to bed and fallen asleep with the light on. I got into my pajamas and switched off the light. Just before I climbed into my bed I did a little jig. No one could have been watching, not Richard, at least. I said my prayers. Just before I fell asleep, the last thing I thought of was that I was the bravest eleven-year-old in the world.

Something disturbed me while I slept. All these years later I still remember the time on the digital clock showed 3:27 a.m. My brother Richard was talking in his sleep again and that might have been what woke me up. I couldn't hear what he said. He may have been practicing a story, or he could have been narrating what he was dreaming about. In any case, he was no longer sleeping his peaceful sleep as he had earlier in the night when I had gone to bed. His talk was too low for me to distinguish what he was saying. Richard did this about twice a week. He had nightmares sometimes. On those nights he would mumble, thrash and squirm around in bed but he would never wake up.

I was thirsty, so I got up and walked to the kitchen for some water. I kept to the middle of my path because I had gone back to not trusting the dark corners and sides where the floor joined with the wall. I was slightly ashamed of this, especially after that practice session earlier that night to help me ward off my fear of the dark. But here, safe at home, my old fear of the dark strangely enough came flooding back. I thought about switching on the kitchen light but left it alone because I didn't want to disturb my parents. Their bedroom door opened from the kitchen and they usually left it ajar. If they woke up, they'd ask dozens of questions I didn't want to answer.

I could see in the semi-dark now. There was enough light coming in from the kitchen window that faced the empty lot next door. I could hear the tree leaves rustling, the branches swaying. I stood still. What was that screechy-scratchy noise? Not Bloody Mary again! Dan had said she lived centuries ago in a faraway place across an ocean. I had proved his stories were all made up. But what *was* that dull screech? It took me a few minutes of listening and watching the shadow of the branches to realize a couple of branches were scraping the outside of the house along the boards and window screen. The noise was like long finger nails on a chalk board.

I had been told that I was tall for my age, but I had to stand on tiptoe to get a better view out the window. The great oak that housed our tree house was swaying madly, its branches twisting over each other in that half light. So was the tree I had climbed earlier that night to reach the empty lot. If trees had arms instead of branches, they were swaying to the rhythm of an unknown song. Both trees looked as if they were ready to uproot themselves and fly away like untidy magic carpets. I worried about our tree house, hoping it wouldn't be destroyed by all the shaking. The smaller trees and low bushes in the back were also quivering restlessly.

I hoped a storm wasn't coming. Lightning and thunder, particularly at night, made me burrow down deep into my bed with my sheet for comfort. When I was ten, a bad storm drove me into my parents' bedroom. I woke them up in the middle of the night, making myself the butt of family jokes for days after that.

I took a good look at the empty lot and thought of my experiment towards the truth and my activities around and in the hole some hours ago. That had been fun, in the end anyway. Why on earth had I been frightened of the hole for all those years after I heard Randy, Evan and Richard's story? I could not imagine. I should have checked a long time ago. Why did I have to build up courage to look towards it now? I held my breath and glanced straight at the hole.

Something moved.

I could put it down to still sleepy eyes, but were my eyes playing tricks on me again? I had to look away, rub them and look back at the hole in that semi-darkness. There it was again! A dark figure standing half in and half out of the hole. What could it be? I tried to match it to something, maybe a dog, large raccoon, or even the neighborhood skunk? My heart kept pace with my thoughts. No, a raccoon would have gotten lost in the three foot depth of the hole. Not even a dog could stand that high.

I backed off from the window and reminded myself how brave I was. Had I not carried out an investigation some hours ago? But that was earlier. It was really late at night now. My mad jumping up and down, the shouting and raving may have awakened something or somebody who was best left alone. I would have to find out for myself, investigate more thoroughly. I would have to go out to the back porch for a better view.

Slowly and hopefully noiselessly, I walked past my parent's bedroom to the door leading to the porch at the back. I swung the unlocked backdoor open. Leaving the porch lights off, I now had a better view than I had from the kitchen window. I could see both the backyards clearly now without having to peer through a high window, but at the corner of the porch I had to get up on my tiptoes for the best view of the back of the empty lot.

There it was again.

I can only describe what I saw as something close to being a young girl. From what little I could see, the girl was unlike any I had seen in real life. She seemed to be standing in the hole, had long unkempt hair nearly down to her waist and was facing away from me. The otherwise brisk breeze seemed to turn much warmer now.

I was again having trouble trying to breathe. My heart was about to pound its way out of my chest. Stray thoughts flitted across my head, I must be dreaming! This can't be real!

The figure started to move in a manner I had never seen before. It flayed its arms and placed long bony fingers on the outside, along the side of the hole. It seemed to be trying hard to hold onto the edge as it hauled itself out of the hole. It managed this after what seemed to be ages, while my mind told my heart to calm down. It crawled on all fours on the ground away from me towards the big oak with the tree house.

Arthur M. Mills, Jr.

The Empty Lot Next Door

It had taken the thing two minutes to crawl from the edge of the hole to the tree. There, it seemed to dig its nails and fingers into the trunk to pull itself upright. It partially managed this while still seeming to cling to the tree for support. I got the impression it had been a long time since the girl (if it was that) had stood on its own legs. I could hear a nasty gurgling sound from the figure. Was it trying to draw in air? I realized it was intent on getting onto the tree house.

Now I faced a worse problem-Duke. Duke is Evan's dog, a large fawn-colored boxer that if he stood on his hind legs, he would be taller than my oldest brother. Because of his size Duke is kept in the backyard of Evan's house that is on the other side of ours. Despite Duke's massive body size and his docked ears, Evan's pet was docile and friendly. But not now. Duke awoke and started to bark and howl franticly. He may have been disturbed by that choked gurgling noise, or else simply sensed something new. The girl-thing by the tree did not exactly turn her head around to look, but snapped her head back towards the sound of the barking dog.

If I drew an imaginary straight line, I was right in the middle between that figure and the dog. All this time I'd been mesmerized and motionless. Now I was more than terrified as the figure seemed to be looking straight at me, seeming to be as surprised as I had been when I first set eyes on it. Now it managed to turn its whole body around. Earlier, when Dan had mentioned her at the dinner table, I had thought of her as the little girl who had once lived next door. Now I felt repelled. Could ghosts and ghouls be true? I could see no color on her. I could only see that disheveled hair, half of which hung down over her face. I couldn't see her face. I could, however, barely make out the rest of her. She was not a skeleton. She was just dirty and patchy, covered in what could have been either tatters or long, dried grassy clods.

She was attempting to walk, with a stumbling, unsteady gait towards the fence between my backyard and the empty lot. She (if it was a girl once) was old enough, but seemed to be learning how to walk all over again. She would pick up and flop one foot in front, drag the other till the last second when she managed to pick that up and flop that down, in front.

Her course on all fours had taken less time. I wondered why she was trying to walk away from the tree now and could only conclude

Arthur M. Mills, Jr.

she wanted to get a better look—at me. But surely this 'thing' couldn't actually see me. My hopes faded as she got closer. My eyes! As I strained them, I felt as if they were going to pop out. I could not see her eyes, but when she reached the fence I sensed a piercing gaze aimed straight at me. The fence was only ten feet away.

I had not wanted a closer look but could now see her better. The wild, disheveled looking girl was about my age. I could still not make out the face or the color of her long hair or what she might be wearing.

Could this be the little girl whom I'd heard about? Was she the one who had died in the fire and was buried in the hole?"

She looked at me and shook her head up and down. Were my thoughts whispering into her ears? Could she hear me? Her frightful, hoarse laugh seemed like an apt reply.

I could not be dreaming because by now it was not just Evan's dog barking, but all the dogs in our neighborhood. They were barking loudly as dogs do, at an unknown intruder. The dogs' response made me think this was real. And that, in turn, made me realize I had to save myself. I must shake myself out of my frozen, horrified state. I jumped, turned and ran for the door. The laughing behind me got louder. She understood. She was mocking me.

In the morning I opened my eyes to a bright bedroom. My mother had just shaken me awake and gone back to her room to get ready for work. Richard was already up and halfway through getting dressed for school. My head reeled. I still had to know. I didn't stop to think before I asked Richard if he had seen or heard anything unusual last night. He gave me an offhand "no" and warned me he would tell Mom if I didn't get up right away. I thought of last night. No, it couldn't have happened. It was all a bad dream. How could I otherwise explain being on the back porch, then waking up in my own bed in my own bedroom?

I got up and went to school as I usually did and spent another normal day not paying much attention to my school work. I know I drove one of my teachers to distraction by refusing to understand the sums she had taken such pains to explain. She eventually gave up and rushed out of the classroom in a state.

All I thought about was my awful nightmare of the night before: the girl's disheveled, faceless staring look; her crablike crawl to the tree; her attempt to stand and walk; her apparent ability to hear the frantic neighborhood dogs; and worst of all, that awful stare through which she seemed to be able to fathom my thoughts.

Would I ever feel as safe as I had before last night? Would I feel as I had before, knowing or dreaming about the hideous horror that could emerge from that hole in the empty lot?

My troubled thoughts swirled over and over in my head right through school. I tried to console myself that it was just a dream, the kind Richard had probably been putting up with for ages. This was no good, because of my clear memory of that dream. So my inner turmoil went on all day, as did the fact that I had proven that Bloody Mary was a fake. What if challenging any bodies in the hole last night had not been a good way to prove anything, even though nothing had happened at the time?

After school Richard said he was going to hold a magic show at the tree house. Most of the neighborhood kids showed up to watch Richard perform. Richard wanted to prepare things for his show and got to the tree house first. All of us were crowding around, avoiding the hole but looking for vantage areas on the ground so as to get the best view for Richard's show. Mark and I walked past the hole. I could not stop myself from glancing in. I need not have worried because I didn't notice anything unusual. It had to have been a dream. I needed the reassurance now and gave in to it. I quickly joined the others, sat down and watched my brother's amazing show.

Adding a special movement to entertain us, he moved like a robot and acted like a mime all-in-one. We were thrilled and were sure he was better than the best TV artist. Richard even raised a curtain to shield himself from the audience. In the next split second the curtain fell and Richard was gone. That was his favorite trick and ours. The kids yelled and clapped.

"How did he do that?" Nolan yelled.

I was still smarting from Richard's lack of response in the morning when I had tried to talk to him. I knew the secret of Richard's homemade stage and could give it away.

"Look, Nolan! We made an escape hatch. He opens it when the curtain is hiding him. When he's off the stage, he pulls this string and the curtain falls. It's really simple."

"Stop ruining it for everyone," Richard shouted at me from inside his hiding area.

Arthur M. Mills, Jr.

I was merciless now. "Here's Richard's hiding area." As I pointed, I slowed down. I had just noticed what appeared to be long blond hair stuck to the tree. I stepped closer and noticed claw marks that looked as if someone's claws had raked the tree bark. I pulled the hair away from the tree and looked at it up close. It was human hair. My hair was blond but short. Hair this long could only mean one thing—a girl. Evan's sister had medium length blonde hair, but she avoided the places where we played. Besides, one of our rules was that girls were not allowed in or near our tree house. So whose hair could this be? It quickly dawned on me that while I'd been telling myself it was just a bad dream last night, here was evidence it was real. The claw marks on the bark were real, too.

I felt the color drain from my face. The girl who died in what was now an empty lot had climbed out of her hole, crawled to the tree and then stumbled towards me! I should not have made that visit to her resting place last night. She had heard me and it must have disturbed and offended her. I had called out to a ghost to show itself. She had done just that. I should not have called her a burnt-out ghost. I deeply regretted it, but too late now.

Arthur M. Mills, Jr.

CHAPTER 7

Andre lived in a house up the street on Ben Howell Drive. He fitted in between my brothers Richard and Felix in age. I didn't know of anyone else in the same grade at Mollie Dawson Elementary, but I did know he was in our school. Andre sometimes walked to school with us and considered himself a friend. But most of the time he would roll to school on a skateboard that belonged to his cousin. That meant he had to take the long way around. It also meant he had to share the road with other traffic. My group of friends didn't know him well, which was fine with us. We were happy to leave Andre to his own ways. He seemed happy enough in the house he lived in with his cousin Edwin. Dan and Felix spent a lot of time in Edwin's house, mostly in the garage. They practiced their music there and talked of getting a band together. We could hear the Pink Floyd type of music wafting across from Edwin's garage and hoped the people in the houses between Edwin's and ours wouldn't complain about the noise of the music, as they did about our games. Edwin, Dan and Felix spent a lot of time together, even though Edwin didn't much resemble Dan and Felix. He wasn't much like Andre, either, as I was to find out later.

Andre rarely came over to our house, which was fine with me because my friends would melt away if Andre ever came over to the empty lot to play with us. He was easily one of the most aggressive fourteen-year-olds in our neighborhood and was known to play mean. He *had* to be in control of whatever was going on, even if it was just a game. He took play seriously and thought he should be the boss every time. Nobody liked to play with him.

After my horrible nightmare, I would keep glancing at the hole in the ground next door whenever we were outdoors at the back, but had not noticed anything unusual during the daytime. I kept thinking back to that long blonde hair stuck in the rough tree bark and the mark of nails or talons on the bark. Those scratch marks on the tree were still there to see for anyone who looked in that direction. The others may have thought of them as cats' claw marks.

One afternoon after school Richard and I were playing in our backyard. He and I had managed to play without our usual arguments, and things were going smoothly. Any time now, one or more of our friends would join us, I hoped. If a lot of them came, I knew Richard would want to get up in the tree house and entertain us.

But it was Andre who sauntered over. He definitely had an attitude, and just now his attitude seemed to put him in charge of the place. He looked like he owned our backyard. He looked mean. Richard and I didn't really want to play with him, but we could not and did not want to just tell him to go home. We reckoned that anything of the sort was likely to set him off and he'd want to start a fight right away.

Andre told us he wanted to play his kind of games and started off asking if we wanted to play with cars. Both Richard and I said no. Most of the imitation Hot Wheel cars that I got years ago have long broken apart.

But Andre didn't listen. His eyes lit up. He dug into his pockets and came up with two of the most beautiful speedy wooden cars I'd ever seen. One was a toy race car, the other a motorcycle carved in detail. I thought they looked like someone had bought them some time ago and kept them really well, unlike the toy cars I had.

"Where did you get these?" Richard asked in amazement.

Andre gave us a sly smile. "Let's say I found them. Or that someone found them a long time ago and gave them to me."

Andre started to play, rolling his tongue to make a loud "Rrrrrr" sound, running the car and motorcycle on the steps leading to the back porch. But after a couple of minutes it became clear it was going to be Andre's turn every time. All Richard and I would be allowed to do was stand and watch.

We tried gentle persuasion on Andre, showing an interest in where he got the cars. Had someone really given them to him? Dan and Felix had told us long ago that Andre's parents didn't live in Austin.

Arthur M. Mills, Jr.

His grandparents, aunt and uncle had taken him in, and that was why Andre lived in the same house as his cousin Edwin. Andre's relatives were good souls and kind people, but having to live away from his parents could have turned Andre into the kind of fourteen-year-old that he was.

Andre glanced at us from time to time. He looked happy now. "You and your little friends think you have everything, don't you?" he said. "Well, my Ma and Pa may not be here and may not be as well off as yours, but I get nice things once in a while."

Richard and I felt ashamed. I had come to believe we were the least well-off as anybody and had begun to feel sorry for myself. But here was Andre with his rough ways. He had managed all right without his parents, although I suspected his good toys may have been few and far-between.

We stopped asking Andre about these particular toys and thought about him, instead. We felt that his situation might be a little awkward. We must have looked forlorn, because Andre decided it was time to give us a little story of his own.

"It's all right, guys. It's just that these cars are a special find and I can't let anyone play with them."

This last remark didn't make matters any better for us. I was dying to get my hands on Andre's toys.

He went on to explain that an older friend of his who had since graduated from Mollie Dawson used to play with a girl who lived in the house that used to stand next door to us. By now it was common knowledge about the house burning down. The girl had lent Andre's friend some of her toys which the friend kept when the fire broke out. Since Andre's friend had not been able to return the borrowed toys, he had given these two to Andre as a keepsake. Andre was pleased to have them. "I can get anyone to part with anything," he bragged.

We could see Andre was going back to being the Andre we knew and feared.

To prove his point, Andre laughed. Through the sound I heard something else. It was unmistakable. What I heard was a slow gurgle from the direction of the hole in the ground. My blood froze. I wanted to tell Andre to shut up and stop bragging about his toys but couldn't get the words out. I then heard a long drawn-out breath from the same direction.

Sheer black fright swept through me. Andre could pride himself on doing what he wanted, but as for me, I was grateful I hadn't even touched those toys that belonged to the girl who lived next door. I thought of her differently now. Before that awful night she was just another boring little girl. Now she was a fearful apparition. What if she hadn't liked all of us handling her toys? What if she had not liked Andre's claim to ownership of her toy cars? He had been brash and loud, like he always was, and she could easily have been offended.

I had fallen into the habit of clenching my fist and steeling myself for any eventuality before I glanced at the hole. I did this now, and to my surprise noticed that Richard was casting furtive looks in the same direction. Both of us took a long hard look at the trophy tree as well. Now everything seemed normal except for a small increase in the temperature.

Andre had made it clear he wasn't interested in whatever baby game we'd been playing. He was a boy with a great many ideas. Now he was asking if we wanted to play hide and seek. Having played this game with him before, we both said no, knowing if we played, Andre would either cheat or bend the rules in his own favor.

But Andre insisted, so we began to play hide and seek. Our hearts were not in the game. We did not play well—just went through the motions without enthusiasm. I told myself I must be tired. Not only that, now that Andre was here, our friends wouldn't come around. I could only hope Mom would come home early from work and call Richard and me in for dinner.

We continued to play an unenthusiastic game of hide and seek in the two backyards, as we always did—the backyard of our house and the one next door. I owned up to myself that I was distracted, but in any case, Andre won every time. He kind of enjoyed it but grew suspicious, especially when he hid in the hole in the empty lot and neither Richard nor I made any attempt to find him. Of course, we could see Andre but pretended not to. I wasn't about to go anywhere near that hole, and I guessed Richard felt the same.

Finally Andre climbed out seething. "Why didn't you come looking for me?" he raged. "What does it matter if they couldn't find a place for that girl in the cemetery and might have put her in there? She isn't there now, is she? That's what you believe right? You believe a girl is buried in there. Ya don't know anything. I know the truth." *What is the truth?*

Arthur M. Mills, Jr.

I felt nervous and awful all over again. If she had heard my thoughts she could very well hear him shout. She could also have heard him brag about her toys. At any moment she might pop out to look for him. The thought cheered me up a bit, but not much. Right now Richard and I had to deal with the hard realities of having the bully come visit us.

Andre finally figured out we didn't really want to play with him. As expected, he got so mad he went up to Richard and hit him in the face. "You don't want to play? Do you want to fight?" he yelled.

Richard tried to calm him down but without success. "I don't want to fight," he said, but Andre couldn't be appeased. He hit Richard again and pushed him. My brother just stood there trying to be uninvolved. He tried to be stoic. He did not even make an attempt to block Andre's blows. I had never noticed this about Richard before, but from this point forward I knew the fight had gone out of him. He had no desire to fight back.

Andre didn't relent and kept at it for about ten minutes. Richard looked more and more resigned, but he refused to be drawn into any sort of retaliation. Even Andre was surprised at Richard's refusal although he carried on for as long as he could. I hoped that at some point he would realize he was hitting a neighborhood friend. Finally he gave in and accepted Richard's passive stance. Without another word he walked off, finally leaving us to ourselves.

Richard went into the house and into his room. He seemed to be brooding, reasoning and thinking something through. When I finally went in, I could hear him talk in a low voice. It reminded me of his sleep talking, the same low rumble. I looked around and decided Richard must be talking to himself. Surely he was because there was no one else around.

That night, except for me, no one in our family noticed Richard's bruises. They were all busy with themselves. By now I knew our older brothers were into all sorts of substances. I knew this because of the counseling talks in school about what was good for us and what was bad. I had made it my business to find out about drug habits and their signs and symptoms.

Richard might try to protect himself from Felix and Dan, but he didn't really have any idea how to stop the bullies at home and among our friends. He had become too passive to be able to stop fights, as he had been just now with Andre. What he did know was that he could still bully me. I had no one to turn to. My father included me when he watched TV but had his own self-imposed image to maintain. Our mother spoke little and was lost in her own world. I didn't know how to do anything about the terrors Richard faced, as well as my own.

That night Richard skipped dinner. He made out that he was working on something and didn't come out of our room until the next morning when it was time to go to school. He avoided company and walked to school on his own, as was his habit.

CHAPTER 8

The next day, Richard and I got ready for school as usual while Dan and Felix got ready to make trouble as usual. Richard looked awful. He had noticeable bruises on his face, but apparently Mom hadn't noticed when she came in to wake us up for school. No one spoke a word about it. No one, neither Mom nor our older brothers, asked him how they got there or showed any concern. Richard left for school. I had considered running to school on the route the cars took, but I saw Mark waiting for me and joined him to walk to school instead.

My day passed without a hitch. I gave little thought to Richard's problems. I figured both of us would somehow find a good way to handle ourselves when and if Andre came calling again. Maybe I could just run. It exasperated me to think Richard would probably not run. What was wrong with him?

My father was already home when Richard and I arrived. He had his serious face on when he asked Richard and me to sit down. He had something to say to us.

At first both Richard and I thought we might be in trouble and through no fault of our own, as usual. Had Andre complained about us? If so, that was totally unfair. Maybe one of the neighbors had complained, but that didn't seem possible because we had done nothing wrong. Even so, I suppose both of us were getting a little worked up.

"Are we in trouble?" Richard asked.

"No" our father said. "Your friend Andre was killed this morning."

We both gasped and looked at each other in horror. Finally I managed to ask, "H-how did it h-happen?"

"Andre was riding his skateboard to school when a Jeep sped up Cumberland Drive and hit him. He died instantly. It was a hit and run driver. The police are still looking." My father sadly shook his head. "He'd been warned. It isn't safe riding a skateboard on a busy street like that."

So Andre was dead! Richard and I spent the evening in a kind of numb daze. Later that night we talked before we fell asleep. Our father had been as shocked as we had been about Andre's death, but our ill-feeling towards Andre the previous day somehow made us feel worse. We could mostly remember how mean he was and how much we didn't like him. But yesterday Andre had hinted about his vulnerabilities and how he felt different from his cousins. I reckoned that boys like Andre felt things more deeply than they let on. Here was something only Richard and I would know. Andre had exposed his soft side. It was something Richard and I had been allowed to guess despite what came later when he beat up on Richard.

We discussed how Andre was being raised with his cousins here in South Austin. Even Felix and Dan had talked about the way Andre had to live, far away from parents. Yesterday he had mentioned how he had learned to manage the little things in life. We wondered what it was like for a boy growing up without his parents. It made us feel guilty and bad in a complicated sort of way.

My father indicated it would be a good idea for us to go and pay our respects to Edwin because he was more or less Andre's father figure. We said we would.

Because I worried about Richard, I had things to ask but didn't know how to ask them. I knew he had been tormented beyond the bruises left for everyone to see. He had sought something . . . or someone, but I simply didn't have the words to ask Richard exactly what was on his mind.

Our talk died down as we slipped in and out of sleep. We were ready for a good night's slumber. *But at least for me, that was not to be.*

Both of us thought we heard a faint knock on our outer door that led to the front porch. Richard's eyes widened. I jumped up to a sitting position. We stared at each other, wondering who it was at the door and which one of us was going to answer it.

Arthur M. Mills, Jr.

Andre had died unexpectedly. I had seen the messed up creature that had climbed out of the hole in the empty lot and was frightfully scared. I told Richard that since he was closest to the other front door he should answer it. He looked out the window that overlooked the front porch to see who had knocked but said he couldn't see anyone. So he stayed in bed.

After another minute or so we heard the knocking for a second time, only this time it was louder. I told Richard again he should be the one to answer the door. This time he found his nerve and got up to answer. He turned on the light and opened the door, but nobody was there. We both looked at each other. We were partly still scared, partly relieved. He closed the door, turned the lights off and went back to bed. He fell asleep right away without bothering about his sheet.

I couldn't fall asleep. Instead, I was lying there wide awake thinking about Andre, Richard, and me when I heard the knock on the door again. "Richard!" I whispered. But either he was asleep or he preferred to keep quiet.

"Richard!" I tried to say his name louder this time, but my throat seemed to have dried up. I tried to sit up but found I couldn't move. Then I saw the front door to our room off the front porch was slowly opening. I stared as it swung open all the way. At first I could only sense the extra warmth on a warm spring night. And then I saw it for the second time in my life.

I could have died. It was the thing I had christened Candle Face, the horrific child I had seen climb out of the hole next door. It was bad enough I had to see her across our yard late at night, but this was a hundred times worse, having her here, inside our house and into our bedroom. *I was going to be proved wrong on this matter.*

I tried to shout but could get no sound out of my throat. She knew what she was doing and she knew how I felt. She approached my bed and knelt in front of me. I tried to close my eyes but couldn't. There was not a thing I could will myself to do. I was not in control of myself. I had been dazed before but now I was paralyzed with fear.

The light from the window closest to my bed shone from behind her. It highlighted a silhouette. I couldn't see her face and that was just as well. I was thankful for small mercies. Since that porch door opened, I had been aware of a smell, the kind that comes from rotting, burning flesh. I recognized it because Mom had once tried to cook some fish, then realized the fish had been stored for too long.

Closer to me, the stench grew a lot stronger. Her face remained a blur, the light shining behind her bouncing off her long dead dreadlocks. Every time I dared to look in her direction, all that I could make out was a blurred face which looked like it was made up of dripping candle wax. I told myself again that if I was forced to see her in silhouette, it was for the better.

I shuddered at the thought of a child with hardly any eyes, nose, lips or ears. I tried to still my mind when I realized the silhouetted shape was trying to show or tell me something. She had drawn in some air. What I heard now was that choking gurgle. I hated it. I wished I could do something to avoid hearing it. She seemed to be able to read my thoughts again, so I had been right about that as well.

She reached to the floor for one of my imitation Hot Wheels cars and one of my wooden dolls and placed them on my bed. I was puzzled. I didn't want to play with her. In any case, I would not want to play with something like her. Again I was experiencing a mixture of repulsion and compassion towards her. I had not meant to be rude, if play was what she had in mind. I just wanted her to go.

But what was this? She placed the car in her right hand and rolled it towards the wooden doll. Candle Face made a sound of a car screeching as she controlled the speed as it braked, "Rrrrrrrrrrrrrr" followed by the sound of a crash as the toy car hit the wooden doll. She laughed her hoarse, gurgling laugh. Her message finally dawned on me. She had heard us—Richard and me—as we watched Andre play with the toys which used to be hers. She must have heard us, and Andre in particular, the day before.

She knew those cars were hers. She had recognized her toys and had heard Andre bragging. I remembered Andre's laugh and Candle Face's response from her place of rest. Andre had made more than one mistake. He, like me, had compounded it by jumping on her resting place out back.

Candle Face had enacted Andre's death with my toys on my bed. Something awful clicked in my mind. She had taken care of Andre. Was I, too, going to die? So this was what Candle Face wanted to talk about. I wanted to turn over, wish her away, but she chose this time to lean over to my ear. I was going to hear her talk for the very first time.

Arthur M. Mills, Jr.

"Watch yourself, you could be next." Her breath burnt my ear. Her voice sounded like she was a two pack a day chain smoker. I wanted to shut my eyes and keep them tightly closed but could not.

I could watch my back, but I would never know when she would choose to strike next. Was there more to what Candle Face was trying to tell me? Or was I again getting tied up in knots of my own making? I could only watch my back by thinking ahead. Did Candle Face know Richard and I had not liked Andre? Even if she did, she had to have known about that tiny chink in his personality that we had been allowed to see. She should have known we would not wish such a death on Andre. At least I wouldn't, but Richard . . . ?

He had refused to retaliate, but that didn't mean he forgave Andre for those bruises on his face. In fact, how could he forgive such bullying? Horrible thoughts began to flood my consciousness. Whom had Richard been talking to that night? Candle Face might be able to read his thoughts as she had mine. Richard *must* have harbored tremendous ill-feeling towards Andre for what he had done. Was Candle Face responsible for Andre's death, and how had she brought it about if she was? *Was Richard somehow involved?*

Candle Face had just worked a racing jeep out from under my covers. She placed it on my bed with my toy car and wooden doll. What was its significance? Who *had* been behind the wheel of that jeep?

From her presence here tonight and what she had shown me, I was left to deduce that Candle Face had been involved in Andre's death. From what she was saying, I knew she was using this horrific fact to threaten me.

Richard shifted slightly in his sleep. I knew he would not wake up and I was annoyed. How could Richard sleep while Candle Face did this to me? Was he simply staying out of a more-than-sticky situation because I had never been able to back him up? Or because I always kept quiet when he punched me?

I had major problems I would give anything to get away from. I had made a mistake but was paying more than my fair share for it. If anyone had asked me, all I wanted was to walk away from Candle Face. Either that or I would like her to go away in whatever fashion she chose. The other thing I would like was for me and everyone in my family, Richard included, to look at each other—really *see* each other—and talk.

The next thing I knew, light streamed through the windows and my mother was shouting it was time to get up. Richard was already up and ready to go to school. I quickly decided I wasn't going to make the same mistake as the time I asked Richard for a hint as to whether he knew about Candle Face. I wasn't that naïve now. As I scrambled to get out of bed, two objects fell from my bed. A melted blob that was once my toy car and the other was a chard wooden doll.

I felt sick at this sight of my once-favorite toys. But in my busy family, it was only I who was affected, *I thought.*

CHAPTER 9

Richard usually walked to school alone, hands in pockets and head down, thinking deeply about his world. I, on the other hand, ran on my own, caught a ride with Evan's parents, or walked to school with Mark. Regardless of how we got there, the only thing we all had in common was that anyone who didn't take the long road would walk through a creek. This involved crossing a small creek using a small bridge and following a narrow dirt path till we came out through the woods onto a regular street. School was then some five minutes away. We simply thought about our picturesque short cut as 'the creek.' *I am told that no one uses that path any more.*

The path by the side of the creek was about a hundred meters long, but the creek itself was known to be rather dangerous. All the same, it was a short cut to school, one we couldn't do without most of the time. After we crossed the bridge, the approach bordering the creek was narrow and high. This was the worst part for anyone who missed their step on the narrow path which was wide enough for just one person. If they did, they would likely plummet down. The creek had a steep bank on its left side. If anyone fell, they would slide down this bank and into the knee deep water of the creek. There was no guarantee that whoever fell would fall feet first. I fell down one day when I had just started kindergarten. I had fallen on my backside and cried noisily. Richard had to walk me back home and get me into dry clothes. We ultimately both got to school late and received pink slips.

Even Randy had fallen once. He landed on his right shoulder, dislocated it, and had to wear an awful harness for a couple of weeks.

We greatly admired his get-up but were doubly careful about that approach to the creek after that.

The approach path and its dangers lasted but a short distance. After another ten meters or so the path got safer. Now it was wider and on level with the water. At this point I often stopped to taste the water, which was clean, clear and cool. Mark's mother had cautioned him against drinking water from the creek, though. She thought it could be polluted and unfit for drinking. This safe walking zone carried on for another sixty meters. After that, the path proceeded to wind through a wooded area and up a hill. We had to turn right onto a tarred road before it eventually led to a dead-end.

Meanwhile, I had decided to stop running on my own to school. It would be better if I had company. Candle Face's warning about watching me had been ringing in my ears ever since that dreadful night. But as the days passed, I grew more confident. She would not do anything . . . . would she? No one deserved what had happened to Andre. If only my doubts about Richard hadn't lingered, if only I knew what Candle Face herself wanted. If only I could be free of my own fears.

I went back to walking with Mark every day, making sure Richard was not too far away. One day he was walking alone as usual. However, we all got to the creek at the same time and noticed another group of children our age from a nearby neighborhood. They had also just reached the creek. This was a rare occasion.

The obvious leader of this group was a large boy name Carlos. The other boys encircled him in the manner of bodyguards. Carlos saw Richard and whispered something to his buddies. These other boys snickered. I was worried because Carlos was a troublemaker and a bully. I suspected he would probably be up to something.

It wasn't too late to back out of this route. We had only just reached the bridge, and I wanted to get my gut feeling about Carlos across to Richard. The creek would be even more dangerous if Carlos were to start a confrontation. Deciding not to care if somebody called me scaredy cat or something worse, I went over to Richard and began in a rush, "W-we should go the l-long way to s-s-school. I think they're going to start some t-trouble."

But as with Andre, Richard wanted to yield to the doom that awaited him. "Jesus will protect us," he replied. He walked off the bridge and headed down the narrow dirt path along the steep bank. I followed him, upset with myself for not having run as soon as I saw Carlos and his gang. Had I done that, Mark and Richard would have been sure to follow. I had just been too preoccupied with that approach path and the dangers that lurked along it. Now the danger posed by Carlos loomed even larger.

I was also annoyed with Richard for what I could now see was close to a suicidal attempt.

Right now I had no option but to hang around and hope the worst wouldn't happen. Mark understood my concerns as the two of us walked slightly behind Richard. We carried on like this through the safe part of the creek. As we approached the last part, Carlos made his move. He began to tease Richard about a girl in school named Maria. She was in the same class as Richard, and I knew he really liked her. He had, however, been a bit of an ass in the way he made his feelings known to her. Maria was a nice girl who was not ready to go out with Richard. She had been sensible. Ultimately Maria had politely but firmly rejected him.

Carlos brought all this up. He dramatized Richard's part in the one-sided romance and made Richard out to be a love-crossed idiot. He also acted Maria's part along the path and made her out to be a giddy teenager. It was the kind of drama Richard excelled in without the silly girl parts. Mark and I knew Richard could have done this a million times better without being half as obnoxious as Carlos. I made a mental note of suggesting it to Richard. Meanwhile, he had to save himself, although at the moment he seemed to be beyond all cares. He was looking steadily at Carlos as if he had nothing to worry about.

Richard made a quick glance towards the sky. I also made a quick glance too to see what he was looking at.

I twisted my neck around so I could look straight up at whatever image was fixed in Richard's eye. I could see the sky, or rather not see it. It was blotted out by formations of low lying, heavy grey clouds, though it was not raining. The cloud formations were joining and merging, then spreading out again and eerily changing at great speed.

Suddenly my insides were knotting with fear. I thought I could see a semi-human face in the largest cloud. It had gaps for sly eyes, nostrils and a laughing, mocking mouth. The wisps streaming away behind it resembled long, flying hair. It stayed that way for about 30 seconds. No one seemed to notice the cloud formation.

Was Candle Face watching us? And was she laughing at our circumstances? Her hoarse smokers' voice still rang in my head, "Watch yourself, you could be next."

Arthur M. Mills, Jr.

I wanted to shout back at that leering cloud shape above me, "Your warning was for me, Candle Face." But it turned out to be Richard who got hurt. Not a word emerged from my lips. The clouds shifted. Now no face laughed at us from above. Even so, I remained frozen with fear, just like when Candle Face visited me on the night Andre died. I began to feel angry. If that hole was Candle Face's resting place, why was she plaguing us in this way? She had grown more powerful since Andre's death. She had somehow wanted to show herself outside, during the day. And she had managed it. She could scare me. I wanted to reassure Richard, tell him this particular cloud formation had no use for him. But how would I know whether I was getting through to him?

Meanwhile, all the kids with Carlos laughed throughout the mini-drama. Mark and I could do nothing except stand there and scowl. I knew my brother was being humiliated, but now things got worse. Carlos suddenly turned and pushed Richard. Richard flew a couple of feet backwards and fell heavily where the path was steep. He sprang up but waited too long on his feet. He was a sitting duck. Carlos pushed him and he fell again. I knew from the start Richard didn't want to fight.

My mind flew back to the afternoon when I had seen Richard in the same situation, when he had refused to fight with Andre. I could see that Andre's one-sided fight earlier and his death the very next day had unnerved my brother. He would never be able to retaliate now.

Carlos pushed Richard again. He tried to keep his balance but the impact of the blow caused him to fall heavily. Carlos found Richard's attempt at holding his ground immensely funny and kept laughing shrilly. It seemed like a charade or a slow dance to me, the way Carlos would hit and push, Richard would topple over, get up and dust himself down. He was refusing to acknowledge Carlos' strength. By now, Carlos sensed an easy victory was within his reach. He punched Richard hard on his lower lip. Again he fell. This last punch had cut him badly and blood began to flow. This time Richard couldn't get up.

While my brother lay on the ground, Carlos and the boys walked off, still shouting taunts. I went up to him, wanting to help him get back on his feet, but he just lay there. Nor did he respond when I told him I would help him get to school. I pleaded with him, reminding him Mark was with us and the three of us could manage to get there safely. Still Richard didn't move. I tried to encourage him, saying he had managed to withstand Carlos' fists some half a dozen times and had got up each time.

Mark and I stayed with Richard for over twenty minutes trying to get across to him that there was no one around anymore to hurt him. We kept pleading with Richard to get up. He did not. A jolt of lightning lit the sky, followed by an ear-splitting crackle of thunder. I longed for my bed at home, but instead here we were totally out in the open. I had heard what could happen when lightning struck trees and living beings. We could be charred to near-nothingness in a matter of seconds! Slender trees surrounded us. Could Candle Face wish death on me from above?

Large, warm drops of rain started to pelt us. I couldn't wait for Richard any longer. The threat to me, maybe to us, had been assembled in the sky but was now falling away. Those clouds had portrayed a being I didn't want to know about. The message had been directed to me, but ultimately it had directly affected Richard. The clouds were constantly shifting and disintegrating. From now on I would ignore any further messages in the clouds.

There was also the matter of being late for school. Mark and I shouted a last-minute reassurance to Richard and ran as fast as we could to Mollie Dawson Elementary School. I hoped Richard would follow us in a few minutes, but he didn't. In fact, I didn't see him all that day.

The next time I saw Richard was at the dinner table that night. He and I didn't speak a word about what had happened. Just the same, I knew Richard had looked hard at that face in the clouds. Mom must have noticed Richard's face and the fresh cut. She seemed detached, as on most days and didn't ask how Richard could have got those fresh bruises and that gash on his face. Nor did our father or brothers.

CHAPTER 10

Most Saturday mornings Richard and I were left alone because our parents would both leave for work at their engraving studios. They worked for different establishments but did similar work. Our brothers would spend Saturdays up the street at their favorite haunts: their girlfriends' and friends' houses. They had informed us their music group, which was supposed to rival the best of '60s music, was coming along nicely in Edwin's garage.

One Saturday morning Richard and I were watching TV when Dan and Felix came in. I noticed each had a loaf of bread in a plastic bag and a can of spray paint. With Felix and Dan that could only mean one thing: a day when they would get high on paint. 'Sniffin' paint they called it, and that meant trouble for us. I had seen them do this before: remove the bread, and then empty the contents of the entire paint can into the polythene wrappers. They made sure the cans of paint were really empty by holding the spray nozzle down till there was no more. Next, they needed a place to hide. Our house was ideal because it had a high foundation that allowed easy access underneath. The three foot gap was a lot more than the foot or so in the other homes they frequented and where they would not have got permission anyway. The height was perfect for my brothers. They could easily crawl under the house and stay there unnoticed till they were done. In other words, until they had finished sniffing the entire contents of the can of paint.

When they entered the house this particular Saturday, they didn't bother to hide their spray paint. The coast was clear, and they were sure they could safely do what they wanted. Our parents were not expected home all day. My brothers laughed as they talked about all this and went into the kitchen to get the bread out and use the bread wrapper for what they considered a more useful activity. Finally they went out the kitchen door to their special place under the house. Their best spot for sniffing paint was just a few feet into the entrance but under the floor boards. This Saturday they remained in the three foot gap long enough for me to practically forget what was going on under the floor. But Richard was uneasy. He suspected that in the more than two hours they'd been there they were doing something more than sniffing paint. He seemed to worry about who else might join them and what more trouble might result. I, however, could see no point in worrying. Dan and Felix did as they pleased. Maybe they slept. Maybe they passed out down there in their hiding place.

Eventually Dan and Felix came back inside, the telltale signs of their habit all over them. Both had black spray paint covering their mouths and noses. These were the parts of their faces they had clamped inside the plastic bag while they sniffed paint. To me they looked like alien beings on a high or clowns in the circus that had come to Austin the year before. We didn't dare tell them this, though. They took themselves and their pastimes seriously and didn't want their supposedly clueless little brothers telling them what they looked like.

They didn't care either about what they said to each other. After they stumbled into the living room, they regarded us with evil smiles spreading across their faces. Felix said to Dan, "She said I could take on the short one, and that I should leave the wavy blonde haired baby for her."

From past experience we knew what to expect when they went on one of their paint highs, so we stood up, ready to run. In a crazy Dan-and-Felix way, our fear made them feel even better. Felix's exchange with Dan could only mean that somehow things would be worse for us. Sure enough, Felix made a bee-line for Richard. Since he was both bigger and taller, Richard found it impossible to escape. He fell to the floor and automatically curled up in the fetal position, expecting the worst.

Richard and I knew this was going to be a lot worse than the fights with Andre and Carlos. Richard had chosen not to fight back both times. Now he couldn't hit back even if he had the slightest wish to do so. Nor were Dan and Felix going to limit themselves to blows on the face or a punch in the stomach, as Andre and Carlos had done. This was going to be a one-sided beating again, only a lot worse.

The hitting began. At first Felix restricted his blows to Richard's legs, then his arms, all the while seeming to revel in Richard's squeals of pain. In the meanwhile, I had to be wary of my other brother. Seeing Dan coming towards me, I sat down on the couch and stuck out my feet to kick him if he came too close. Then, oddly enough, when Dan saw me getting ready to defend myself, he stopped and watched Felix beat on Richard instead. *Why did Dan stop? Did he stop because I was prepared to defend myself?*

When Felix finally quit beating on Richard, the two of them went off to their bedroom laughing wildly. I hated them both for relishing what they had done to us, both now and in the past. I especially hated Felix for what he had just done to Richard, telling myself Dan wasn't as bad. I didn't know what to do to help Richard. From what I had seen and heard, he could have done with medical attention.

Richard managed to crawl to the couch and sit down. His legs were covered in fresh bruises. He obviously had no words for what he had just endured. We turned to face the TV and sat there like puppets, behaving as though nothing had happened. There was nothing else Richard and I could do. I could see Richard was in a state of shock.

What we didn't know was that the next round from Dan and Felix was going to be still worse. Their high-pitched laughter when they went off to their bedroom was only partly because of a job well done. *In reflection, some of their laughter was on account of what they were going to do next. Something that Richard and I did not have the slightest notion about.*

Just half an hour later when Dan and Felix returned to the living room, my instincts told me if we had not been able to run earlier we should run now.

Felix held something behind his back. Richard and I knew something was up. Too late we realized Felix was still high and would still try to draw pleasure out of inflicting pain on a brother less able to defend himself. We were properly scared this time and tried to think ahead to how much worse it could get. What other tortures could he be planning to try on us?

Felix faced Richard and whipped out his secret weapon: a paper airplane. Richard and I first flinched and then looked at each other relieved.

Was that all? Just a bit of paper? Maybe his paint high had fuddled him. Felix couldn't even attack a baby mouse with that paper airplane!

But Felix was getting busy with his new weapon. He drew his arm back, pointed the paper airplane at Richard and threw it. Even though he aimed with deadly accuracy, we thought Richard could easily avoid a paper airplane with a pointy nose. He pulled his feet off the floor and put his head between his legs as he sat on the couch in front of the TV. He wasn't required to fight back, just block this seemingly harmless paper airplane from zeroing in on him. Even so, it made its mark on the outside of Richard's thigh.

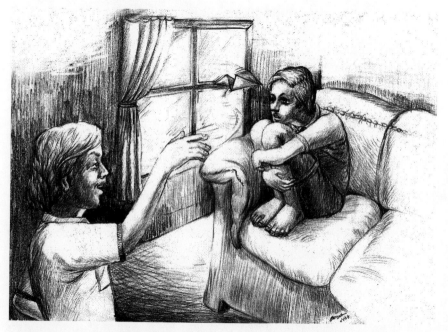

I was puzzled when Richard screamed in pain. Dan and Felix also let out a long-drawn scream. Their screams were screams of delight. Richard knew what had just happened and so did Dan and Felix. I was the only one who couldn't figure it out.

Felix lunged forward to retrieve the paper airplane. Richard shrank back with his knees drawn up. I wondered why Felix had to pluck it out. I could see a steady flow of blood trickling down Richard's leg from the spot where it had made its mark. Felix jumped up and down like someone whose experiment had been successful. To confirm this, he continued screaming. What I heard him shout was, "It worked!"

Arthur M. Mills, Jr.

Richard was in pain, his blood now running onto the couch he was sitting on. Again we both looked at the paper airplane which seconds ago had been stuck in Richard's flesh. Blood showed at the tip of the airplane in a long thin line. Now we could see the airplane had been devised with a sewing needle poking through the pointy tip. We could see it clearly now. Felix whooped and turned the weapon toward my face. I blocked it with my hand, but it still drew blood from the spot on the back of my hand where it hit. If it had found its mark, I would have matched Candle Face in looks. Somewhat? Well, I supposed not. Her face would always be worse.

Richard didn't wait for another missile hit. He ran to our bedroom and tried to slam the door behind him. Dan easily stopped that, called Felix, and the both of them forced it wide open by using their combined strength. Richard desperately tried to get away. He turned and ran towards his bed but not before Felix threw the deadly paper airplane at Richard's butt. The needle stuck to his skin, but the paper bit fell to the floor. By now Richard was begging them to stop. His panic only added to Felix's fervor and he carried on for another five minutes in the same fashion. Dan watched. *All I could do was watch too.* I wondered if I was as bad as my two older brothers because I had not defended Richard, although I had joined him in begging Felix to stop. But Dan and Felix could easily afford to ignore the pleas from this defenseless eleven-year-old. I thought about fighting back, but what if they turned on me? Our parents were miles away. There was no one to help me. But I felt awful because I hadn't helped Richard. In my own mind I was as bad as Dan and Felix.

By now the paper airplane was soggy with Richard's blood. The needle could no longer be put back, so Felix devised a newer torture. He began to stick Richard with just the needle. Richard managed to drag himself off the bed and even managed to run for the door. Again, Dan blocked the way and effectively stopped Richard's escape.

Richard grew ever more desperate. He recognized it was not his life that was at stake, it was his entire being. He wanted to be a twelve-year-old like any other without having to contend with sadistic elder brothers. And then there was the pain, a threshold he had been forced to cross to the other side. What could Richard do except get back behind the bed and use it to shield himself?

What had worked effortlessly when Richard created magic for us had disappeared. Richard the performer was gone. He could have used his bag of tricks, but all he had left now was fear and panic. He made a quick jump to get behind the bed but wedged himself between the wall and the headboard, facing the wall and exposing his butt to his tormentor.

As Richard helplessly squirmed to free himself, Felix relentlessly poked Richard with demonic intensity. By now Felix had overstepped all limits and scared Dan as well. Dan joined Richard and me as we asked Felix to stop, but he seemed devoid of all feeling, intent on torture for its own sake.

By now Richard, too, had reached a state where he was beyond screaming from the pain. He also knew that showing how much he hurt would have no effect on Felix. His screams died down. Dan pulled Felix away and they left. I moved the bed a little away from the wall so that Richard could free himself, but instead of doing that and emerging from captivity, he crawled deeper under the bed. He was in the same fetal position on the side he had started in. Now he hugged his knees and began to rock with his head moving up and down on the floor, mumbling something incoherent.

This sight scared me. Would there be no let up in what I was forced to watch? I wanted to talk about the conversation Felix and Dan had been engaged in when they entered after two hours of lying under our house. Had a girl given him the go-ahead to take Richard on? But Richard was silent, as he had been the time Carlos beat him up at the creek. He stayed under his bed for the rest of the day.

Deep in my mind I had the answer to my own questions. But it was just a suspicion and I needed proof. Richard was the only person I could have talked to, but right now he was completely traumatized. Our older brothers had just damaged him horribly. Richard and I could only hope and pray for some kind of solution to this horrible situation. As it was, Richard must have come to the realization he could not stop himself from being someone's target and there was no way he could free himself from pain.

When my parents got home, they remained unaware of what had happened because they had got so accustomed to Richard staying in the bedroom. Besides, even if I had tried, I could not have described to them what Richard had to go through on account of my mother's older sons.

Arthur M. Mills, Jr.

CHAPTER 11

It seemed to me that sleep for most people, including my family (*I am still not sure about Richard*), was a break away from the stresses of life. They could rest and dream their peaceable dreams. All of us needed this to be able to recharge, to be able to face the next day. But as for me, I was deathly scared about going to sleep. I could not put up with Candle Face's visitations well after midnight. Under these circumstances I had nearly come to accept that for me, falling asleep was one sure way to wake up to torture.

I could not go to sleep because I didn't dare sleep, nor did I want to. It had dawned on me we weren't like other families, that my brothers weren't like other people's brothers, and Richard and I might not be able to find a way out of the mess we had to accept as our lot. Sleep was for others. I had not slept more than two hours at night for the last couple of days. And that, too, was only because I was too exhausted to be bothered by my private terror.

Earlier I had given in to small stresses and adopted one elaborate habit with the idea that making myself comfortable could help. I made sure I slept with a sheet on, even in the middle of a Texas summer. I also made sure this sheet was tightly wrapped around and tucked in at the sides, making myself practically airtight and covered from the bottom of my toes to my neck. You could say I looked like a mummy to whoever was looking my way as I slept, or tried to. However, my best arrangement could get undone. I never did stay this way the whole night. By the time I woke up the next morning, I would usually be lying on my left side and find the sheet by this time was covering me loosely. Richard was different. He woke up the same way he fell asleep. *Was this a progression that I had still not attained?*

If I did sleep, it would take at least two hours of struggling after I had got into bed. It didn't help that I kept trying to keep the sheet and myself in position during these two hours I spent trying to fall asleep.

In the old days, before the advent of Candle Face, I could wake up in the middle of the night, quietly scope out my bedroom, then go back to wrapping myself tightly and go back to sleep. But not since Candle Face. Sometimes I would be so overwrought I would not sleep at all till daybreak. When that happened I would not be able to go to school. I could not have explained to my mother or anyone else that I had not slept a wink at night. She would want to know why, and that would have only made matters worse. So the only way I could cover up was to pretend to get ready for school and then, as soon as Mom left for work at Sears, I would get back into bed. Richard, of course, threatened to tell, but he never did. All I knew was I could not go to school in the state I was in on those mornings, whether my parents found out or not.

My daytime sleep was good for me; there were no visitations from Candle Face in the morning and no one at home to disturb me. *My staying away from school was perhaps better for my teachers as well.*

I carried on in this manner, managing my nights and managing my daylight hours as best as I could. But I slowly came to understand I was just making Candle Face more frustrated and angrier. I came to the conclusion I had to be miserable for Candle Face to be satisfied. I drew a parallel with Richard's beatings. It was the same as Felix when he imposed pain on Richard. I thought about the strange ways of the world, ghosts and all. There was no getting away from it, though I did try.

Actually I no longer craved sleep. If I dropped off, which, as I have explained, would not occur before at least two hours had passed, I would wake up in the middle of the night at least two nights a week with a sense that a hateful presence wanted something of me. My eyelids would fly open, and there would be Candle Face kneeling on the side of my bed, staring. Ours was considered to be a safe part of the city. My parents were not unduly worried about locking doors

Arthur M. Mills, Jr.

and windows, something that Candle Face had learned to take full advantage of.

At first sight, I would only see the crouching figure by my bed in silhouette. As before, she would be outlined by the street light outside the window closest to my bed filtering through. I would never be able to make out the geography of her face in this light, but I could sense she didn't have many facial features anyway.

Had she been trying to read my dreams? *Or create them?* Her face would be just inches from my face, making me feel more and more vulnerable. Candle Face's ability to invade my personal and private space increased by the day (mostly night). I no longer felt safe, whether at home, in my room or outdoors, like the day Richard got beat up by Carlos.

As soon as I would become aware of Candle Face by my bed, I would become petrified with fear. I could never make a sound nor move in the slightest. Her presence was way beyond all that I could deal with. With her face just inches away from my face, I could smell the heat of burnt flesh radiating from her skin. I could feel her flame filled breath strike mine. Candle Face now devised newer ways to retaliate when she sensed any resistance from me. She would sometimes poke my eyes with her index finger or close my nose and mouth to stop my breath. She seemed to do this for fun, to see what happened. I knew what would follow when I stopped breathing. My eyes rolled backwards. This alarming sight would work her up and provide her with more thrills and excite her even more. This I could tell from her increased movement, heavier breathing and noisy gurgling.

At the last moment she would let my nose and mouth go, but I was not going to be let off that easily. Candle Face wanted to have the last word. There was one more gesture, an "Uhhhhh" sound. She would pat my hair before she left. I had to be teased. I had to be mocked. I had no choice but to let her do what she pleased. She controlled me.

Needless to say, I didn't want to open my eyes to that crouching figure. I didn't need that burnt-flesh stench. I wished someone could protect me from that breath-stopping exercise which was fun for her. I didn't want to wonder if this was the end, whether I would ever be awakened by my mother in the morning again. I didn't want her bony fingers and long nails touching my face and hair. Everything about her made my stomach churn. I no longer thought of the times when I was half sorry for Candle Face, back when I tried to think of her as a girl who once lived next door.

Was she after my life? *Not just now.* She could have contrived to kill me soon after Andre's death, at the time she had warned me. It may have been the fact I had not helped myself to her possessions as Andre had. What she now wanted was her kind of teasing, her kind of fun.

Richard would move occasionally during Candle Face's torture sessions. I would notice and so would Candle Face. She would quietly

Arthur M. Mills, Jr.

glance back towards him, turn her face back towards me, lift her index finger towards where her mouth might have been, and respond with an exaggerated "Shhhh." It would be the only time she seemed to comply with my silent wish because then she would get up and leave.

Richard was carrying on with his own life and his own sleeping habits, talking and thrashing around in his sleep like he always did. As for me, I was just not able to go to sleep the way I used to. Come to think of it, I was no longer living my life the way I used to.

I was beginning to realize since the first night when I disturbed her peace, Candle Face had singled me out. I didn't know about Richard . . . . *would never know whether Richard knew.* My brother slept his own nightmare-filled sleep just about five feet away. His sleep was obviously disturbed, but he never awoke.

When Candle Face left, she would crawl to the window of my room; appear to cling to the window sill with all the strength in her fingers, hands and arms, then pull herself upright. Next she had to reach up. She appeared to claw at the window mesh while she looked for something to open the window. Eventually, she would find a handle and ultimately haul her body through and appear to slither away. Of course, any and all of this exercise was flesh-crawlingly horrific. The only reason I kept my sight glued on her was to make sure she was leaving.

Where did she go? The thought once occurred to me just as she left and I could feel sleep descend. Maybe I didn't know or care. What did it matter to me that her home during the day had to be that accursed hole? But maybe it did matter because on most such nights I could not go back to sleep at all.

Worse still, it wasn't only Candle Face who kept me from my sleep. Richard's habit of talking, twisting and turning through what were obviously more and more frequent nightmares, was steadily getting worse. I told myself that despite his restless nights, Richard at least was getting some sleep without having to face Candle Face. He was far better off than I.

The long nights gave me more time to think strange thoughts. At some point I could no longer say I didn't care where Candle Face came from and where she went. I went back to sorting out and reasoning with myself the way I used to. If I could solve the riddle of what Candle Face wanted, I might be able to save myself *and Richard?*

It slowly dawned on me maybe I could lock all the doors and windows. The problem was, if the others knew I was going around the house locking up for the night, there would be questions and more teasing. But maybe I could quietly lock up and not tell any of the others.

Another question I had was: where did Candle Face go on the nights when she wasn't looking for me, the nights I would spend only half asleep, waiting, sweaty and nervous? What about the nights when I could get no sleep because I didn't want to fall asleep, didn't want to feel vulnerable enough for Candle Face to disturb? Was there anyone else she was terrifying? And even more interestingly, was there anyone else she could be conferring with? By now I had my suspicions about Dan and Felix. They would do anything for a lark.

I became obsessed with these thoughts, so one night when I couldn't sleep I crept to the kitchen and its high window. If anyone asked, I had decided to say I had come for a glass of water. Just like that first night when I had seen Candle Face, I stood on tiptoe to look through the kitchen window. It was like stepping back into time, but only up to a point. As on that long-ago night, it seemed to be windy outside. The trees and shrubs were rustling and waving around. Were they wishing themselves elsewhere again? I carefully looked around. Evan's dog began to whine. Dogs in the far distance barked. I steeled myself to gaze towards the hole in the empty lot next door—and saw something.

No, my eyes weren't playing tricks on me. I knew what that was, the thing that was climbing out of the hole. She seemed to crawl and slither. She seemed very tired, her movements slow. She had her back to me, as she had on that fateful night. Candle Face flopped down on the even ground when she was out of the hole and seemed to wait awhile. This time, she didn't look in my direction though the dogs were still barking. She had grown used to them, but they had obviously not accepted her presence. She seemed to pause and think awhile. Then she did something I hadn't expected. Candle Face crawled her crablike crawl but took off away from me, around the far side of her lot, down Ben Howell Drive.

Her strange action gave me some new insight. She had not bothered to look in my direction, hadn't bothered to read my thoughts. Apparently she didn't think I would want answers to those questions that crowded

Arthur M. Mills, Jr.

my mind at night. But what was this? I could see a distant crablike flurry crawling down the curb back towards our house. It passed the corner of our house. There, on the other side, was my parents' bedroom wall, and my brothers' bedroom beyond that.

I went back to my own bedroom and looked out through her favorite departure window. Now I couldn't see her on the curb. She had either stopped by the front of our house or cut across the road to the other side. I waited awhile. Some fifteen minutes later she emerged and took the same route back. I quickly walked back into the kitchen and watched her from the window. I watched as she came to the great tree in the empty lot next door. She must have had some practice, because she climbed up and went into the tree house with ease. The sight made me shiver, made the hair on my arms stood on end. No sense standing there. I forced myself to go back to bed.

Of course I couldn't sleep knowing Candle Face must have stopped by our house. What could she have wanted and what did she do here? The more I found out, the more questions I had, like why didn't Candle Face ever wander far from her home in the ground?

As before, the next morning I wondered whether I had dreamt the whole thing or if it was real. On the nights Candle Face chose to come and crouch beside my bed, my brother would wake up and say, "Mom burnt breakfast again this morning." Richard always looked directly at me. Deep inside I knew what that smell was. But there was no way he could know what I knew. *He* was not a mind reader. Or so I reasoned to myself.

CHAPTER 12

As time passed, the whereabouts of Dan and Felix became increasingly odd. Most of the time, even by their own admission, they went to their friends' homes. Their friends, however, would go to school, so the mystery about what Dan and Felix were doing remained. Earlier, they would at least come home for dinner, but now they were hardly ever at home.

I didn't care because I didn't want them around anyway. I think I can speak for Richard when I say he was downright scared of them as this earlier Saturday had proven. This other Saturday would be worse in a different way because they had Richard's active participation. Even our parents didn't seem to mind when Dan and Felix weren't around.

Richard and I could presume what kind of young men Dan and Felix would turn out to be. The term for it was 'out of control.' Felix was not only fighting mean, he would storm out of the house if our mother gave him any chores. He got Dan to follow him and used words I hadn't heard before, not even from the mean kids in school. Our mother could not ground him anymore. He just left if she tried.

Dan and Felix's lack of hygiene was apparent to us younger boys. They hardly ever used the bathtub. Their longish hair and sloppy clothes were such a disgusting, filthy mess I couldn't figure out how they managed to get that way just from spending time at their friends' homes on Ben Howell Drive or sniffing paint.

I was becoming more aware of what was going on around the house. Not only Richard and I stayed out of our older brothers' way, so did our mother. I noticed she was asking less of them, although she was there, quiet as always, but talking less to us and a lot less to Dan and Felix. I had a suspicion that she was aware of Richard's inability to protect himself and his failed fights. They had to be obvious because of the marks the fights left behind. Dan and Felix's slovenly appearance was obvious, too, and she couldn't have overlooked their huge appetites. But Mom's response remained the same: she ignored them.

I continued being favored by our father and still sat with him through our favorite stuff on TV. He still talked to me about matters that interested him. Richard still stayed out of everyone's way and stayed in our room. But our mother was drifting further away.

If anybody asked, I don't know if I could have told them what I knew. Dan and Felix were getting themselves involved in both alcohol and drugs, both of which our counselor at school had warned us about. I had told myself my brothers would be my favorite 'un-role models,' and that when I was a teen I would definitely stay away. I also told myself their drugs and dope were what were making Dan and Felix into walking horrors. Sometimes I saw Mom looking at them keenly. She may have thought as I did but didn't get much of a chance to see them because they were hardly ever home. Wherever Dan and Felix were, they now spoke openly and often about wanting to drink beer and smoke marijuana. I guessed most of the time they were doing their bad deeds up the street at their friend's house. Richard and I didn't talk about it. I was curious to know if he thought as I did but didn't know how to bring up the topic.

What Richard and I knew was that on some weekends when our parents were at work, Dan and Felix would smoke marijuana in our backyard and play drinking games in the house.

One Saturday Dan and Felix brought home marijuana, chewing tobacco, and two cases of beer. The amount and variety were a lot worse than what they had indulged in before. They were planning a day of drinking games, discussing it with great glee. Occasionally their eyes slid sideways towards us, so I reckoned I would be asked to roll those marijuana cigarettes. My brothers claimed they were fussy about how these were done and would holler for me to come and do it. It may have been apparent that I did not want to. It was also apparent to me that I had no choice. It was an order.

Two cases of beer! I couldn't help thinking that kind of money could have fetched us a lot of toys, like the carved wooden speedy toy cars Andre had shown us, the ones he said belonged to the kid who had died in the house fire. So where did the money come from? My older brothers talked a lot about their music and rock band, but so far, fame and fortune had eluded them. They had yet to play for money.

In the meanwhile, on this memorable Saturday, Richard and I shifted uncomfortably on the couch remembering that other Saturday when Felix and Dan had unleashed their vindictiveness on poor Richard. I thought surely they'd had enough of tormenting him, at least for another couple of months.

Richard was probably thinking along similar lines. He had been caught up in not being able to save himself in a number of ways and with a number of people, my brothers included. But he wasn't stupid and was probably considering the best way to save himself from today's difficult situation.

Later I found out he had indeed thought up a plan: he asked Dan and Felix if he could play the drinking game with them. They may have been surprised but were mostly thrilled to have a third person play. I was horrified.

Dan then asked me if I wanted to play, but I had no interest either in drinking or joining a gang of brothers with such interests in mind. I remained pretty shocked about Richard joining in and just sat around trying to understand them while I kept watching TV.

My three brothers sat around the dining room table. They started with a game called 21. I didn't know this game, and was sure Richard didn't know it either. He had possibly thought he could figure out the game as he went along, but either he couldn't work out the rules, or he was getting fuddled too quickly. Dan and Felix, however, didn't mind because they were discovering the hilarious side of their younger brother.

At first, Richard had to drink an extra half a can of beer because he had brought up a number out of turn. Then he got it totally wrong and had to drink more. I found their game boring and only watched because I was worried about Richard. But the three of them hadn't a care in the world and went on to other drinking games for over an hour.

I perked up when Dan suggested a game called 'beer pong.' Did he have to live the part? I wondered. By now an unmistakable cloud of a beer smells surrounded him. The game had to do with tiny half glasses of beer, with ping pong added. Dan and Felix's main target continued to be Richard. The ball would literally land in his glass and he would have to drink it up. Of course Richard was not accustomed to drinking beer, or any kind of alcohol, and I could see he was getting very drunk. I was glad when they decided to take a break from the game, but when Richard got up from the table, his legs gave way and he fell straight down.

Dan and Felix thought of Richard's tumble as the funniest thing that had happened around there for a long time. They howled at his inability to prevent himself from getting drunk. They found it funny that he couldn't hold his liquor. The sad part was, Richard decided his fall was extremely funny and joined in the laughter that was entirely at his expense.

After that, Dan suggested they go out to the back yard and get busy with the marijuana joints I had been made to roll. All three of them smoked pot in a storage shed out in the backyard. I stayed on the back porch. When they emerged from the shed, I could see Richard wasn't just drunk, he was stoned as well.

Where was this going to end?

Not soon enough because Felix now offered Richard some chewing tobacco. Richard played into his hands by showing he was more than willing to try some for the first time. Felix showed Richard how, and Richard did his best to follow. Despite the state he was in, Richard put a larger-than-necessary wad of the chewing tobacco into his mouth. Dan, Felix and I held our breath. Within a few seconds Richard seemed to hold his breath as well. Then he spewed it out and threw up all over the entire dining room floor.

My brothers laughed and laughed. It was deafening. Richard fell to the floor, passed out in his own vomit, and my brothers kept on laughing. But they knew our parents would be home soon and they had to get things back to normal as much as possible. Dan and Felix picked Richard up, dumped him in the bathtub and turned the tap on. They were also looking the worse for wear. I now had some clues as to how they got dirty. I had heard about how people drowned when they were too drunk or too stoned or both, so I stayed in the bathroom to make sure that didn't happen to Richard.

Later, I asked my brothers for help in getting Richard to bed. Dan and I hauled Richard out of the bathtub. Dan held him under the armpits and I held him by both his ankles. We got Richard to his bed. He groaned when he hit it, so I knew he was going to be all right.

I also asked Dan and Felix to help me clean up the house. They ignored me, so I cleaned it myself because there was no one else. I did my best, starting to mop up the floor where Richard had thrown up, but I kept gagging on account of the smell. Eventually Richard came to, crawled out of bed and helped me clean the dining room floor.

Dan and Felix also did some tidying up. That consisted mainly of gathering up the empty beer cans and going off to their friend's house. When Mom came home, she knew something was wrong. She looked suspicious but couldn't figure out the mayhem that had taken place in our house. Richard stayed in our room and didn't come to the table for dinner. Dan and Felix didn't come home or return for dinner either. They had stayed on at their friend's house. I watched *All in the Family* with my father. The three of us had a quiet dinner before we turned in for the night.

When I went to bed that night, I couldn't go to sleep. Instead, I lay in my bed wide awake and thought about the day. Richard had surprised me when he showed how willing he was to join Dan and Felix in their drinking and drug taking. Now I understood what it was Richard tried to achieve—he wanted Dan and Felix to approve of him, wanted them on his side. He had no desire to be one of the good guys and had finally proved, or so he thought, that he could be just like his brothers. They had played along with him and now knew Richard would do whatever they wanted.

What Richard had managed to achieve that day was to play right into my brothers' hands.

Arthur M. Mills, Jr.

CHAPTER 13

Dan and Felix came back on Monday. Richard and I saw them the minute we got back from school. They told us they'd been waiting for us and looked as if they'd been busy in the bathroom and got cleaned up. They regarded Richard with new interest. I guessed Richard was wondering how quickly he could get to our room and hide.

Of course, Dan and Felix had anticipated Richard's reaction by telling us they had a new story to tell and a new game to play. Right away we smelled trouble. The only question was how much trouble their presence meant. Dan and Felix had anticipated our suspicions as well. They were actually trying to soothe our fears.

"Come on guys . . . you have to grow up." Felix said.

"You can have some thrills with us," Dan said with a wink. "Right, Richard?"

Richard avoided his look, but we knew there was no getting away. Felix, who always took the lead, said, "Remember that Bloody Mary game?"

I was dumbstruck. How did he know thoughts of Bloody Mary had weighed heavily on my mind?

Felix carried on, "I first learnt about Bloody Mary in English history. She managed to become the Queen of England only because her father, the King, died. But she was an evil woman who had many people burnt at the stake and loved to kill. She was cursed and now roams the world. I told you how anyone can flesh her out through the bathroom mirror."

I wondered if any of this had been going on in the bathroom today, besides their overdue baths.

Dan cut in, "Well, we've left all that stupid school stuff behind. We found a newer story yesterday. It is still about Bloody Mary, but this one's different."

Dan began the story. Felix joined in and the two of them alternately regaled and terrified us with what they called the 'true blue' incidents.

"There was a beautiful young woman by the name of Mary Worth who lived in England in the 1890's. She lived in the village of Painsley, which is somewhere up north, far from London. The people who lived in Painsley had never been to London except for one or two young women who had married well and moved to towns near London. When it was time to have their babies, they would come home to their mothers. They would then stay on in the village for nearly a year before they went back to their lives and husbands.

"Now this Mary Worth had passed her marriageable age, though she was still very beautiful. The reason for this was that she had turned away all suitors. Her family despaired for her and wondered what would become of her, how would she manage her life, especially when she grew old.

"But Mary wasn't bothered, or so it seemed. She loved Painsley and the surrounding woods, but most of all, she loved herself. Never mind the Queen of England, Mary was the uncrowned queen of Painsley and all the villages around, and she was determined to keep it that way.

"On one of Mary's walks in the woods she discovered a coven of witches. They asked Mary to join them on moonlit nights, to chant and dance to a one-line song called, 'I killed your baby.' They promised that in return Mary Worth would be immortal. She was interested, not only in immortality but in preserving her looks. The witches were old, and showed it."

"The witches did their best to persuade her because they needed one more person to join in their midnight dancing. They told Mary her beauty would be well preserved if she bathed in the blood of young children. They would help her to do this if she could bring them the children. But the problem was, Painsley was a small village, so there weren't many around. Mary wanted the few that were there, though. She had been supplying the only sweetshop in the village with sweets which she cooked at home. Now, using the sweets as a lure, she would take the unsuspecting victim for a walk in the woods.

Arthur M. Mills, Jr.

There, the evil witches would be waiting. They would pounce on the child and hold it captive.

"Later at night they would skin the child alive. They would collect the blood that flowed and Mary would bathe in it under the moon, surrounded by silent, watchful trees. The witches tried it themselves, and Mary could see that they were beginning to look younger, as was she.

"Of course the people of Painsley grieved for their lost children, who had been disappearing one by one. Try as they might, they could not stop any child over five years from walking away, with what seemed like a young woman, never to be seen again.

"Now it happened Mary was close to two little babies whose mothers had come to Painsley for their birth. One rainy afternoon when she thought she was alone, she lifted a six-month-old from her crib, hid the child under her shawl, and ran toward the woods as fast as she could. She knew the witches would be waiting for her under a rock ledge balanced on two tall rocks.

"But the baby's mother had entered the room in time to see Mary's skirt swish out the door, and hear her baby's pitiful cries trailing away in the direction of the woods. She quickly gathered her fellow villagers. Enraged, they took whatever homemade weapons they could find and charged off in the direction of a noise in the woods, a noise which came from the witches cackling and chanting, "We will kill this baby." They were getting ready for their weird dancing and bathing-in-blood ritual."

"The villagers got to the clearing in the woods just in time. They rescued the baby and killed the evil witches, as well as the evil but beautiful Mary Worth. When she died, her well-preserved face disintegrated before their eyes into a mutilated face. The villagers ran back with the baby to Painsley. They didn't bother to bury Mary of the mutilated face or the ugly witches."

"After that, they weren't bothered by evil goings-on, except when they lit their candles in front of their small mirrors (it was before the advent of electricity). They cursed Mary Worth for all they were worth. But one man found by accident that when he stood in front of his mirror at night, with a lit candle and cursed Mary Worth saying "Bloody Mary," three times, there slowly appeared in the mirror the same ghostly face he seen in the woods."

Dan and Felix claimed this tale of horror had been proved right. In fact, my brothers had been to a sleepover party the previous Sunday where they had experimented with the game. It had worked. Dan said they could see bloody nail marks on his thigh after they had performed the ritual in his girlfriend's bathroom mirror late at night. That was why he took a bath when he came home—to wash off the blood. They now suggested that we try it too. It would be fun, they said, to prove it was true. It was only Bloody Mary who had died, they reminded us, not the person on our side of the mirror. I knew this, but I couldn't very well tell them I had already tried it. I hadn't died, but the ritual had led to the release of something or someone who may not have been buried as other people were. I couldn't tell them she had last visited me just a few nights ago, that I knew where she came from, and where she went most nights.

As usual, there was no stopping Dan and Felix when they got hold of an idea. They said this time they would show us how to do it. So Richard and I put our school bags down in the bedroom. Along with Dan and Felix, we crowded into the bathroom, which was small, messed up and noisy by now. I stood near the entrance, hoping to be able to run. It seemed like a long time ago when my father was outside this door and I inside, trying my hand at Bloody Mary. How I wished he could be here now! He would have made sure I stayed out, just as he had then.

Felix lit a small candle he'd brought and propped it up on the bottom of the mirror frame. Dan rushed to switch off the light. He was not going to bother with counting his steps as I had done; he was just going to bluster his way through. But now my older brothers decided there were too many of us in the bathroom, so we could do without them. They pushed me in front of the mirror and ran out; slamming shut the bathroom door and laughing on the other side.

I asked Richard if we still had to go through with it, since we could always fool Felix and Dan and come up with a story of what we might have done. But Richard's eyes were gleaming in the candle light and in the bathroom mirror. He looked determined, as I have seen him look before. Our brothers, too, must have realized by now we were up to something. Through the door, they urged us to start, and then threatened us with dire consequences, worse than what Bloody Mary could do, if we backed out of playing the game as it should be played.

Arthur M. Mills, Jr.

Richard was not going to waste any time. I was right in front of the mirror. He was just behind me. He spoke loudly and quickly, "Bloody Mary, Bloody Mary, Bloody Mary." I saw Richard's reflection go down, in the same way that he fell when someone hit him. But how could that be? There were only the two of use here in this small bathroom.

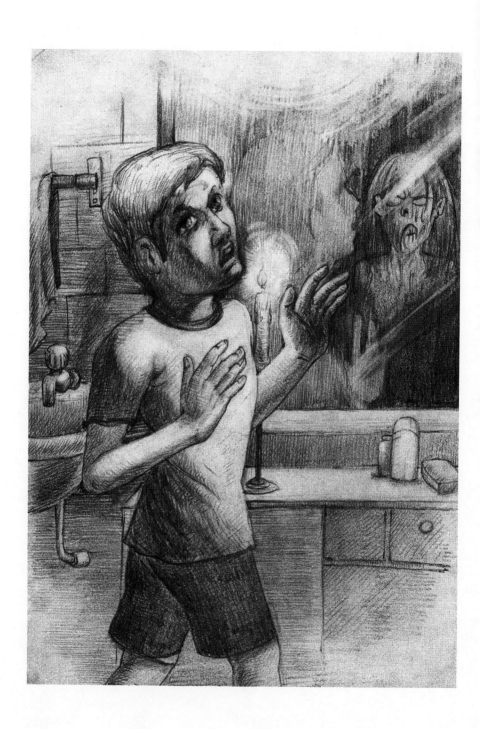

Arthur M. Mills, Jr.

And then, in the candlelight, I saw a face materialize on the mirror. It was not the face of Bloody Mary. It was Candle Face, with gaps where her eyes, nose and mouth should have been. There were pinpoints of light in the center of those eye sockets which reminded me of the gleam in Richard's eyes. I was looking at the face I had not seen clearly before. She still looked like parts of her face were melting and merging, too damaged to become stable even for a minute. It was clearer than the face I had seen in the clouds that day in the creek. I thought that something was trying to stifle me in that tiny bathroom.

I didn't remember anything after that until I awoke the next morning and I was in my bed. Richard was lying in his bed with his eyes on the ceiling. It looked as if he had just woke up and would soon get out of bed to get ready for school. What did Richard see this time right above his face? I wondered. But Richard was now getting out of bed. As he walked towards the closet to get the first choice of clothes, I saw something down the outside of his thigh. It looked like fresh claw marks over the nearly healed trail of the needle that Felix had plunged into Richard days ago.

CHAPTER 14

Our parents worked hard and conducted their day-to-day life between their places of work and home. They ran the household of six with barely enough money, which meant we did without the extras. Spending on outings and entertainment was a no-no. Our parents rarely went out and gave us the impression that they didn't need nights out. If they did go out, Dan and Felix saw it as an opportunity to go out as well.

On days or evenings when I was the only one home, I felt I was lucky. I had my privacy and my independence for quality time on my own. I could watch TV or do whatever I wanted when I was not being crowded by the rest of the family.

On one such evening I was talking on the phone with my friend, Nolan. He lived a couple of blocks away so we didn't see each other in the morning on the way to school. Nolan was as keen a soccer player as I was a runner. We were trying to agree on when and where to meet for a class project. Since I had the house to myself, I tried to get him to come over. Also, I needed some clues as to what the project was about. In other words, I needed to pick Nolan's brains. He and I had started out together in Kindergarten, and his grandparents had encouraged him to be a good student. Nolan was on top of the class and I was on the bottom so I needed to know what he knew about the project.

Nolan was a worried boy, though his concerns were not about content for the project, as mine were. He told me there was something amiss on Ben Howell. He mentioned what Evan had told him, that Evan's dog was not well and barked all night if he had to stay out. The dog was old, and should have been set in his ways, but now he wanted to be a house dog. That meant that guarding the outside was not for him anymore, as far as the dog could tell Evan. He scratched and pawed at the entrance doors and whined till he was let in.

Now Evan had a theory about this. He thought Ben Howell was no longer a safe place, that burglars were afoot down my street and had plagued his dog into wanting to stay indoors all night. Nolan objected to coming over because he worried he wouldn't be able to get home before it got dark. Nolan's grandparents were concerned for his safety, Nolan explained apologetically.

I felt like swearing in the same fashion as Dan and Felix. I knew what plagued Evan's dog and that he was a wise dog for preferring the inside of Evan's house. But I still needed to get my project done. Dared I sprint across to Nolan's house now and back after we finished? If I did, it would be a waste of an empty house as well as the independence I had earned.

I was still on the phone when I heard a knock on the window that faced the street and wondered why anyone would want to knock on the window instead of the door. I had to hang up the phone, hoping Nolan would do his bit of the project all right. I also hoped he would do a bit for me, too. I had to answer the knock on the window.

It had taken a little time to get off the phone and to get to the window. I ran across, but by the time I got there, I stopped in my tracks. Was that another knock I was hearing, on the window next to this one which faced the street? There was no one and no more knocks on the first window anyway. That could be fixed. In two long strides, I was at the second window but found no one there.

Within seconds, the pattern repeated on windows farther away. I heard it on all the windows around the house. The knocking had now taken on an urgency with what seemed like one or more people knocking in a frenzied way on all the house windows repeatedly. None of my friends could run that fast from window to window.

I stopped running helter-skelter. There could be only one set of pranksters for something like this. Recently my brothers had done their best to get Richard drunk, stoned and senseless. Dan and Felix would find this funny, this knocking and hammering at high speed on one window at a time, then the next and the next and so on. They had left the house earlier in the evening at the same time as our parents did. They now probably thought trying to confuse and frighten me would provide better entertainment that night.

Arthur M. Mills, Jr.

It was typical of Dan and Felix to do something like this. Now there was repeated loud knocking at the kitchen window. Strange. None of my friends could reach high enough to knock on that one. I remembered I had to stand on tiptoe to look out the kitchen window on the first day of Candle Face's emergence.

I decided to ignore the noise, but the pranksters didn't want to be ignored. I heard the back screen porch creak open and slam shut. I walked towards the back door to the porch expecting to see Dan and Felix. That was when I noticed the back door chain lock was in place. As I reached to unlock it, my hand outstretched, a protective instinct must have cautioned me. Midway through, with my arm stretched in an exercise pose, the door came loose and the chain stretched taut. I stopped, and then froze. A dark and dry, fibrous and skeletal skinny arm suddenly shot towards me through the gap between the door and the door frame. I jumped back. Now I was sure who it was.

She was the prankster—or the intruder, as I now saw her intention. As far as she was concerned, my reflexes were getting better. I could see that bony arm snake through to the other side of the door. I could see she intended to grab my arm and I had jumped back in the nick of time. She pulled her arm back, and I quickly shut the door and shot the bolt. She had been trying each of the windows all this time! *I am now glad I had been secretly locking the doors.* But I was not sure if I locked all the windows. I heard the back porch screen door creak open and shut. Candle Face was on her way out. I also heard a scuffing sound along the dry leaves at the side of the house facing the empty lot.

Could I let out a sigh of relief? *Not really.* Candle Face hadn't left. She had just crept around the side of the house. From what I remembered about her run that night when I got up and watched unnoticed, Candle Face by now was familiar with the outside of our house. Next thing I could hear was her climbing onto the foundation of the house near the kitchen window. She had come back and was scraping the window screen with her hands and raking it with her nails. It was a lesson learned from the way she had clawed at the tree trunk some months ago. I rushed to insure the kitchen window was locked and managed to do so just in time. But that didn't stop her because by the time I was done, she had jumped down and headed for the next window.

I frantically ran there because I knew what she could do when she was determined to harass me. By now, she had probably got used to easy access into our house. I knew her many means of torture and knew I didn't want her inside. Time and time again, I could see her hands scraping the wire mesh at the windows and her nails clawing to get in.

I managed to get to every window a split second before her and close and latch it before she got in. We carried on around the house in this fashion. I not only beat her every time, but I knew I had won for the first time since my ill-thought-out visit to her resting hole in the ground. That night not only did Candle Face stay outside, I was learning how to best deal with my problems.

I felt elated at the start of my investigation to discover any ghost, which, of course, resulted in the emergence of Candle Face. That was a mistake and I had occasion to regret what I done as a result. Could I feel satisfied about having won some kind of a weird game with Candle Face that night? *I could, but I could never be too sure about anything any longer.* I remembered my resolve to lock all our doors and windows before our family retired for the night. It would work. It would keep Candle Face out.

I went back to my next best pastime when the family was out. I sat down to watch TV and settled down to *All in the Family,* my favorite program. Archie was bullying a fellow worker. He did this very effectively. Archie had got good at rolling his eyes and looking incredulous. The man appeared to be intimidated. So far so good for Archie. But when his opponent was nearly finished, he began to have second thoughts about giving up. Archie's opponent turned into his enemy. His enemy contrived to grow in stature and began to steal the show in terms of work-based efficiency.

Archie showed signs of exaggerated worry. I supposed he was worried about the fact that someone he had considered puny could get back at him. Archie was right to be worried. He had aired a couple of opinions, all of which turned out to be wrong. It turned out that Archie's opponent had been right. In the end, Archie graciously made it up to him. The plot had a happy ending.

I sat on the living room couch and thought this story through, all the time wishing my parents would return. I felt good because I had spent an evening on my own feeling independent, acting quickly when

Arthur M. Mills, Jr.

I felt the need. As far as Candle Face was concerned, I had won some sort of a game. For the first time I'd been able to assert myself with her, had managed to keep her outside the house. She would not be able to horrify or harass me tonight. *Or ever again, I thought.*

I was feeling content and floaty, which was just as well because Richard told me the next day that when he came in late that night he found me asleep on the couch with a smile on my face. He woke me up and made me go sleep in my own bed. I slept well that night without having to get my sheet wrapped just right. When I awoke in the morning I found I had slept without changing into my pajamas and without my sheet. I wondered how I had happened to be smiling when Richard came home. That was because I seemed to remember a dream from last night. It involved Dan and Felix and Candle Face and it was not nice. Dan, Felix and Candle Face? The dream came back to me in bits. It was a lot like what I had watched on *All in the Family*. The dream seemed to be from inside Candle Face's head! This was a change. It meant I'd got a chance to see what she was thinking. Candle Face had spent an early evening around our house. She just wanted to come in and have some fun. She knew me and loved waking me up. She loved my horror stricken eyes and the delicate way in which I wrinkled my nose. She did not have a nose herself, but ever since she'd come back, had taken care to present her silhouette to me.

She was going to present herself at each window of the house where we lived. She had some inkling of Richard because she could burrow into his dreams. She had found Dan and Felix when they were sniffing paint under the house and found she could talk with them on their level (they were a foolish pair of boys). But I was the best.

Perhaps she thought she could get at me earlier than usual that day. That would provide more mileage for her evil ways. She could take maximum pleasure in my fear and then go back to her nest before she set out later at night. Candle Face was going to have an evening of fun. She knew I would be at home but wasn't sure if anyone else would be there with me. She began at her usual window but didn't know about it being the window I knew she most used to get in. I had been talking to someone when she knocked, so she thought I must have company. She was looking forward to this.

She laughed her cackling laugh to herself at the thought of how befuddled I would be. It was a high pitched laugh, not her usual growl.

I ran to the first window as expected, then to the next which she was knocking insistently on one, then again on another. By now Candle Face was feeling slighted because I thought it was those foolish brothers of mine. They had told Candle Face their names were Dino and Poncho. That was a silly subterfuge, because I always thought of them as Dan and Felix.

Worse still, Candle Face had overdone her scare tactics with her knocking and her gorgeously long nails. I carried on in a confused manner, but when I realized it was her, I managed to lock each and every window. I locked them one after the other in the same pattern in which she had knocked on them. I had actually been able to avoid her arm when she managed to snake it through the gap in the porch door. She would have liked to grab me by the hand. She would have had a field day frightening me witless.

Candle Face reasoned that tonight had not been a good night. She had been left on the outside and had not been able to enter. She also figured I had been alone at home. It was a pity, but she was sure she would get at me sometime soon. She would leave Richard for now. There seemed to be too many others getting at him. Some of what Poncho (or was it Felix?) did to Richard, Candle Face could not do because of her lack of substantial form. She might as well get back for that long deserved rest. Later she would go looking for Dino and Poncho—*or was it Dan and Felix?* She was sure to find them drinking that stuff out of those cans, or else smoking those strange smelly cigarettes which drowned out her own rich smell.

It had been a regular night for Candle Face except she had underestimated me. I had made the right moves such as clicking the windows shut one by one and snatching my arm back just in time. There was more to me, she had to admit, than just a frightened youngster who could not get his child's voice to work when he needed it, or his muscles coordinated enough to run when she was around.

This was my dream. *Was it a dream?* Candle Face had acknowledged I had won, that she had not been able to enter my house. I felt scared all over again when I realized that now, since Candle Face's entry into my world, I should not enjoy as I used to an evening alone. I wondered if I would have been better off with Nolan if he had come over to my house. I would not know now, but I reveled in my new-found confidence about being able to repulse Candle Face's entry. But as

Arthur M. Mills, Jr.

before, this one insight was giving rise to a host of other questions. Were Dan and Felix throwing in their lot with Candle Face? Would they do as she told them to?

Richard came home from wherever he was and woke me up. I had fallen asleep on the living room couch. I got up from the couch and went straight to bed.

The next morning before heading to school, I walked to the side of the house facing the empty lot to look for evidence. All I could see were a great many small hand smudges and scratch marks on all the window screens. She had been here all right. Had she been to see Dan and Felix later, as my dream had revealed? Right then I had to get to school early and find Nolan. I had to know how far he got with our project. There was work to be done. Maybe I could break out of my 'no homework rule' and do my bit for the project. If I had been able to successfully do my best where Candle Face was concerned, I might be able to do my best for the other bogey—school work.

Arthur M. Mills, Jr.

CHAPTER 15

Richard liked a girl from school. Her name was Maria. She was Richard's age and they were in the same 6th grade class at Mollie Dawson Elementary School. We could see that Maria was a pretty Latin-American twelve-year-old. She was tall, thin and willowy and would be truly beautiful in a couple of years. Right now, Richard could not take his eyes off her. He worked it out so that he could sit near her during class. Maria would just look back and smile. Richard, however, noticed that Maria smiled at everyone. She was a good, quiet, friendly girl.

It would be an understatement to say Richard liked Maria. He really liked her a lot.

Richard had furthered his creative talents. In addition to his magic, stage shows, story writing and storytelling, he also wrote romantic poetry. On occasion he would take part in the school elocution program with poems he had written. The children would listen enthralled. His teachers loved the way he read poetry; in fact, they loved anything he wrote. He would sometimes offer his poems to me to read at home. I thought they were brilliant.

Richard came out of his shell to show our parents the notebook where he wrote his poems. Our father only pretended to read from the notebook. On the other hand, Mom would read a couple of poems and tell Richard he was very talented and keep up the good work.

I thought Richard's poems were also a good way to express his feelings. Everyone could see Richard wrote his soppy romantic poems with Maria in mind. At least he was wise enough not to present them to her in class. That would have frightened her. But he wanted to make

Maria see how much he liked her. He would have to go about it in the best way possible.

The problem was that Maria was not grown up enough to like Richard in the same way Richard liked her. She wanted to get this across to Richard without hurting him. Richard didn't know this, though, so he lived in hope, still doing everything he could to get her attention. He kept watching carefully for any sign of interest. If only she had let him know!

This was when he made his first mistake with Maria. He had been hopefully waiting, so keen on impressing her he was now going to bring matters to the fore. One of his ideas was to get Maria to come to a magic show where he would be the master conjuror. It would it be a performance in which he would conduct magic with finesse in front of our group of friends. He was also confident about the clapping and cheering he would receive from all of us and thought Maria would notice how his friends put him on a pedestal. Exposing Maria to their admiration would notch up a plus point for himself. She would know how much all of us admired him, and then, of course, be proud to be associated with him.

That settled, Richard considered how to approach Maria. He would, of course, ask Maria in the nicest way possible, so he decided he would send her a written invitation. A simple invitation card was out of the question. Richard had been getting better and better in the romantic type poetry he wrote. He knew poetry was his specialty and that he excelled at it. Would this be turned into an advantage with Maria? He thought it would.

It was not that he was going to present an ode or any silly piece of romantic poetry to her directly. In one brilliant stroke, Richard decided he would send her an invitation composed in poetic form. He penned it carefully, corrected and rewrote it. It turned out to be a poetic invitation to Maria asking her to a magic show he intended to conduct at the tree house in the empty lot.

Richard was very proud of his creative stroke of genius, his poem. He was sure once Maria read it she would understand him better and surely attend the show. Getting her to accept him would then be easy. His invitation went something like this:

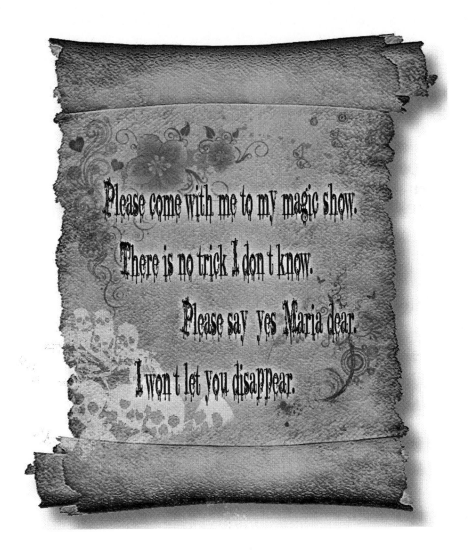

Please come with me to my magic show.

There is no trick I don't know.

Please say yes Maria dear.

I won't let you disappear.

He wondered how he was going to give it to Maria. She had a brother named Chico in the third grade, just a year junior to me, so Richard wondered if he could use Chico to get his message to Maria. At this point, Richard had to ask me if I would get to know Chico. As it happened, I already knew Chico. He was a cheeky little boy who liked to run with me. The only drawback was that running was all we had in common; it was mostly all we talked about.

The next time Chico called, Richard wasn't home, so I told Richard we had to hang around together if he wanted to meet Chico. Richard did, although he grumbled about it. I pointed out it was for his own good, then wondered if I had said the right thing. There was a city run the following week on Saturday, so I knew from the year before that the TV crew looked for young kids to film and talk to. Chico and I both planned to be there. Richard wasn't a runner, but he figured he was almost out of time, so he made me promise that afterward I would bring Chico by the house.

It was late by the time Chico and I walked back to my house from our run at Saint Edwards University. Richard was waiting for us on the front porch. He was unusually animated, greeting us with, "Hi ya folks. How's the running going?"

I introduced Richard and Chico. Richard was boring holes into Chico with his eyes, but Chico just gave him an impish grin back.

"So you're Maria's brother, huh?" Richard asked as if he didn't already know.

Chico shot back with, "And you're the keen one in her class, aren't you?"

Richard appeared nonplussed for a second, then moved back to his planned topic. He had mentioned Maria, and he was direct. "Chico, can you give Maria a school note for me? It has some school homework that she won't know about. She left early on Friday."

"Is that so?" said impish Chico, not buying Richard's story. "Let's see what it says." He made to tear the envelope open.

"No!" said Richard jerking the note from Chico's hand.

"Maria is out with her friends," Chico continued. "Give it back. I'll be going to bed early tonight because of the city run, but I'll just give it to our parents to pass on to her."

At this point, Maria's father drove up to our house to pick up Chico, so Richard hastily stuffed the invitation back in his pocket. We waved

　　　　Arthur M. Mills, Jr.

goodbye to Chico, then Richard turned and glared at me. As if things had gone wrong and it was my fault! Our parents weren't home yet, so I worried I was in line for one of Richard's beatings. But instead, he busied himself with making sandwiches—one for him and one for me. So I knew he wasn't going to react as he usually did. For once, he wasn't going to be the old irritable Richard.

I knew Richard felt embarrassed that both Chico and I knew he was desperate to get his message to Maria, although only I knew about the invitation to his magic show in the four-line poem. I certainly hadn't let on to Chico what Richard's message was about. This latest was a setback for Richard all right, but it made him all the more determined. Now what could he do? In another flash of inspiration Richard decided he must come out of this charade of secrecy. He would give Maria her invitation in public!

If his classmates were going to worry about being left out, he would ask them as well. After all, there was no shortage of seats at the magic show. Our group of friends was comfortable sprawled on the ground at the back of the empty lot.

Richard had decided he would give Maria the invitation in full public view, but now he needed to get his nerve up to carry out his plan. He was going to practice what he had to say to Maria, and how to say it in front of an audience. The only way to get such practice was in front of the bathroom mirror, so Richard spent long hours in the bathroom. When I heard him through the door, I asked what he was saying and who to. Richard being Richard, told me to leave him alone, but I knew what he was up to. The family noticed Richard was in the bathroom a lot of the time. That included Dan and Felix, although they were spending even less time in the house now. My father noticed but my mother did not.

Dan and Felix teased Richard by imagining scenarios about what Richard did in the bathroom in all the time he spent there. Our father finally threatened to whack him if he didn't get out that very instant. Richard got out. I just waited.

Richard finally perfected the art of inviting Maria and handing her the poem-invitation. After a final rehearsal before school, Richard went to school and told his class he had an announcement to make. With a flourish he gave the invitation to Maria in front of everyone in his class. She glanced at the invitation, turned red, and held her breath for quite some time while she looked at Richard. He was thrilled, thinking she was taking her time to word her acceptance, but when Maria finally found her voice, she told Richard she would not be able to go.

Richard's classmates informed him that the way in which he'd presented the invitation was all wrong. They had loved his dramatics on stage, but now they made fun of him. He had always been confident of his skills while on stage, but now he felt his confidence draining away. His classmates informed him he was an ass. They also told him there was no way she was interested in him.

Richard was devastated.

Maria had understood what he was trying to get across but was too nice and polite to be rude. She had come as close as she could to telling Richard directly she wasn't interested, but he just didn't get it and was going to carry on living in hope. He would do everything he could to draw her attention. He figured maybe she'd respond favorably some day and he would just give it a break for now.

I didn't know Richard had been rejected until I got home from school and saw the expression on his face. Immediately I guessed what had happened. Since I didn't have the heart to tease him about it, I went to our bedroom and pretended to do some homework. Pretty soon he came noisily into our room and announced that he was going to take a bath. Waiting for the bathtub to fill, he thought of Dan and Felix's long-winded rigmarole about Bloody Mary. He could remember both the stories perfectly well, the one about the Queen and the other about Mary Ward.

After he climbed into the tub, he started thinking about the mirror trick, just as I had, and it aroused his curiosity. He decided he had to try it in order to find out what the near-future held for him. He jumped out of the bath and looked around for Dan and Felix's candle stub. He found it, along with a box of matches on top of the medicine cabinet which our brothers must have left behind, possibly when they'd smoked in the bathroom when no one was around. Richard lit the candle, switched off the light switch, and walked back to the mirror. Since Dan and Felix's rules stated this should be done aloud, Richard spoke Bloody Mary's name three times, but he did it in a whisper, "Bloody Mary! Bloody Mary! Bloody Mary!" He looked into the smudgy depths of the mirror. Thinking about Maria, he was also formulating words for his most fervent wish at the same time. Finally he heard what he thought was a hoarse laugh. A face slowly materialized in the bathroom mirror. It looked like a girl who was deathly pale. The white of her skin looked like dripping candle wax, the face not looking much different from the candle in front of her which was now burning low. She carried on sniggering softly. Not knowing about Candle Face, Richard thought it was the face of Bloody Mary—any one of the Mary's. Or maybe it might be Bloody Mary trying to evoke the face of Maria.

Later, when Richard told me his story, he was awkward and uncomfortable while relating the horrifying details. He said the moving vision in the mirror seemed to read his thoughts. The face, if it was a face, grew and expanded, seeming to rush at him at great speed. It was so sudden Richard feared she might crash right out of the glass. He instinctively moved aside, and the blob did just that—gave a mocking gurgling laugh then sped out and away, cracking the glass mirror.

By now, Richard was terrified. He opened the bathroom door and ran to our bedroom. Panting with fear, he told me what happened. I, of course, knew he spoke the truth. Richard had a scratch on his nose where the glass, or Candle Face's quick exit from the mirror, might have cut him.

When my father came home, he was annoyed because the bathroom mirror had broken and pieces of glass were scattered on the bathroom floor. He demanded to know why none of us had cleaned it up. Still scared, Richard didn't want to go back into the bathroom and neither did I. We didn't say anything. By now Richard wasn't sure if what he had seen was real or whether he'd imagined the whole thing. I had felt the same in the early days after I had just seen Candle Face, and after her first few visits. But what about the broken bathroom mirror? *That was my proof.*

I instinctively thought of our older brothers. They were spending even less time in the house, which of course I blamed on their drinking and drug habits. I even suspected Candle Face may have managed to become an associate of theirs where advice about torture was concerned. On the other hand, it began to dawn on me that her haunting our house may have been the reason why they wanted to stay away.

Candle Face had not been able to enter our house at night because I'd made sure the windows were latched. But tonight she had learned the art of entering through our mirror.

Later that night I thought about latching all our outside doors and windows. But my family were bustling around, and in any case, I knew Candle Face could be hiding somewhere inside the house. I closed our bedroom door and the windows, and when I went to bed I wrapped myself in my sheet as I usually did, with my face exposed. When Richard got into bed he made his usual preparations and covered himself in his sheet with even his face covered.

Richard slept as he usually did. I stayed awake as was my custom nowadays, tossing and turning and re-wrapping myself into my sleeping position. I stayed that way for ages, my eyes wide open in the dark, the street light from one window my only aid as I picked out all the shapes in my bedroom. As I turned towards Richard's bed, my senses sharpened. There seemed to be something white under his bed which was changing shape, growing and elongating even as I stared at it.

What looked like a large white bed sheet with a form hiding in it came slithering out from under the bed. I managed to tear my eyes away to glance at Richard. But he was still on top of his bed, still completely covered from head to toe and presumably asleep. I looked back at the thing on the floor which was now billowing towards me. It crept up close. The hand I had seen at the back porch door emerged from one side, clutching and creasing the white sheet. It crept upwards in this fashion, clutched the top edge and pulled it down. Then I saw Candle Face's visage, which I had still not got used to. Her gurgle started low, then reached what I thought was a roar in the middle of the quiet night.

In her horrible, harsh voice she said, "I got your brother scared today, didn't I?" I maintained a stunned, frightened silence. Richard stayed asleep. "It won't just be the mirror next time," Candle Face went on. "Like I told you, watch your back, little boy. I'm not going yet."

Please do, I thought, regretting it the next instant when I remembered she could look inside my head. Meanwhile Candle Face was tittering and settling down at the foot of my bed. She no longer crouched beside it as she had in the past.

Arthur M. Mills, Jr.

I was back to being starved of my voice and was immobile, as I always had been with Candle Face around. But she thought it was a good time to start a conversation. "Who is that girl Richard's so bothered about?" she asked.

I didn't answer.

"He hasn't a hope. Tell him to give up," she commanded.

Richard started to stir in his sleep. Candle Face glanced at Richard, then back at me, placing her bony finger where her lips would have been. She said, "Shhhhhh . . ." in an exaggerated way, and then turned expectantly in the direction of the noise Richard started to kick up. She opened the window and crawled out in her customary way. I was thankful for Richard's commotion since it ultimately propelled Candle Face into leaving my room and allowing me to sleep.

When my mother came into our room in the morning to wake us up for school, she was annoyed about one of her sheets lying on the floor. She picked it up and found it was filthy dirty. "Who's responsible for this?" she demanded.

Richard didn't know. I knew but couldn't tell, so we both kept quiet and she grounded us for the rest of the day after we came home from school. Even so, I was thankful for having been allowed a little bit of sleep after Candle Face left. Richard didn't look so good. I could tell from his face he was either still mourning his rejection from Maria or still feeling the aftershock of Candle Face's entry, or both.

CHAPTER 16

Ever since we moved into the neighborhood, Richard and I had regularly attended church at South Austin Baptist Church. Only the two of us went. My parents didn't attend, although they encouraged us to go. Eventually Richard and I realized our parents sent us off to church so they could have a leisurely Sunday morning with a few hours of peace and quiet after a week of hard work.

Dan and Felix didn't go because they preferred to spend most of their weekend at their friend's house up the street. Their girlfriends would also be there because Dan's girlfriend, Silvia, was his friend's sister. When our parents were away at work on Saturday, Sunday or both, Dan and Felix preferred to stay home, so Richard and I reckoned it would be better to be away on Sunday. The church gave us a nice feeling. We felt safe there. Also, I thought Sunday school was good for both of us. In fact, I could see Richard was becoming very devout.

I also thought our religious teachings may have inspired Richard to turn away from fighting Andre and Carlos. They may even have caused him to turn the other cheek when our older brothers inflicted their cruel pain upon him. Turning the other cheek had to be good for Richard in the long run, according to the scriptures.

In the early spring of 1984, the Sunday school held a Bible verse competition. From start to finish, the competition was to last two months. We were not given a fixed target but were told we had the six days of the week between Sundays to memorize as many Bible verses as possible. For Richard this was easy. He had already committed verses to heart on subjects as diverse as angels and atonement, forgiveness and non-retaliation. I, on the other hand, had to start from scratch. I had changed my attitude. Not bothering about lessons and not doing my homework was one thing, but this was different. I wanted to learn the verses for the church which had been a mainstay for Richard and me in the years while we were growing up. This was the least we could do. One week I chose:

Psalms 72:5 He will endure as long as the sun, as long as the moon, through all generations.

Psalms 76:7 You alone are to be feared. Who can stand before you when you are angry?

Psalms 85:9 Surely his salvation is near those who fear him, that his glory may dwell in our land.

The verses made sense to me when I was mugging them. I even went as far as reciting them in front of our new bathroom mirror. But on the Saturday before our recitation, I couldn't get them right. I got the 'endurance through generations' wrong. If I had to endure what I was enduring at night, I hoped my children and their children wouldn't have to. At least I knew what I feared. Besides Candle Face, I also feared my older brothers. How was I going to analyze these verses as they should be analyzed?

The week's recitation would be held the following Sunday. The student who could recite the greatest number of Bible verses correctly was going to win a sticker for his or her Bible. Our Sunday school teachers had given us lots of clues and references and spoken about a number of present day situations which were similar to those that happened in Biblical times. Fellow students were busy looking for relevant or favorite verses to memorize. I pretty much knew what was going to happen.

Richard got a sticker in his Bible the very first week and managed to get new stickers in his Bible every Sunday after that. As for me, I found my interest fading as the weeks wore on. I knew Richard would do better than my best. He had found it easy to memorize most of the verses during regular Sunday school, something that fitted in well with all his other talents. He never missed a line in his school, church or home theatricals.

Richard was growing in stature in the eyes of the other children in Sunday school and the church as he made sure he won the stickers. At the end of the second month, the student who won the most stickers would win the grand prize, a brand new Bible.

Richard won the Bible.

He was proud and so was I when he was awarded that grand prize. When he brought it home, for once our parents and older brothers couldn't take their eyes off Richard and his Bible. My mother claimed she hadn't even known about the competition, but now that he'd won, she was proud of her son.

All the kids in our group dropped in that Sunday. They could see that the Bible was Richard's most cherished possession. *Now it's my cherished possession.* Everyone in our family saw it, too. Our parents were proud of him and I suspected even Dan and Felix thought better of Richard for attending Sunday school regularly, joining the competition and winning the grand prize.

By now Richard wanted to make another attempt at reaching out to Maria, to make her see how much she meant to him. I could see this from the way he looked at her when we entered the school on Monday and found Maria standing with a group of classmates in the corridor. She immediately seemed aware of Richard's presence and must have realized he would approach her once more because she looked distressed. Obviously she hadn't changed her mind and was hoping Richard wouldn't embarrass her again.

But being a quiet, introverted girl, Maria kept her feelings to herself. So Richard got all the signs wrong. All he was aware of was that Maria still smiled back at him from time to time. He told himself the kids in his class were just being mean when they told him Maria had no interest in him at all.

I had guessed all this not only from the looks Richard gave Maria but from how he talked in his sleep. I had listened carefully and found even his lowest key mumbling could be deciphered. I remembered Candle Face's cryptic remark when she had left the last time. "He hasn't a hope. Tell him to give up." But how on earth could I tell Richard that? How could I tell him the message came from a frightening source that might have seen the future and got it right? I might have succeeded in cautioning him, but I would also bring back the fact of the dreadful face in the mirror and the fact that it might be true.

Arthur M. Mills, Jr.

I kept quiet.

At least I hadn't died after Candle Face warned me about watching my back. I had managed to outwit her the time she tried to jump in through our windows and had been stopped. I could only hope Candle Face was wrong about Richard not having a hope.

Richard told himself that, just as before, he would never know Maria's feelings for him unless he showed her how sincere he was. One day he took the Bible to school. I could see the kids were impressed. They asked Richard for details about the church contest. The ones who already went to church with us backed up Richard and doubly confirmed with the others how good Richard had been.

Maria stayed on the fringe of the crowds who wanted to be Richard's friends, but Richard lost his nerve and didn't talk to her. Having major doubts about what he wanted to do and what he was doing, he brought the Bible back home. As was his custom, though, he pondered hard, rehearsed the giving again in front of the bathroom mirror. He convinced himself Maria had realized what that prize meant to him. Therefore, it would mean the same to her.

The next day Richard took the Bible to school again and offered it to Maria. He told her he had won it at Sunday school, but of course Maria already knew that by now. She said she knew how much it meant to him but could not accept the gift. She did try to soften it, though, by telling him he was 'nice.'

Once again Richard was devastated. But this time he took the blow a lot worse than during the invitation for the magic show.

Even his fellow classmates were kinder to Richard this time around. Like me, they thought he should never have made such a major mistake. Nobody teased him, though. They knew what a great guy he was for winning that Bible.

By that evening, I knew the outcome of Richard's gamble. Judging from his mood and the fact the Bible was back in the house, it was not a difficult guess. How could I not know when I saw Richard looking at the window with anguish written all over his face? His lips were moving as if he wanted to invoke something, or someone. At least he didn't repeat this little performance in front of the new bathroom mirror.

Later that evening, like a flutter in the cool evening breeze, I heard a choking, gurgling titter from the direction of the back yard. This was going to be another hell of a night, I told myself. I took care to lock all the doors and windows.

Richard made his preparations for bed after dinner, after he'd forced me to help Mom with the washing up instead of himself and after he'd finished his school work. I marveled at him for not forgetting all his responsibilities, which included bullying me. Despite his troubles of the day, Richard went to sleep as usual while I stayed awake as usual.

Soon, as I knew it would, the window to the street creaked open and the filthy rotten smell drifted in before she did. Here she was. This time she had chosen to slide a long fingernail in to unlatch the window and had hopped in, one leg at a time, over the windowsill, toes first on the floor. Her gash of a mouth changed shape. The message she sent me was, "Told you so." She actually did a little dance around the room, not crouching nor sitting nor slithering on the floor. She went up to Richard, pointed her index finger at his sleeping form and turned her head towards me. She cackled loudly enough for me to hear, but Richard slept on.

Now Candle Face dashed up to me. I would have leapt out the window if I could, but as always I was immobilized in her presence. Candle Face dashing around was more alarming than her slow creeping and crawling. She hovered over my face, exhibiting how jubilant she was. "I went to see Maria," she said in her horrible voice.

I didn't answer, but she must have seen my eyes widening in horror. "Maria didn't know I was there," she continued, "but I got a good look at her. Tell me how Richard could like someone so insipid, so goody-goody?"

Again I remained silent.

Candle Face looked annoyed but didn't pursue the subject. Instead, she began to talk about her family. She had never mentioned them before, so I listened carefully despite her dreadful voice.

"I was in my room," she said, "and my eight-year-old brother was in his room when the lightning struck. Then my parents woke up and knew something terrible was happening. At first they didn't know what it was, then realized the house was on fire. They rushed out with my brother and left me in my room alone.

"We had a large lawn outside. A lot of people were standing on it, drawn because of the fire. They put my brother down on the grass and

Arthur M. Mills, Jr.

were talking to the people they knew. The firemen arrived. My parents told them I was still in the upstairs room and had to be rescued. But the firemen couldn't get back inside. My brother wandered off and went back inside the house. We both were lost that night."

I was astounded. That boy who I thought might be in Mollie Dawson Elementary School had died! What a lot of versions there were concerning the empty lot next door. I wanted to ask Candle Face what happened after that. Reading my thoughts, Candle Face said that since her brother was an innocent child, he went around looking for innocent souls like himself. This was as close to personal as Candle Face could get.

She came back to the present and reminded me that she *had* warned me about Richard losing out. *Why could I not have communicated this to Richard?*

She carried on by telling me she didn't care. Richard deserved the worst. He deserved what he got. "Maybe my brother will befriend Richard," she added, "since I never would."

Why? was my silent question.

Candle Face turned her wrathful face towards me. "Why should everyone watch him perform with their backs to me?"

What I could make of this strange utterance was that Candle Face had watched unseen when Richard performed up in the tree house. We would be facing Richard when he was on the stage, so of course our backs were turned to her while she was in the hole. What about my glances in that direction? I had always checked the hole out before we started. I always gave it a 'clean' chit because I never noticed anything unusual on these occasions.

Was Candle Face jealous—first about Maria, then Richard? She must have realized how absurd she was because at this point she yanked the window open and stepped outside like a ballet dancer. She left in a huff, no longer the tired old Candle Face. She was stronger now.

After that night, Richard never mentioned Maria. He chose to sit at the back of the classroom and didn't steal looks at her any more.

Arthur M. Mills, Jr.

CHAPTER 17

Richard's dark and somber mood didn't last long. Soon he was back to being a quiet and serious boy who spent time on his own and had a passion for drama and poetry.

I had witnessed our brothers using and abusing Richard. I had seen him when he thought that giving in to their ways might help him win their favor. I had seen Andre getting at him. Quite a few of us were aware of the Carlos incident. We knew of the occasions when Maria had politely turned away. However, after her dramatic entry through the mirror, Candle Face had left Richard alone. I remained worried for him on that account because Candle Face had voiced her opinion about him. I hated to see Richard being picked upon by so many people.

Richard had been able to face up to each situation as it arose. Obviously he would never retaliate, no matter how anyone treated him. But he managed to collect his wits and his feelings and bounce back on his feet each time. He knew where he was going and knew what he was good at. He maintained his grades in school and returned to taking part in school and church plays and conducting magic shows. His creative side flourished. The stories became more extempore, weirder and sympathetic towards the ghost family who had by now found their skins and original looks.

Richard was back doing what he did best.

But then came the next sudden change. This must have been long after he had won the Bible which Maria declined to accept. It was sometime after I thought he had gone back to being the twelve-and-a-half-year-old that I knew.

My friends and I noticed this next big change. We were bound to because Richard suddenly lost interest in what he did best. He didn't want to hold magic shows anymore! Mentioning something about how easy the tree house had become for anybody and everybody to get to, he said he wanted to tear it down. As it turned out, it took more time to bring it down than it had to put it up. Richard carried on single handedly and doggedly, a determined expression on his face.

As far as I knew, Richard had reasoned his one sighting of Candle Face had been his own imagination, brought on by his heightened emotional state at the time. Meanwhile, Candle Face still came in at night, harassed and horrified me. I spied on Candle Face one night, for a change (rather than she on everyone else including Maria). I suspected she may have visited Dan and Felix, but if she had, they stayed put in their room for the rest of the night. I saw her return to her lot, then go up into the tree house, sure no one else saw her except me.

Any mention of Candle Face today reminds me of the helplessness I felt as an eleven-year-old. I was never prepared for her evil presence. Did Richard know what I was putting up with from Candle Face? How much did he know?

I did worry about Richard's comment about the tree house. Did he know who had been going in there, or was it a guess? I greatly wanted to ask him what he had meant. But as before, I didn't want to bring up matters which I knew he might want to avoid.

Richard at this stage was changing again. He was a different Richard than the boy he was a month ago. He still went to school and did his lessons, though he followed his class work mechanically. He no longer raised his hand when the teachers looked for someone to answer a question. After school he came home and stayed in his room. This, at least, was usual. We still went to church Sunday school, but Richard's participation became like mine. He listened if he had to, grew bored if he felt the topic had been discussed before, and did not participate a hundred percent, as he used to. This wasn't like the old Richard.

At least he kept on writing and narrating his stories to us. I found the stories had become darker, the situations in them more impossible and more fantastic. There was a mystery story about a family who disappeared. The story ended with a more than intense fire, as at a

Arthur M. Mills, Jr.

crematorium. Listening to the story made all of us in our group very uncomfortable, something that had never happened before.

The story was about a family: mother, father, boy and girl. They were Mexican by birth and used to live in South Austin. The girl was a great beauty and her family worried about her, except the younger brother. He knew his sister would be able to take care of herself, but her mother was worried enough not to want to go to work, even when she was offered a really nice job at the ice cream parlor at the local mall. The mother was happy to stay at home, drive her daughter to school and look after her children in every possible way.

Well, someone cast an evil eye on the family. It was a powerful evil eye because all of them just got more and more sick. A kindly doctor at the local clinic found out what had taken hold of them. He said they would have to move out and have their home exorcised. Nothing else would get rid of the evil eye.

Since real medicine wasn't working, the family asked the priest from their local church to come and take a look. He came, went over the house with a special exorcism tool which could tell that a spell had been cast. He confirmed their worst fears and said he would be back the next day to do what was necessary.

But the priest died in his bed that night. The family didn't know what to do. They felt awful about the priest who died. Even worse, his death seemed to be a confirmation their home was cursed. They reasoned the evil spirits in their house must have resented the fact that they would have to leave and had killed him. They wondered what they should do next and decided they would stay on in their house just a little bit longer.

The friendly doctor received a call late at night to say that the mother and father were ill. By the time he arrived, he found the house had gone up in flames and everything in it had been incinerated. He never found any signs of the family or their house.

No one ever saw the father, mother, girl and little boy again. People wondered if they had really burned to death along with their house. Now Richard added a twist to the story. The boy had a friend who had borrowed some of his toys to play with. When the family disappeared, this friend kept the toys for a few years, then gave them away to his sister.

I was amazed, at the story and at Richard. All around me my friends stared down at the ground while they recalled which of their toys were truly theirs and which were borrowed. I was also surprised because Richard had given the people in the story no room to escape, unlike his earlier stories. I could not bear to think about the other parallels to real life situations because it came to me in a flash—these were people he knew!

And that ending about the toys Richard had taken from Andre's conversation with us. We had not spoken of Andre since the day he died, but I knew that through his story, Richard was telling me he would never forget the afternoon when Andre came to play.

As time went on, Richard would retell the story with special additions and alterations. Like his other stories at this time, people went into situations over which they had no control. Then they died at the end. Unlike Richard's old stories, there was never a way out for them now. This was a definite change that I couldn't make head or tail of.

Richard also continued writing poetry, but his poetic style had taken a 180 degree turn. Earlier, the themes centered on love and peace. Now he changed his focus to death, destruction and the lack of peace. The poems became all-consuming for Richard.

He still wanted his poems to be read. I read them, as I always had, but didn't like their new tone. He sent his poems to a number of magazines and entered a great many poetry competitions. He entered a national Boy Scout poetry contest and won first place with a poem that gave away his innermost concerns and hope. It exposed Richard's soul at the time. It spoke of this world and its lack of peace. Here is his poem:

There was peace on Earth,
At its birth.

But things have changed,
Everything is rearranged.

Peace is gone,
Everything is wrong.

Arthur M. Mills, Jr.

People did it,
But they won't admit it.

If we help one another,
And work with each other,
We can change the Earth,
It can be a second birth.

Although Richard was happy about winning first prize for his poem, our family showed less interest than when he won the Bible. Father said he wasn't in the habit of reading anything, poetry or otherwise. Mother read the poem, congratulated Richard, and went about her business. Richard and I thought maybe Dan and Felix could set the poem to music—their Pink Floyd type rock band was going to be launched soon. But Dan and Felix took this information from us with glazed eyes and a marked lack of interest.

Our friends were happy enough. Richard recited his poem for them, and it reminded us of the way things used to be. Maybe we, too, were outgrowing a lot of our interests. The bicycle hop and clover picnic were definitely things of the past. But when I look back now, I can see the change in Richard led to the rest of us changing in little and large ways. *It is called growing up.*

Then there was my friend, Nolan, with the short blonde hair. We rarely met these days outside of school. He was topping my grade at studies and was working hard to keep it that way. I complained, but not much, because he had helped during that project. Candle Face had interrupted that discussion by knocking on the window. Nolan was ace. He wanted to be the best in everything and had less time for me or the group because he was doing his best in academics and at soccer. Nolan said that his main focus now was his grandparents who were bringing him up. He was going to have some sort of a top class university job and his grandparents would live with him when they were really old.

Evan still played with Richard and me but invited us over to his house next door less and less. Richard wouldn't go in any case. I did, but felt I was under the scrutiny of his parents, his sister and his dog. His dog was an old dog that had reacted to Candle Face that first night. The dog would now look mournfully at me as though I were to blame. *I suppose I was.* Well, Evan was still worried about his dog and was spending more time with his family which included the dog. I had heard them sing along with each other in the car on the way to school, but now they sang together at home as well. I could hear their melodies wafting across to our house. My mother would hear, too, and stand still for as long as the song lasted. Sometimes the dog would wail or howl while the rest of the family sang.

Mark and I still walked to school together. I supposed we would until we graduated. Maybe we'd travel to the next school together, since we were in the same grade and best friends. Mark, like Evan, was paying more and more attention to his sibling. Mark wanted the best for him and his older brother, Sean.

Randy was more Richard's friend. He was older, broader, and shorter than Richard. We never got to go into his house, except that one time when I saw the fish aquariums. Instead, he always had to come outside to play with us. His mother always looked at me and my brothers with a strange expression, like she wanted to ask, "Who, or what could you boys be doing here?" I could see that Randy was preoccupied. He was trying to get away from home and Ben Howell. He was another troubled soul.

I was changing. Earlier, there were all my older brothers to be scared of. But I could now understand Richard better and could see why he was the way he was. I always got on with my Father. I could also sense some of my mother's frustrations and could see how swamped she was, not only with her engraving work and housework but having to pretend all was well with Dan and Felix. I could see how helpless she, too, felt from time to time.

I was spending more time with the changed Richard. Besides what I saw, there were more changes in how Richard related to his world. He got himself a new good friend. But the friend was not there.

CHAPTER 18

Richard had turned from an extrovert into an introvert. This transformation might have been going on for a while, but I hadn't caught on to the little changes. When I finally did, it seemed as if he had changed practically overnight. He was the same quiet Richard but now a lot quieter. I was never sure why. Perhaps the cause was Maria, or perhaps his changed interests, or that our group of friends was loosening up. Maybe Richard thought he had no one to turn to. There was me, of course, but I could easily be overlooked. Richard was quickly becoming a stranger to me and possibly to himself as well.

Other than the evening of his brush with Andre, a long time had passed since I heard Richard talk to himself. But now I would sometimes see him sitting alone the curb in front of the house talking into thin air. One night after we'd gone to bed, I plucked up the courage to ask Richard who he had been talking to on the curb.

130   Arthur M. Mills, Jr.

"Griffin," he answered.

Although the name sounded familiar, I couldn't connect it to anyone I knew. "Griffin? Who's that?" I laughed to cover my embarrassment at not knowing.

"You know, Griffin," my brother replied. "A Griffin is a creature that has the body of a lion and the head of an eagle. We're friends."

"You're crazy," I retorted. "There is no such thing as a Griffin."

Richard shrugged and paid no attention to my ridicule. He was used to it after his brush with all the others.

I didn't want anything to do with Richard's Griffin, but I looked it up in the school library the next day. The dictionary told me it's a legendary creature. Its description was identical to the one Richard had given me—body of a lion and the head and wings of an eagle. The griffin was thought to be an especially powerful and majestic creature. Griffins are normally known for guarding treasure. The illustration showed a griffin with its legs like an eagle's legs with talons. Richard had probably researched his friend better than I had. The old Richard would have taken all this information and put it into a story to hold us spellbound. The new Richard had simply taken the Griffin in as a magical new friend.

Right then I changed my mind about not having anything to do with Richard's Griffin. I now wished I had one. The creature sounded magical enough and majestic enough.

And then I saw Griffin. He was not a figment of Richard's imagination. He was real.

It happened after dinner one evening. I was in the kitchen helping Mom with the dishes. Richard said he wanted some fresh air and had just stepped out to the back porch. We heard him talking to someone whom I presumed was his imaginary friend, Griffin. I looked at Mom. She had her hands in soapy water but had stopped scrubbing. She had her head to one side and was listening intently, the way she would listen to Evan's family singing. She must have known something was up. Had she noticed the change in Richard as I had? But Mom went back to the dishes. We wiped up and headed towards our bedrooms. By then, Richard had returned to our bedroom, got his writing notebook out and was furiously scribbling away, totally focused on his writing. After a while we both turned in, with me wrapping up like a mummy like I always did. Surprisingly Richard didn't cover himself. He fell asleep, I thought, because there was no movement from his bed.

I stayed awake, lying on my back with my eyes wide open and kept checking our room out in the half light. It was getting late, but I was restless, as I usually am early in the night. I turned towards Richard's bed and froze. It was like all those other nights when I saw something I should not have seen. My mind worked furiously, but I couldn't make sense of what I saw.

Richard was sitting bolt upright in bed, legs bent at the knees, feet planted firmly on the floor. He was holding his arms and hands in the most unusual way: both his arms stretched out in front, parallel to the floor, with his hands flopping at the wrists. His hair tousled, his eyes wide open, he appeared to be a spellbound zombie.

Richard rose slowly from his bed and shuffled forward noiselessly. He did not blink.

I would have loved to burrow down in my bed and forget about Richard turning into a ghoul. Then I figured Richard was sleep walking. I had seen that on TV and heard that if children could sleep talk they could sleep walk as well.

Richard's feet shuffled forward. He was headed for our bedroom door. He could be in danger if he walked out, and I knew I'd either have to do something myself or get someone else to help. What about our parents? Should I dash across, rouse them from bed and enlist their help? I thought not. It would take me too long to explain what was happening, and besides, they would surely doubt my theory he was sleep walking. No, I decided. Trying to involve our parents was not a good idea.

Richard would have to manage with just me. I walked though the kitchen to the back porch, a little behind Richard. Fearless in sleep as he had always been when awake, he went to the door to the back porch from our back lot. He stopped. I stole a glance at our trophy tree. It looked neglected and forlorn, with just the one board across its base of branches. My eyes, as always, slid to the hole in the back lot next to ours. Now I kind of knew what to look for.

But it wasn't Candle Face who emerged. It was a real life Griffin.

It looked similar to its picture in the dictionary in our school library, but different at the same time. It was small and furry, not much bigger than Evan's dog. Its front paws and middle bit were like a lion. A pair

Arthur M. Mills, Jr.

of wings like eagles' wings rose from its middle. The eagle effect was carried on to its back legs which ended in long talons.

The Griffin trotted up to the tree, flapped its wings and took a short hopping flight through the night sky before it landed at our back porch door steps. Richard smiled in his sleep, opened the door and stepped out. All this time I had watched the strange form, its description in the dictionary ringing in my ears. But that had made it sound majestic and somewhat frightening, like the other form which arose from the hole in the back lot next door. In contrast, Richard's Griffin looked cute and friendly. Not only that, it talked.

Richard spoke to his friend in low tone. The Griffin talked to him in a human voice. It was not only Richard's Griffin, I now remembered where I had heard that name before. Candle Face had spoken of her brother. His name was Griffin.

Now I knew this was Candle Face's brother in front of me. Candle Face was humanoid in the worst way possible—her form, hair, rasping voice and movements. Griffin, on the other hand, was like a little person in its playful manner and its ability to talk and play like boys. Richard and Griffin were playing out in the grass now, with Griffin hopping up, flapping its wings to soar up briefly. The next instant, it dived down to nuzzle Richard's hair with its beak. I don't know if Richard was awake or in a state of sleep. *Or if I was sleeping-dreaming.* His eyes stayed wide open. He used his arms in play, but they stayed in front of him, hands flopping down. Richard still adopted the stance of a sleep walker, even if he was a sleep walker at play. I watched from the back porch, unabashedly jealous. I could do with a griffin of my own.

What was it that Candle Face had said about her brother? I gave myself the answer. She had said that he looked for other innocent souls like himself. And so Griffin and Richard had found each other. The two souls were happy. Richard didn't feel picked upon at any point. He was not in danger of nasty pecks or pummeling. There was no question of his friend wanting to inflict pain of any kind on him. Richard in sleep was finally free. *If he was sleeping.*

Why had I not been able to see Griffin before tonight? Why had no one been able to see Griffin? Someone had read my thoughts, because I heard a chirrupy boyish voice say, "I keep myself hidden and invisible in the day. My sister does too."

I was happy that Richard had not been talking to the air around him. Never mind if the others didn't know that. But Candle Face on the loose and invisible? It made my flesh crawl to think that I would not know if she were around. It also made matters more dangerous for me.

I went down and sat on the back porch steps as the night wore on. Richard had his friend in Griffin. I hoped that Candle Face didn't think I had chosen her for a friend. Why did she bother me so? I was ready with my answer. I shouldn't have bothered her that night many nights ago, when I had gone in search of one or more ghosts—I had been searching for the 'truth', as I had told myself.

I kept telling myself my thoughts would invariably invoke Candle Face. That was how it was now. I heard a loud choking gurgle from the hole in the back lot and what sounded like a barking command. Griffin turned to Richard, said goodbye and flapped back home. He carried what looked like a golden egg in his beak. Richard turned back towards the steps where I sat. I waited for him and both of us walked back to our bedroom in comfortable companionship. We went to bed, and this time Richard covered himself from top to toe as was his habit.

Richard slept on. I stayed awake for a while thinking about what I had just seen and heard. I remembered the dull gold of the egg in Griffin's beak as it glinted in the moonlight. That was when I remembered the other description in the dictionary, that Griffins were associated with treasure. Richard had found his treasure. What about me, I wondered?

When I awoke the next morning, sunlight was streaming in from the window next to Richard's bed. It was bright, golden sunlight near his feet. Richard sat up, collected some glittery stuff from where the rays of light fell. He walked to the closet and dropped it at the back of a clothes shelf.

Mom came in later and said she was glad we were both up because she had to go in early today. She then glanced at Richard's feet and her mouth fell open. "Did you play in the grass outside last night?"

Richard and I did not answer.

I wanted to ask Richard about what he put on the back shelf. As before, I felt awkward voicing the amazing sights from last night, the remains of which Richard had stored. But when I did, I realized this

Arthur M. Mills, Jr.

was the changed Richard. He leaned forward and told me Griffin had promised to take him to a distant land tonight. I could not go, but Richard would let me read the story of that adventure after he had written it.

Needless to say, I couldn't wait, but I was back to worrying about Richard flying to a place far away on the back of Griffin. It turned out that Richard couldn't wait, either. I fell asleep early that night. Richard and Griffin met in sleep or wakefulness, I don't know which.

Richard's story of his adventure with Griffin was written as soon as he returned. In life, Griffin was an eight year old. The long sleep of death gave him and his sister a great deal of time until a young boy came and disturbed their place of rest and invoked their spirits. Griffin's sister had taught him to read, and he loved to visit the Mollie Dawson library as he remained invisible.

At first Griffin was greatly interested in dinosaurs, those beasts which roamed our earth millions and millions of years ago. Among the many types of dinosaurs, there was one called Protoceratops. These beasts had beaks and laid eggs which appeared golden. Their bodies were part terrestrial beasts and partly birdlike. Griffin liked the lineage. He would like to trace his ancestry to this particular dinosaur which had lived some 70 million years ago in central Asia. Fortunately, Griffin was able to choose his form from the mythical griffin, evolved from Protoceratops when he revealed himself to Richard. *And later to me.* His sister was not able to choose her form. She was stuck with what she had. I did not ask why.

Griffin held Richard in his talons when they took off for the land of Griffin's ancestor's ancestors. Richard reached forward and gripped his ankles. They were safe till they reached Mongolia. Griffin and Richard could see the Protoceratops' graves from above before they landed. Their fossil outlines were unmistakable. Richard did a little skipping run during landing. Griffin felt he was home.

At first they walked around the outline of the huge beasts, noting their beaks with a kind of frill along the place where their necks would have been. They then set off to look for their fossilized eggs in their fossilized nests. Griffin said that it was thought that Protoceratops always lined their nests with gold. It was a soft metal and gold always appeared magically near Protoceratops herds. Their huge eggs were safe in these nests which were tough yet soft enough for the

Protoceratops mothers to rest their bellies. Griffin's research in our school library had revealed that when humans arrived here some 70 million years later, it wasn't difficult to make the connection between the huge dinosaurs which had grazed here built their nests, laid their eggs and stayed close to gold. If a human found a Protoceratop fossil, he knew he would find gold nearby. The connection endured. Their early drawings gave birth to mythological stories about the griffin.

Richard and Griffin left the same way they had come. Airborne once more, they could see a land below a mountain which looked as if it was made of molten gold. Across this mountain and the valley of the great beasts and their nests, was a hillock of red sandstone. The sun was setting. Richard would never forget the beauty of that evening and the joy of being with Griffin who was a true friend.

In the next few hours, Richard came back in time to go to bed and to go to school. Griffin had an irate older sister waiting up for him. It was lucky for me, because Candle Face had counted the hours anxiously for his return. She had not bothered about anything else. I begged Richard for more details after I read his story about his flight. I didn't know this was to be one of the last stories he would ever write.

Arthur M. Mills, Jr.

CHAPTER 19

I remember it as being a holiday. I was doing my usual at home, which was not a lot. In fact, I was lolling in front of our TV in the living room. Some movement at the edge of my line of vision must have first alerted me. When I looked in the direction in which I had first spied it, I could see a blurred image on the other side of the glass panels of our front door. I got up to take a better look. It was a teenager, a girl, and she was standing there looking like she was not sure about whether she should knock.

The girl must have been about sixteen or seventeen. I had never seen her before, but she seemed to be waiting expectantly, looking around. She saw me and shot me a quizzical look.

"Hello." I said.

She did not reply. I was wondering if she had heard me. When I looked at her, I realized that she was lost in thought, studying the outside of our house with some keenness.

"Hello?" I said again, stressing the query. I opened the screen door and stepped outside. She had taken a quick peek inside in the time I had taken to open the door and walk out. I now stood on the porch with her. She turned to me and spoke for the first time.

"I used to live here," she announced.

I quickly did my sums. "It must have been a long time ago because I've lived here for over six years."

"I used to live here in this house but that was when it wasn't here," she said.

I didn't know what to make of her proclamation. My only question was, "What does that mean?"

"This house used to be many miles away to the east, on the outskirts of Austin. Someone bought our house when I was little. I was eleven and remember my parents telling me our house being relocated by the new owners. I remember the men in overalls who came and did the relocation. It's something I won't forget." She paused here, rummaged inside her handbag and found what she wanted. "Look, my dad took pictures of it being plucked out and put on the huge truck that drove off with our house."

This was a new view of our house for me. There were men in orange overalls. They seemed to be leveraging our house from its foundation onto huge steel pipes. There was another photograph of our house, as tilted as it could get, the whole of it on a huge flat board which fitted all the floors. The men seemed to be rolling the steel pipes off, and a crane was hoisting the flat board foundation onto the biggest truck I had seen. None of my fake Hot Wheels toys had a copy of this one. Randy had the newest Hot Wheels, but he didn't have anything that looked like this truck either, and this was some six or seven years ago.

This was another view I would probably never see. There was another photograph of our house being driven off in that monster truck. A girl of about my age stood in the foreground waving at the house. I looked back at the girl in front of me. It looked like her when she was eleven. It was our house all right. I smiled at her and handed back the photographs. But she shook her head, saying I could have them. She said she had another set and had brought these because she wanted to give them to whoever lived here now. I shuffled though the pictures and stopped at one picture that showed my house as it stood in its previous location. She looked back at me with the same quizzical expression she had when I went out to say hello.

"Notice anything different?" she asked.

"No," I responded.

She laughed and took me outside by the elbow to our front yard. She was the same height as me, but then I was tall for my age. The girl pointed to the roof of our single story house. "Notice anything now?" I had to. The house in the picture had a small duplex room stuck above the bedroom I shared with Richard. I realized now about the second entrance door from the front porch, and why people tended to think of our house as a duplex.

I wondered why our house had been remodeled and that little room knocked off. It could have been a playroom for me or a writing den for Richard.

I was still wondering what happened to that duplex. *Was it really our house that the girl had lived in?*

The girl had no such doubts. "I've thought about our house so often since it was sold and driven away. I'm glad I found it!" She was close to crying. Finally she stopped, let go my elbow and wiped her eyes. We were quiet for a bit, as she thought her thoughts and I thought mine. What I was thinking was, this explained the mystery of the high foundation under our house. It must have been built separately, and our house slid off the huge truck by those men in orange overalls, to be positioned where it was now.

But I had more questions—what was here before our house arrived six years ago? Was it an empty lot as well, and did it join with the empty lot next door? I would not wait a couple of years this time. I would ask my parents tonight. This was a mystery that needed to be solved as soon as possible. It was more intriguing than the duplex and what happened to it.

The girl had composed herself by now. I wondered how I would feel if someone bought our house and either lived in it here, or took it somewhere else to live in. *I wondered how I would feel if I were to visit our house with its new owners many years later, as the girl was doing.*

"Your parents must have had this house brought here. I lived in it before the house was moved here," the girl was saying. I had already figured this out.

She asked me if she could come in and look around. I said yes and she walked in and recognized little details inside the house right way. She pointed to my bedroom and told me it used to be her parents' bedroom. The room above had been a storeroom.

We walked around the house while she exclaimed at all the features she could remember. She was traveling down memory lane. I kept imagining myself many years later, trying to relive my life in this house. It was a weird feeling and a new line of thought, something that thrilled me with its new set of wondering what it would be like if . . . .

I told her about my family who lived in it now—my brothers, my parents and me. It was fun talking to her but I was feeling a little unsure. Was I giving too much away? I asked myself later whether it was the girl or whether it was the fact that currently Candle Face dropped in whenever she felt like it. Right now I felt instinctively that I should hold back, if only just a little bit.

My instincts were right in a way. But they were off track. After we had walked around a bit she took a step closer to me and asked, "Have you ever seen anything weird in this house?" Her question came unexpectedly, but because of all that I had seen and heard, I could have answered her right away.

I could have said "yes." She had given me a cue. I could have told her about Candle Face and her visitations to this house, to what used to be her parents' bedroom. I could have told her about my most recent discovery about Griffin. I could have described my older brothers' torture sessions inflicted on my brother Richard. Instead, I took a deep breath and said, "No."

She looked at me and seemed to heave a sigh of relief. She left and I never saw her again. I have thought of her often. At the time, I heard her with disbelief. That morning I wondered why she would say that, when the weird thing inside and outside the house was only because of the empty lot next door in this neighborhood, not her own.

Richard came back that afternoon looking exhilarated. He looked as if he'd had a busy morning. I told him about our visitor, what she had said and showed him the photographs. Richard was ecstatic. He thought what I had to tell and show him was material enough for one long story. I heard him talk to himself again *(or was Griffin there and invisible to me?)* "Wait until you hear this, Griffin. It's going to be like another of your researched stories."

My older brothers were at the table during dinner that night and strangely subdued. I steeled myself to ask the many questions I had. I told myself I was older now. I had asked about the family next door many months ago and my family had found it funny. I had to hand to them the fact that they *had* answered my questions as far as they knew. Now, as then, I looked at my father and told him about the girl who had dropped in this morning and how she had said this used to be her house, except that it used to be some miles out of town. It was my father's turn now to look subdued. He and my mother exchanged glances. I was surprised when Mom spoke first. "Yes, we used to live in the projects. You were only five or six years old, Ray, when your father and I bought this plot. We bought the house separately. It was somewhere in East Austin, if I remember right. The owners were going to tear it down and build a new house. We got it at the right price, moved it here and got the package at a price we could not otherwise have afforded. The original house even had a duplex. But we were advised against it because the foundation we had to build here on Ben Howell would not have been strong enough for the whole house."

All this was news to my brothers. They were quiet. They were listening for the first time.

Our mother had explained the remodeling and the missing duplex. She had explained the foundation, which I had half guessed. But there was a lot more I wanted to know. "But Mom, b-but Dad, w-what was here b-before that? Was this another e-e-empty lot?" I had to know.

Mom looked over at my father again. She had said her bit, she seemed to indicate. It was now his turn.

He was not usually at a loss for words. But now he looked at us, chewed his food slowly and cleared his throat before he spoke.

"It was an empty lot all right, but it was a large empty lot. It was part of the empty lot next door. The City must have decided to split the large lot into two. They sold ours to us first. As yet they haven't been able to sell the one next door."

He gave no more explanations. We ruminated over what he had said and ate in silence. The next question was inevitable. Dan asked first, in a voice lower than his usual loud and brash self, "You mean our lot was part of the lot next door?"

Our mother answered, "Yes, they had a garden here. I believe they had started digging a pool closer to their house when the fire broke out." She did not look at us.

We had nearly got used to our parents communicating as little as they could. But we now had more questions. It wasn't just me who had to know. Felix asked why they had bought this plot when they knew about the fire that had killed at least one person in the family. Richard asked why they had moved all of us here if they knew at least one child had died and may have been buried in their back lot by the City. I, of course, asked about the hole in the back lot. I was braver now than I had been some months ago.

Our parents answered us with infinite patience. They knew only what they had been told by the realtors, they said. This was the same as what our father had told me many months ago—that there had been a fire and that one person had died in that fire, a girl. They had heard snippets from our neighbors after they had arrived, but each new story conflicted with the other, and there may not have been any substance in the garbled gossip that everyone had to offer. We knew this to be true.

We finished dinner in silence. Richard helped Mom for a change. I brought out the photographs again and passed them around.

My father and I watched TV for a while after this. Richard and I prepared for bed as we used to earlier. I made my mummy-like preparations and Richard covered up. I could hear Dan and Felix as they left for their friends' house to stay over. They told Mom that the rock band was at a crucial stage and they needed to work on their music. Mom didn't say anything. Dad told them he intended to have a good night's sleep undisturbed. My family went their usual separate ways.

CHAPTER 20

I still hated going to sleep. I had won once when Candle Face had to stay outside, looking in and venting her frustration from the other side of the window. She had learnt many skills since that memorable evening she had managed to come in and go out, most of them focused on how to give others the worst time possible and me in particular. Despite everything, and Richard's preoccupation with Griffin, I could see that everyone else looked forward to a good night's sleep. The only thing I could expect was a nightmare-filled night. But then again, I could never be sure about these nightmares.

Richard and I were always told when we had to go to bed. It had turned into a little family drama of its own. My mother or father would point to the living room clock when it said eight o'clock. At first we would ignore the summons. Then we would refuse or plead for more time. After a lot of whining, we would finally comply. By now it would be half past eight and our in-between time was up.

Richard was always the first to get into bed. As usual he liked to sleep on his back and would be completely wrapped in a sheet, head upwards. I often thought that what I was looking at wasn't my brother asleep but someone who was dead and had been covered in a white sheet.

Now he regularly talked in his sleep and walked out as well. I had a sense of all this in my trance-like situation. Sometimes I would follow him. Griffin would join him. It made me sad to watch the two of them play in the back yard because as before, I felt completely left out. They wanted no one else. Was Candle Face listening? I stopped going out to watch.

By the time I came into the bedroom to go to sleep, Richard would usually be in his ready-to-go-to sleep arrangement. This meant I had to turn off the light before going to bed. I hated it when he put me in this situation because I hated having to turn off the light and then make my way to bed. The light switch was on his side of the bedroom. If I turned the light off, I would have to run across the room and dive onto my bed. I was scared to death of the dark. *No one could blame me for all the nightmares I had and the visions I possibly saw.*

One night I stood in the middle of the bedroom mapping out my path from the light switch to my bed. Our bedroom was in a particularly untidy state with our clothes, toys and books littering the floor and our beds unmade all day. My mother had lectured us just that morning, but we still left this chore undone. This meant I would have to clear the clothes and toys lying on the floor of this path—the way back to bed. I had a short cut for that as well. I simply pushed them out of the way and walked up to the light switch.

Deciding to practice, I checked under my bed and Richard's bed. I wasn't going to forget that form in a sheet hiding under Richard's bed. I pretended to turn the light off, then ran and jumped several feet before I landed on my bed. I had taken a new interest in long jump in school and could do this perfectly. I had to start the jump several feet from my bed. I had checked underneath, but the jump gave me additional security, just in case she had materialized in the few seconds when my back was turned.

I have to admit I was always afraid of Candle Face trying to grab my feet from underneath my bed. It was old and squeaky, and the sound I made crashing onto it must have echoed around the house.

In my self-conscious state I felt everyone in the house must have known what I was up to, but I knew my family didn't care, even though I was afraid of the dark and had reason to be. I guess I wasn't as brave as I would have wished. Was my fear making me as wily as my nocturnal visitor? I was telling myself I would have to match her wits if I took seriously her threat—*to watch my back.*

I practiced hard with the light switch. But not everyone thought it was necessary. "Just turn off the light!" Richard yelled at me from under what I thought of as his shroud.

His muffled dark voice startled me. I knew I wasn't brave at all because by now I was crying in fright. "Richard, can you please turn off the light?" I asked, with tears rolling down my cheeks.

Arthur M. Mills, Jr.

"No. If you need me to get up now, you need a punch. What you really need is to grow up and do it yourself."

"You do it!" I was panicked.

"No, you do it," Richard said loudly.

"You do it!" I nearly screamed.

I heard my father yell he didn't want any more shouting and we had better get to sleep. Practice hadn't made me brave. Richard had gone back to the old, uncaring Richard. I would have to turn off that light myself; otherwise, I could try getting into bed with the light on, and that meant another beating from Richard, which might turn into another round of discipline from our father. There would be no end to it.

Fingers quaking, I turned off the light and ran straight towards my bed for the final jump as I had rehearsed. I leaped in the air and landed perfectly on my bed. As quickly as possible, I wrapped the sheet tightly around myself and tucked the sides tightly under my body, as was my habit. I must have looked like Richard but with my face and head exposed. I lay there motionless, my senses on full alert for any signs of that evil presence. My breathing was heavier than after running several miles. I think my heart beat was even louder.

"Go to sleep." Richard mumbled.

Everything was dark—too dark. My eyes had still not adjusted to the darkness. They probably wouldn't for several more minutes. I knew sleep was out of the question, whether Richard or my father dictated it or not. I wouldn't go to sleep because for me this period of time was crucial. My eyes were still wet. I was completely vulnerable to any evils that might lurk in the darkness. I told myself that in my life, evil lurked everywhere. I couldn't stop feeling sorry for myself. I couldn't stop feeling scared.

My heart and breathing hadn't gotten back to normal before I heard a faint noise from the closet. I wished it away but should have known nothing stayed the same. In my house and anything, once noticed, would only get worse. The noise grew more curious. There was a shuffling, then a creak. Then it dawned on me.

Oh my God, I had forgotten to check the closet!

The closet door was slowly opening with a long drawn out creak. I could only guess who was behind it. So all that practice had come to naught. Checking under my bed and Richard's—counting my steps from the switch—jumping and targeting my bed—it was all useless. Earlier I had cried in fear, but now, just as before, I couldn't alert Richard because not a sound came from my throat, as was usual in Candle Face's presence. In any case, Richard might have refused to help as he had earlier.

The creak from the closet door as it opened was accompanied by the smell of burning flesh. I waited with bated breath, my thoughts racing around, my compounded fear building up the sound of my heart beat, my eyes straining to see in the dark. My ears picked up the sound of a choking, gurgling, mocking sound. I could still not see any part of her. All I could sense was her presence.

The presence pressed down on my mattress towards the end of my bed. Scratchy, skeletal knees pushed my feet apart, one on each side. Candle Face was making herself comfortable. I needed help and I needed it now. I got none. My sense of helplessness was total. Was she not going to be the slightest bit distracted, as she had last time? Was she not going to consider others whom she could confer with in her evil deeds this time? Did I have to be her only target? I couldn't believe what was going on. This had to be way past my worst nightmare. *But that was just what she had in mind.*

Arthur M. Mills, Jr.

She hadn't chosen to crouch or kneel near my bed as she had in earlier days. Back then I could make out her silhouette from the street light. Tonight was going to be a lot worse. I recalled an observation I had made from her last visit. Candle Face was stronger. I reminded myself about Griffin. Could his interaction with Richard have driven her towards this stage of harassment with me? Didn't she understand she and I didn't have to be close in the sense that Griffin and Richard were? They were friends. She and I were not.

Maybe this thought infuriated her even more. The growl coming back from her indicated "why not?" *I would soon find out.* The stench came closer. She had climbed on, I knew, because of the depression in the mattress. Now her knees were just below my knees. My eyes were now starting to make out shapes in the dark. I heard a low, evil laugh and felt her inching her knees between my legs. I wanted to kick at that foul body. I wanted to get away but couldn't move, as usual.

I couldn't stay like this. I had to do something. I tried to yell "Help!" but my voice stayed frozen. She began to laugh at my obvious fear. She moved some more, aware I couldn't. She was closer to my face, sitting on my stomach. I felt suffocated, unable to breathe. I couldn't take in any more of that dreadful smell of rotten flesh cooking. I could even hear her dreadful skin sizzle. She would have known this but leaned forward, her face inches from my face, forcing me to inhale that burning flesh stench.

I could have renamed her now. Her face wasn't just covered with melting, burning blobs like wax. The gaps were worse. Now a blue colored flue circled the burning bits. A rotten smell streamed out. I thought of holding my breath. Could inhaling water and drowning to death be worse than this? And then I saw what looked like maggots on fire deep inside the top waxy layer of her face.

I wished I could stop breathing. I wished I could pass out, die, anything to get away, but right now this was where I had to be. I had to inhale her dirty rotten smell. I had to stare at the glowing maggots which had long since eaten her flesh. Candle Face yelled, "You do it! You do it!" mimicking the words I had uttered some minutes ago. She pointed to the light switch and smiled her broad, vicious, open mouthed smile. The maggots inside seemed to be waiting.

Richard moved slightly and mumbled, "Go to sleep, you baby," as Candle Face snapped her head towards Richard's bed. Richard had actually heard her! Could he not distinguish between my teary voice and her throaty mimic? How could he think it was me, when I had only done what I had been forced to do?

Candle Face returned her attention to me. She was getting down to serious business. She started to poke my chest with her bony right index finger. I heard her rasping whisper as she continued on the same theme, "You do it." I still couldn't move and knew I was paralyzed with fear. I could feel her bony fingers stabbing me in the chest. She started to use both index fingers and repeat, "You do it, you do it, you do it."

She must have gone on like this for I don't know how long before I passed out from the pain. It seemed like hours. *Passing out had its advantages.* I no longer had to be terrified and in pain. I remember a feeling of falling, of getting caught inside a whorl inside a dark tunnel. The tunnel smelt different. I no longer had to stop breathing because of that foul smell. It was a smell of fresh cut grass and I somehow knew that I was younger . . . . eight years old, maybe?

I fell onto soft earth and heard a chirruping voice and the swish of a long tail. It was Griffin. He looked at me indulgently. I hoped *she* wasn't around, but Griffin moved aside and there she was, standing on her long spindly legs. A light shone behind her and a breeze ruffled her dreadlocks. She was in silhouette again. Candle Face had a story to tell. I couldn't help being curious.

She began by telling me how she awoke when the smoke from her burning house had streamed in through her nostrils and into her lungs. She could hear voices calling out from a distance through the thick black smoke. Her throat, nose and lungs ached. And then there wasn't anything, just black space. She knew she had died, but the fact was she had also been cremated inside her own room. She remembered the house and its garden. She remembered her parents and her little brother.

She was tired. She missed her home and her family. She wanted to be close to them and knew she was near when she heard voices. She found a huge grassy hole near her house, lay in it and slept.

The hole became her new home.

Arthur M. Mills, Jr.

After that, she heard children's voices each time she awoke. They were busy around her garden, playing and making things. Sometimes she heard her brother's voice. One day she saw him. He looked like a mythological creature she had seen pictures of. She remembered his name was Griffin and now he was a Griffin. She remembered him from his voice, his eyes and his name. The grassy hole was their home, but no one could see them.

She would like a form for herself. It didn't matter if no one but Griffin could see her. She realized that the way she was—no face and a burnt body, wouldn't do. She wanted to keep her long blonde hair. She would find the person she wanted to be. One night there was a great disturbance. Someone, or a number of people, was dancing on their home, jumping in their place of rest. Until that moment she had found a sort of peace, but after that, everything changed. She vowed to get that person who disturbed her peace.

At first she didn't know which direction to go. Then she heard a dog bark and whine. She looked towards this disturbance and saw me, the person who had forced her out. She had no arguments with any of the things that had happened to her up till now. But when she saw me she knew what I had done; she knew what had happened to her. She decided I was the cause . . . of everything, and she was going to get me.

I tried to tell her I was sorry I disturbed her and that I was just trying to find out about her lot on our street and what happened to her house and herself. I asked her not to blame me for everything that happened. "There's Griffin," I said. "Look at him. He has found a friend. He's happy."

But Candle Face wouldn't relent. *You gave me a nasty name*, she seemed to say. Griffin was different. He could keep himself occupied even before I saw him and before my brother found him. Griffin went to my school and learned a lot more than I ever did.

I had sensed that Griffin was in my school and wondered how I knew that. She continued, saying my brother Richard found Griffin the day she had created that cloud I saw in the creek.

"I've been tired for a long time but think I'm growing stronger now," she said. "I'm not a goody like Griffin. You disturbed me, and I'm going to get you." It was the same old threat.

So there was no way out for me. She had been telling me this from the beginning. I was the culprit and was going to be her victim. I

Arthur M. Mills, Jr.

would have preferred to stay in the condition I was in—unconscious and not knowing.

The sun rose to a new day. My father got ready for work and left. My mother got ready to wake us up. When I awoke, I was partly still terrified and partly glad I had passed out into nothingness, that happy instant when I didn't have to stay aware of her.

Although I was vastly relieved last night's ordeal was over, when I tried to get up, I found I couldn't. Feeling a burning sensation. I looked down and saw severe dark blue and green bruises in the center of my chest. Richard saw the bruises, too. He smirked. His eyes lit up, seeming to say, *That should teach you not to go where you weren't asked.*

I jumped out of bed and covered up before my mother came into our bedroom.

CHAPTER 21

Severe, fast and strong storms are a common occurrence in Austin. The city is well known for its spectacular storms. These can start with one flash of lightning like the one that burned down Candle Face and Griffin's house. High winds are possible, as are tornados during stormy weather.

All of us in our group of friends had found out in school what to do when a severe thunderstorm watch or severe thunderstorm warning was issued. They told us what to do when lightning filled the sky and how a lightning strike could be fatal.

One Saturday in late spring, thunderclouds gathered and the sky turned completely gray. My parents were not at home because they worked on Saturdays. Richard and I had several friends over including Nolan, Mark and his brother Sean. Even Randy was there. We all sat on our large front porch and watched the fast moving thunderclouds roll in. All of us were talking about the weather because these clouds seemed to fit the typical weather patterns which preceded Austin's spectacular storms.

It wasn't raining yet, but we knew it could at any time. Wanting to find out if the weather would put on any shows for us, Richard turned to the local TV news channel. Tornado alert! The weatherman was advising viewers to prepare an inside room, preferably a room without windows, where we could take shelter. The news gave the possible tornado a lot of coverage. Storms past and present were shown and analyzed. All of us were greatly taken up with the impending storm and could talk about nothing else. Finally we got bored of being shown the same disasters over and over and returned to the front porch. We didn't want to miss anything.

The wind picked up and at first small hail started to pound the ground. There was still no rain. We got our nerve up to run into this falling hail and pretended to be dive bombers with our arms spread out and tilting up and down. Randy and Richard stayed out of this type of play, I noticed. They were older. *Well, Richard wasn't too old to play with Griffin, I thought, so why not me and why not us?* The rest of us were jumping up and down. We were thrilled and excited. Rushing out into the hail and then rushing back in was great fun. The hail increased as did the winds to the point we had to retreat back to the safety of the front porch.

Richard went back indoors. After a while he walked out carrying the Bible he had won in the church competition. He slowly walked down the porch stairs and into the driving hail storm with his prize.

"Richard, what are you doing?" I yelled.

Richard paid no attention. He walked to the middle of the yard in the hailstorm and sat on a garden seat in the front yard. He sat to one side of the seat, facing the road, leaving a place next to him.

This was madness. I wanted my brother on the porch. If we couldn't get to that inside room the weatherman told us about, we could at least sit inside the porch. After all, it was more fun than being in a windowless inside room. We could follow nature's show from this vantage position, though I knew this was more dangerous than being in that inside room. It would do for now, I thought. And I wanted my brother in here with us. By now we were all shouting at Richard to get up and come back to the porch. Richard's best friend Randy was with us. He would have to play safe, since he didn't want his parents to know he had been out during a hailstorm and an impending tornado. He too, was trying to persuade Richard.

In the middle of all this noise, we heard three short attention-seeking beeps from the TV. We ran indoors where more weather news awaited us. Richard stayed outside. He continued to be pelted by tiny hailstones.

In the house, the weatherman announced he was elevating the tornado watch to a tornado warning. He mentioned that several callers from the Gillis Park neighborhood in South Austin had reported seeing a twister heading south. Mark yelled out, "Gillis Park is only a mile from here. The tornado is heading this way!"

Richard must have heard him. We had just heard Mark's warning when we heard a loud roar. The wind picked up even more. I could see our trophy tree through our back window. Its branches were weaving madly, its leaves flying and the board knocking, making a sound like a gunshot. The leaves in all the trees around our house seemed to be screaming with the wind blowing them any which way. The trees were straining to stay on the ground. Was Richard still out there?

We all ran back onto the porch. Richard still sat outside on the same seat and in the same position. He still had his back to the house and now had his Bible open. I stepped off the porch with the idea that I would have to drag my brother in, but Mark pulled me back on to the porch.

I yelled out to Richard, "There's a twister headed towards us! Get in now."

Richard turned to look at me. "As long as I'm reading the Bible, nothing can happen to me." He turned calmly back around and carried on reading the Bible. The weather was carrying on doing its bit. Piles of hail would build up, then scatter in the next gust of howling wind. I noticed that the spot next to Richard stayed dry. There was no hail build up there. An invisible car wiper *(or tail)* seemed to swish to and fro, keeping the back of the bench dry at that spot as well. As for Richard, there wasn't a thing we could say or do to get him to come inside.

After another minute or so, the wind died down. Richard stood up and walked back into the house and went to his bedroom. He lost interest in the TV report about the storm. Some of us ventured out. When I came to where Richard had been sitting, I saw a large dry patch, big enough for two. I could guess who had kept Richard company. I went back in when the phone rang. First my father, then my mother called to ask if we were all right.

Richard didn't speak to us and we left him alone. I had no idea about Dan and Felix. They must have been in their friend's house up the road but didn't come home even after the storm passed. About an hour later, the news reported that a tornado had struck and damaged several houses nearby. We ran around to find out where it had happened. It was on Stacy Lane, a few blocks away.

All of us were still in a state of high excitement. When we heard where it was, all of us ran there as fast as we could. Richard stayed home and in our room. I will never forget the sight at Stacy Lane. We had seen similar devastation but only on TV. The five of us stood in front of three double storied homes, except now not a single one was left standing. Wooden boards and splintered sides were scattered everywhere; some lying haphazardly in the next street. One house had its front wall ripped off and we could see broken furniture inside, furniture which looked like something brought in from the furniture dump in the empty lot next door. Many trees had also been uprooted in the tornado. One had cracked near its base and lay across the length of the road, its branches strewn all over. The tornado had decided to zero in here. The adults and children who lived here had luckily heeded the weatherman. They had all gathered in a house which had the inside room. This house stayed intact and people in this area were able to escape the worst effects of the tornado.

I thought I heard the swish of a gliding bird and a chirruping voice telling me to hurry home. We were happy to leave. After a day like this we all needed our homes, dinners and families.

Later, when we spoke about this day, all of us admitted feeling apprehensive as we headed home. We hoped none of us would ever again be as shocked as we were when we witnessed the devastation in Stacy Lane.

When I got home I walked straight into my bedroom. Richard sat on his bed scribbling something into his notebook. Without looking up, he told me he couldn't have deflected the tornado without Griffin. I believed him but said I had no idea how Griffin could have done such a thing. Richard still didn't look up. He seemed to be speaking to Griffin, even though I couldn't see him.

"You can show yourself now," Richard said. Griffin materialized, front paws and beak snout first. Richard spoke to him again. "Tell Ray how you prevented the tornado from ripping across our drive."

Griffin told me that since they had opted to sit through a hailstorm, I had to understand about hail. He knew I knew he was there and had seen me look hard at the dry spots on the seat and at the back where he had wiped up the wet puddle with his tail. He explained how hail is produced inside storm clouds (we had all focused on those) and is made of solid ice. Hailstones had to be seen to be noticed, he said.

Griffin went on to explain that ice pellets falling from the top of the cloud collect a film of moisture as they descended. He had been to the tops of such clouds. Both he and Richard felt that to be in contact with hail was to be in touch with something that was pure.

Then Griffin talked about the tornado. The thunderstorm that had so thrilled us boys was the engine that fuelled the tornado which had ripped through South Austin. A bulge of warm moist air had crashed through into an upper layer of cool dry air. It had risen at a speed of 150 miles per hour. The moisture condensed out into a solid looking cloud. We had seen this but didn't realize it was the beginning of the tornado.

How on earth did Griffin know so much? He reminded me that his sister had taught him how to read, and before he and Richard became friends, he used to go to the Mollie Dawson library. That library was a treasure, he said. He had his ways of entering, and there was hardly a night when he wasn't there.

Arthur M. Mills, Jr.

Richard had done some reading, too. But his wasn't all in the school library. He knew the Bible quite well and now quoted from it.

Ecclesiastics 43:17 "The noise of the thunder maketh the earth to tremble: so doth the northern storm and the whirlwind."

Richard explained to me that in Biblical times a tornado was described as a whirlwind. "When we heard the thunder this morning we knew a naturally caused calamity could be on its way." That is how it is best described even now. He said that what he had done was to concentrate on the solid looking cloud that Griffin had explained. He focused on it and prayed with his Bible.

I finally understood, but I knew the others were still mystified. They might think that mere chance had redirected the tornado when it twisted onto Stacy Lane. I wished Richard had explained all this to our friends as he had to me, but he had chosen to hold himself apart from all that was going on around him. He had worked with his friend on what he believed to be true. *Did Richard's prayers, or Griffin, or both, prevent the tornado from reaching our block? I still wonder.*

When we got back to school on Monday, studies were pushed aside. Everyone in school had special stories to tell about the hailstorm and the tornado. A couple of children had trailed the tornado with their eyes as it shuddered across its path. But it was only my group of friends who had been curious enough to want to see its aftermath.

A couple of sixth graders asked Richard for a story. Richard hadn't done a story for a long time. But that afternoon, with friends from school and from the neighborhood listening, Richard came up with a beautiful story about a colony of mythical beasts called Griffs who could fly on eagles' wings. They were called beasts, but were not really so in that sense, Richard said. He described them as being more like friendly four-legged, winged magical creatures. *He should know, I thought.* Well, Richard's magical beings lived with others like themselves. Richard let on that their herd was never far from the largest deposits of gold, which for them were like any other pretty stuff. They didn't think of it as something to be hoarded or stored in secrecy or demanded of others. It was just there. They lined their nests and used gold as best as they could. Nature had seen to it that their mothers laid eggs covered in gold. Their babies emerged from golden eggshells.

Richard described the magical beings at birth. They emerged by pecking through the soft gold with tiny beaks. Their front half was like a lion except for the beak which was like an eagle's. The back half was like the eagle, particularly the back legs. The only leonine part was their tails, which were long, thin, and ended in a tuft of lion's fur. The babies' wings were folded inside their golden eggshells, but they unfurled them for flight as soon as they were able to emerge.

But there was a downside to these gorgeous beasts (Richard reminded us again about such a description not really fitting what they were). Not far from their colony in the lofty mountains lay a village of one-eyed humans called Arimas. Being humans, they were greedy for gold. The Arimas knew that Griffins' instincts about where the gold ore lay, were correct. What they also thought was that those golden eggs they laid were solid gold. They didn't know about the perfect half lion—half eagle offspring who waited inside.

The Griffs wouldn't lead the Arimas to the hidden fields of gold. They saw no point in it. So the greedy humans stole their gold lined nests with the golden eggs intact. For the Arimas, it was a shortcut to getting rich. For the magical animals, it spelt doom. Their mothers cried in chirrups of lament. They wondered what they could do. Should they go down from their mountaintops to the human village and try to retrieve however many of their eggs that they could? No, said the mothers. The eggs might break and their children die.

The elders of the tribe of Griffs put together a master plan to go down to the village and retrieve their eggs. Humans were lazy, as everyone knew—had they not asked to be just led to the fields of gold so that they could grab what they could with little effort? Their Griff raid would therefore be conducted at night, when it was darkest *I felt guilty about the laziness and about the described darkness.*

The animals prepared, and honed their pecking, punching and tail swishing skills. They swooped down on the village after nightfall and located the areas where the eggs were hidden. They would have to cradle each egg carefully in their hind leg talons, cushion them with their front paws and fly quickly back to their mountain eyras. Here, Richard stopped to explain an eyre. They were the mountain nests of birds of prey.

The forward batch of Griff soldiers had just lifted off with their precious cargo when the first human awoke, disturbed by the air

Arthur M. Mills, Jr.

around him as the gliders took off. He was befuddled and thought he was dreaming before he realized what was happening. He alerted the other Arimas and they rushed to gather the eggs left behind and move them to a still more secret hiding place. But when the Arimas set about doing this, they didn't know what to make of it. Their golden eggs were cracking, tiny beaks appearing through the cracks and little feathered and furry creatures were hopping out. The baby Griffs flapped their carefully folded wings and in the next instant, soared off, behind the adults who were carrying the first batch of eggs. Richard added that it was a magnificent sight.

The Arimas made do with the gold in their nests and the gold in the eggshells. The Griffs got their children back. The Arimas became wilier because their greed for gold wasn't going to stop here. The Griffs became more vigilant in guarding their eggs.

The Griffs didn't resent all humans. In celebration of the day on which their babies had been retrieved, they held a grand occasion. Their leader would fly up above thunderclouds with tiny golden pebbles in his beak. Richard talked about the currents of warm and cold air inside the thunderstorm. He said the strong updrafts of warm air and downdrafts of cold air worked on each pebble, the same as with icy droplets. They were carried well above the freezing level, became heavy and fell to earth in sheaths of ice around the gold. It was for children to find the tiny sparkly bits of ice.

Richard told everyone that the next time small hail fell, anyone could collect the tiny sparkly bits of ice. He couldn't guarantee there would be golden pebbles inside, but we could give it a try.

We loved the images he evoked. The younger children told us older ones that they were entranced. Chico cheered for Richard and said he would try to bring Maria next time.

I need not have worried because Richard knew by now what he could achieve, and what he couldn't. He ended with a poem written by someone who had died some hundred years ago, named John Milton, writing in Paradise Lost. Milton knew about the legend of the Griffs. He called them Gryfon. This was what Richard recited:

As when a Gryfon through the Wilderness

With winged course ore Hill or moarie Dale,

Pursues the Arimaspian, who by stealth
Had from his wakeful custody purloind
The guarded Gold [. . .]

Richard recited this in a loud, booming voice. I thought I heard a tinkling chirrup. Some of us understood the poem, some didn't, but it sounded great all the same. Everyone clapped and stamped their feet.

Arthur M. Mills, Jr.

CHAPTER 22

Word of Richard's great story got around. It had somehow connected to the hail storm, if not the tornado in Austin. But that tornado would be in our minds till the next one gave us more to think and talk about. Richard knew not everyone was pleased about the kudos his hailstorm story had won for him. I was hoping he would go back to being the old, outgoing Richard who would think up such stories for our entertainment. On the other hand, I didn't want the same old Richard who used to beat and bully his younger brother.

The school year was winding down. My teachers seemed pleased with me for a change. They had indicated that I was taking some sort of an interest in studies and in projects to do with storms and the natural world. I was expecting a better report card at the end of this semester than I had ever had before.

The trees along our walk to school had turned glorious and leafy green. Mark and I had a great many matters to discuss and a great deal to see on our morning walk to school. One day Mark and I caught up with Richard at the creek as we walked to school. Richard still walked to school on his own on most days, but on this particular day he was walking with Randy. It was going to be a good walk with our group. *Or so I thought until I literally stopped in my tracks.*

The others with me stopped as well. I didn't want to believe my eyes. I could see Carlos, the unofficial lead bully ahead of us. This reputation had won Carlos a couple of younger and smaller sycophants and underlings who reveled in his glory. They were standing in the "safe part" of the creek. Carlos' friends were grinning and chattering. They didn't have a great variety of subjects to discuss. I thought everything they said or did was centered on Carlos, the power he wanted to wield, and ways of enhancing this. This "conference" didn't augur well for anyone outside his group. From what I could tell, Carlos' gang seemed to be egging him on.

I hoped this wasn't going to be a repeat of last time when Carlos had pummeled Richard to the ground to such an extent he was near senseless and didn't make it to school. Richard, Mark, and Randy probably had similar thoughts.

My brain worked frantically. Could I do anything? Last time this happened I tried to persuade Richard to turn around from the creek and take the long route to school. By now I had run that route a great many times and thought it would be good for all of us, especially today. I suggested it to Richard. He said no and headed straight towards Carlos' group.

Carlos walked up to Richard, his heavy shoulders and arms swinging back and forth. I cast desperate looks around me. Could no act of nature emerge to stop Carlos in his path? His face held a mean expression, jealously mean. He must have heard of Richard's success with story writing and telling and probably had heard about his newest round of storytelling and poetry reading.

Carlos didn't hesitate and gave Richard a great shove. Richard fell down but scrambled to his feet. He stood there, not wanting to hit back. Carlos now looked meaner and more confident. He was going to have his type of fun. He brought up the topic of Maria, sneering and mocking Richard because she had rejected him twice. All the kids crowding behind Carlos laughed. Of course Richard just stood there expressionless, his arms hanging by his side. Mark, Randy, and I stood by helplessly, not knowing what to do.

I thought if Richard wouldn't fight he'd better pray. His prayers may have worked wonders during the storm, so why didn't he use them now? Carlos took a step back, giving himself the momentum he needed before he stepped back up and hit Richard in the chest this time. Richard fell to the ground but got to his feet as quickly as he could. Carlos had just confirmed the general pattern of what Richard would and wouldn't do. It was exactly the same as last time. Carlos didn't need anyone telling him he was the greatest. He knew as far as Richard and the three of us were concerned, he was invincible.

Randy decided it was time he encouraged Richard into action. "Hit him back!" He didn't know about Richard's resolution about the only way to achieve peace.

Some of the children repeated Randy's words but in a mocking manner. They presumed he would remain a weakling in the face of mighty Carlos.

Richard seemed to have gathered strength in his own convictions since the tornado, though this wasn't going to work now. He responded with, "The Bible says to turn the other cheek."

Carlos laughed and said, "Okay," then hit Richard again on the other cheek. Richard took the hit without resistance, fell and stood up when his feet allowed him to. Carlos kept hitting Richard on each side of his face. Although he nearly keeled over from the force of the blow, my brother wouldn't retaliate. Some of Carlos' punches landed on his chest with the same effect. Richard fell every time but didn't stay down for long. He would get up and get the same punishment all over again.

I was infuriated even more when one of the children with Carlos asked him if he could have a try. This child approached Richard and hit him in the face. As before, Richard refused to fight back. Eventually the crowd got tired of the fighting and turned away. They may have realized their jubilation was ill-founded. Everyone had done what they had set out to do. Both groups continued walking to school.

I was miserable about having to keep quiet about Carlos attacking my brother. As usual, I told no one, either at school or at home. Mark and Randy didn't bring it up either. No one wanted to recognize Carlos' bullying and cruelty. Had it not been for the bruises on Richard's face and chest, we might have convinced ourselves the depressing event never happened.

I wasn't the only one who'd seen Richard's bruises. One of Richard's teachers noticed them as well. Richard and I had always denied the goings-on at home if one of our teachers (who may have had an inkling) asked us. This time his teacher asked Richard if he got hurt at home, school, or in-between. Richard told him he'd walked into a closed door.

I knew, as Richard did, that this had been his big chance to tell on Carlos. Instead, Carlos got away with near-murder yet again. Why couldn't Richard express himself when he needed to? *Why couldn't I?*

He was the same person who had told us that wonderful story about the Griffs. And that had been taken from something that was real . . . *or was it? Where did reality begin for Richard, and where did it end? I would have also liked to ask this for myself.*

That day Richard and I walked home together from school. We talked, albeit desultorily at first. This was a small improvement, I thought. I brought up the topic because it had troubled me all day. "Richard, you d-d-don't have to t-turn the other ch-cheek all that l-literally, y-you know."

At first Richard was silent, then explained, "I heard Randy when he told me to hit Carlos back, Ray. But I didn't want to. It would go against what we were taught in church."

Now I was angry. I reminded Richard he had cast aside all that nonsense about peace and love in his poetry and also in his stories which came before the Griff story. I told him he knew all that love and peace stuff hadn't worked for him. Why had he refused to retaliate when a boy with an ugly soul, the most insane bully, had hit him for no reason? I asked him why he couldn't answer his teacher truthfully.

Richard had no answer for me. I clenched my teeth and looked up. All I could see was blue sky and some fluffy white clouds. Suddenly it struck me that one of those white clouds was in the form of Richard's friend Griffin. Richard looked up as well and smiled. In a couple of more seconds, Griffin had swooped down to materialize near our feet and was trotting along beside Richard on the narrow path of the creek. Griffin knew Richard was in no mood to play. He stuck to talk.

Griffin endorsed what I had said. He told Richard that he needed to talk to someone. He said that no authority would expect Richard to literally translate any dictum about turning the other cheek. Annoyingly enough, Richard paid more attention to Griffin than he had to me. I guessed that as with "turning the other cheek" Richard wanted to believe. I was impatient again. I wanted a formula which Richard could safely use, something that would work for him. Simple dictates wouldn't do.

I had come to accept that our lives—Richard's and mine—were full of surprises. The bushes by the right side of the creek began to rustle, followed by the offensive odor I had grown familiar with. Candle Face appeared briefly and appeared to talk to Griffin. She told him she expected him home. My terror was somewhat offset by the fact that she hadn't been looking for me. Richard didn't seem to have noticed her presence.

Candle Face turned to me before the two of them took off. She smiled her malicious smile and said, "You don't have to watch it at this instant. I will see you soon."

What had she meant? As usual my thoughts were crashing around, trying to make some sense of what she had said.

Richard and I slowly returned home, each of us with a great deal to think about. Richard had shown a few days ago that deep down he still was the extrovert story teller. It had worked, and we thought he was brilliant. But not every idea he tried his hand at came through as he intended. Neither he nor I would ever be sure how much he had achieved on the day of the tornado. If he had tried to apply the same sort of thinking today, it hadn't worked. Of course Carlos wouldn't even be aware of the mysterious ways in which Richard's mind worked.

Was Richard doomed to flashes of brilliance, but failure overall? Had this ever occurred to him?

CHAPTER 23

Richard and I reached home without any other impediments or surprises. We walked through the front door together and were only slightly surprised to see Felix at home alone. Dan was nowhere to be seen. Such an occurrence was rare. On his own, Felix was less of a threat than the two of them together.

This was, in fact, going to turn out to be a good thing.

As we entered, Felix took a long hard look at the fresh bruises on Richard's face. He stared at both of us for awhile, appearing as if he was searching for the right words. Finally he asked what had happened to Richard's face, the first time anyone in our family had cared enough to ask.

Richard took Griffin's advice and told Felix the whole story of how Carlos had confronted him and beat him up. When he finished, Felix had a lot of questions. He wanted to know if Carlos had hit me. Richard said no and told Felix of his decision not to retaliate. Although Felix was normally a mild-mannered teenager into silly jokes and tricks, now he looked seething mad. I had never seen him this angry. Normally he didn't think very hard about anything, but now that he realized someone outside our family had willfully hurt Richard, he wanted to get back at Carlos and formulated a plan.

Felix told Richard he would go to the creek the very next day and "Take care of it." He would wait there for Carlos. He would make sure Carlos would mend his frightful ways where Richard was concerned. Richard couldn't believe his luck. He was thrilled. I looked at Felix in a new light and I, too, was thrilled.

I still didn't understand many things about my family, though. Why was Felix mad now when not so very long ago he'd joined Dan in roughing up Richard? I seemed to remember Felix had been the main offender. Maybe he'd become aware of the pain he'd inflicted with the pin on the paper airplane. Maybe he realized how he'd trapped Richard and how Richard had felt there was no escape for him. Maybe Felix was just trying to make amends.

But whatever Felix's motives, Richard was as close to ecstatic as he could get. He was glad for his new friend, Griffin, and glad his brother had taken it upon himself to see that a bully would stop terrorizing him. *What about me?* What we had been taught about 'turning the other cheek' when faced with a vicious assault was about to come out right. My muddled thinking over, I could say I was proud of Felix already, just picturing what would happen tomorrow. That evening, dying to share the exciting news, I ran out to tell Randy, Evan and Mark about our mini family conference about Carlos. All of us quivered in anticipation just picturing the various horrendous fates that awaited Carlos and his friends after Felix finished with them. We had a good many laughs and couldn't wait for tomorrow.

But Candle Face came to visit me that night. I had been so happy and my imagination so wild that I forgot about Candle Face when I went to bed. I forgot to fasten the many entrances she used. It must have been way past midnight when my eyes opened to my darkened room with orange streetlight streaming across the ceiling. As in the past, I knew Candle Face was there because of her frightful fumes. She strode from the middle of the room to the side of my bed. Holding my breath, I wondered if she was going to climb on and hurt me again with her bony digits. Was I going to come as close to drowning in rot and fumes as I had last time? For now, she sat demurely on the side of my bed with her legs slung over the side and her feet on the floor. Her long tousled hair covered the top of her face and where her eyes might have been. I shuddered at the thought of those glowing maggots which dwelt deep within the shifting sockets of her eyes and nostrils.

"Please," I said to myself. "I have seen you briefly this afternoon. I thought it was over for the day."

She laughed her evil, gurgle laugh. "Who cares what you think, boy?" She reminded me that she had said she would see me soon. She sat very still, but I knew she would unleash her terror any moment now. The one thought that flashed across my mind was that she had said, "You don't have to watch it at this instant." I had dwelt on that briefly on my walk home, then forgot about it because of the many exciting developments since then.

My problem was I could clamp my hands across my mouth to stop my words, but I couldn't do something similar to stop the thoughts in my brain. Candle Face had read these thoughts and was laughing again. I saw the glint of eyes through the matted hair. "Did you think it was his idea?"

My thoughts were stuttering as my talk sometimes did. "You? B-but w-why . . ." I had to stop. Then Candle Face told me.

Griffin had encouraged Richard to open up. He wanted better for Richard—better than that awful bully and his tactics. Griffin and Candle Face had conferred on the matter. Candle Face said she knew Felix liked a good fight, so she had planted the idea about fighting in Felix's head when he was busy being horrified about Richard's face and what could have caused it. Had she? I doubted that. I still had my suspicions about Felix (and Dan) and Candle Face but still clung to the idea that fighting Carlos was Felix's doing and no one else's. All of us were spoiling for a fight. All of us, that is, except Richard.

I looked across at Richard's bed to see if he was listening to all this or whether he was sleeping. Richard's bed was empty. Candle Face smiled at my lack of awareness about what went on at night and said, "They are out playing." She said she was going to go, but there was something she wanted to do before she left. This was a new one for me. I couldn't help but be surprised all over again.

Candle Face said that my sleeping sheet had come undone and that she wanted to tuck me in. I definitely didn't need her to do this. But Candle Face was insistent. She rolled me over to my right side so as to slip in the left edge of the sheet. But what she did now was to slip her right arm under my back. I should have known she would try something sneaky and nasty and both combined. She dug those nails into my back as she had on my chest.

I wanted to get away but couldn't move. My head screamed, *Richard! Griffin! Mom! Anyone there*? All I felt was burning pain as she raked her talons down my back. What was all that about not having to watch it till Richard and Felix's adventure with Carlos was done?

Arthur M. Mills, Jr.

I had been taken for a ride once more. Now I remembered her threat that I should watch my back. I wished I wasn't eleven, not gullible, smarter than I was. I wished I could remember when someone like Candle Face warned me about something like watching my back. I wished I wasn't stupid enough to turn over along the right side of my body to expose the whole of my back knowingly to her and those talons she had.

She was enjoying this. I could hardly bear the pain, but as before, I was paralyzed. And then I heard the back porch screen door open with a creak and slam shut. Someone had entered in a hurry. Candle Face heard it too. She hastily withdrew her arm. I was on my back on my bed once more. She took a flying leap and was out of the window before the hurrying footsteps entered.

"Did you call, Ray?" Richard asked as he ran into the room. Had he heard me? Was this another kind of his magic?

"No," a faint voice in my head said.

The faint voice continued, "He heard you all right. You brothers are going to bond in times of distress."

I knew then that Felix's concern for Richard was his own. Candle Face might find out about Felix's intent tomorrow morning, probably because I had rushed around telling everyone, but it was Felix who would confront Carlos all on his own.

Richard had told me about his secret friend. I hadn't been able to tell him about the fiend who visits me, but he must have had some inkling. Better still, if he could rush in like that he must have known. I wondered how our parents could sleep through everything, including Richard's creeping outside at night as well as the noisy way he'd run in here.

Richard and I decided to turn in for the night, or whatever was left of it. We both looked forward to tomorrow. Richard covered himself with his sheet and must have knocked off right away. I wrapped myself tightly in my sheet. My back still burned, but I didn't care as much as I had while Candle Face was inflicting pain. Tomorrow couldn't come too quickly.

The next morning my mother was again horrified at the dirt on Richard's feet. She made him promise to wash them before he left for school. I sprang out of bed as soon as my eyes opened to bright sunlight. I looked at the sheet I had slept on top of. Little blots of blood had leaked out of the long scratch marks on my back. I told myself I couldn't care, not today.

By the time we went in for breakfast, Felix had left for the creek. We hurriedly ate and went off to collect all our friends. They were ready and waiting, and we all started walking towards the creek to witness Carlos' demise. Randy, Evan, Mark, Richard and I didn't walk fast as we headed towards the creek. Instead we lingered, waiting for Carlos. When we reached the creek, we craned our necks and tried too obviously, Richard said, to see where Felix was. Richard was annoyed about this. He said Felix was obviously around but we shouldn't look for him. If Carlos and his gang realized what Felix was up to, it would ruin the plan.

The wait had wound me up so much I started to doubt whether Felix was really hiding somewhere around the creek. Was this a cruel trick Felix was playing on Richard?

Carlos and his friends arrived at the creek and saw us hanging around. As before, Carlos made Richard his target and yelled out, "Hey, Richard, are you waiting for your daily beating?"

No one said anything. Carlos approached Richard and pushed him so hard he fell down. Richard got up, as expected. But he, too, wondered if Felix was around. I had so wanted Felix's plan to be successful. I wanted to see Carlos beaten so badly he would never bully Richard again. But where was Felix? Richard was a sitting duck right now. Unless Felix showed himself, Richard would get hammered again.

I frantically looked around, but couldn't see Felix. Richard was no longer looking at Carlos. He was looking around, too.

Carlos asked loudly, "What ya looking for?" and pushed Richard again. Just as I was about to give up on Felix, he appeared on the other side of the water! *Gave him points for hiding in the best possible place.* If there was a pedestal around, Felix would be on it. He jumped the stream and walked straight up to Carlos as his gang of friends watched in horror. We watched in pure glee.

Carlos froze with his fist in mid air. He couldn't believe what his eyes were telling him. His gang was silent. They must've been wishing themselves elsewhere. Felix was older and bigger than Carlos, much bigger.

Felix said to Carlos, "So you like to pick on younger kids? So do I." He pushed Carlos with all his strength, hard enough that Carlos fell hard to the ground. It was a funny sight. Carlos was too shocked to say anything. He just sat on the ground on his haunches and looked up at Felix towering over him. He made no attempt to get up. His friends made no attempt to come forward and help him up.

Carlos was plain scared. However, we, the kids on and around Ben Howell Drive, were greatly enjoying this. Carlos stayed on the ground, not wanting to get up. His friends were no longer laughing, but Richard had the biggest grin I had ever known him to have. I even hoped Griffin was around, being invisible and watching this satisfying spectacle. He had given Richard some support yesterday, urging him to get his nerve up and talk to somebody. It had worked. Felix was here now, defending Richard.

"Get up, punk," Felix commanded. Carlos remained on the ground. Felix decided to help Carlos get up. Once he was up, Felix pulled his arms backwards, twisted and held them towards his spine with one arm. Carlos was immobilized. Felix used his free hand to hit Carlos at full speed and strength on the lower lip. Down Carlos went again, blood spurting from his mouth.

The other kids abandoned Carlos and ran for their lives. Feeling the warm blood trickle down, Carlos tried to clean it off with the edge of his shirt, but the blood kept flowing. Now the damage was clearly visible. The impact of Felix's fist had caused Carlos' bottom row of teeth to cut through his lower lip. I could see his teeth sticking through, a sight I will never forget.

We laughed all the way to school, adding to Carlos' humiliation. This had been the best fight ever. Felix walked nonchalantly off, sticking his hand with the bloodied knuckles into his pocket.

All of us were in high spirits that day in school . . . in fact we stayed in high spirits for a couple of days. In school that day I saw the sixth grade teacher who had asked Richard about his bruises walk up to damaged Carlos and talk to him. Carlos quickly pointed to where we were now crowded around my brother. The teacher looked towards us, shook his head, and stared back hard at Carlos. We had got the sense

Arthur M. Mills, Jr.

of this charade. Carlos had tried to blame us, and the teacher hadn't bought it. The teacher strode away.

Strictly speaking, none of us were responsible for what had happened to Carlos. He had brought it on himself. Richard may not have been the kind of boy to retaliate, but that didn't mean Richard would do nothing about it. We ran out and whooped for joy.

That night Dan and Felix were at the dinner table. During the meal, our father noticed Felix's bruised knuckles and asked, "What happened?"

Felix answered, "My knuckles came down on a set of teeth that got in my way."

My brothers and I all laughed. Our father looked relieved while our mother looked upset. Everyone must have thought Felix was joking, but Richard and I knew he was telling the truth. No one ever talked about it again.

Richard never had a problem with Carlos ever again. I liked to think this incident drew Felix, Richard and me a little closer. I thought that Dan would follow soon enough. *Where is my savior?*

CHAPTER 24

By this time I was in fourth grade. Richard, a year and a half older than I, was in sixth grade. We were old enough to manage our early morning schedule quite well without our parents. As always, they worked hard and long hours and would have to leave for work on most days before we left for school. My mother would leave cereal out on the dining room table for us. Dan had a large appetite. If he got to the table before Felix, Richard, or I, there wouldn't be anything left for the rest of us. There were times I had to go to school hungry because Dan had eaten everything. My mother, in the meanwhile, put my lean looks down to my running.

One day I noticed Dan had got to the breakfast table before me. I groaned inwardly but then noticed there were still plenty of Rice Krispies in the box. I poured the cereal into my small bowl, then poured in the watered-down milk. My mother forced us to drink watered-down milk in an attempt to save money. I placed my ear near the bowl just an inch from the top because I loved to hear the snap-crackle-pop of the cereal.

During the 1970 and 1980's, Rice Krispies commercials suggested the cereal had something to say. This was the reason why I would always try to listen as carefully as possible to the milk and the Rice Krispies in the bowl. My brother Dan saw me doing this and moved from his chair to sit next to me. "Do you know what they're saying?" Dan asked. *Was this Dan warming up to me as Felix did with Richard?*

"No, what?" I asked feeling pleased. I had always wanted to believe the cereal could really talk. Now that my eldest brother had asked about what the Rice Krispies were saying, I was closer to that belief.

Dan kidded along with me, and then lost interest. He had just thought of something . . . that maybe he should make sure I got to school in the absence of my parents.

"Hurry up and eat, or you will be late for school," Felix said as if he wanted to be in charge. In an act of defiance, I placed my ear back near the rim of the bowl. All I could hear was the snap-crackle-and-pop.

"You have to pay close attention," Dan said. "Listen real hard."

I kept my ear where it was. My doubts about cereals talking started to flood back. Dan *had* to be fooling me. The Krispies by now were getting soggy and silent. The snap-crackle-and-pop was going out of them.

I dug my spoon into the cereal and tasted it. It was still slightly crunchy. I put the spoon down and placed my ear back just inside the bowl. The snap-crackle-pop came back but with less gusto. I listened hard for any sounds from the "talking cereal." Success. I heard a faint, tiny "hello." I quickly lifted my head and looked straight into the bowl but could only see a mess of milk and cereal. What was that? I went back to one ear near the top of my cereal and milk.

There it was again: A small voice saying, "Hello?"

"Hello?" I answered. My brothers looked at me as if I was crazy. I wondered if maybe I was. I didn't want to make a big deal of my discovery when the three of them were looking at me like that. I raised my head and brought my face closer to the cereal inside my bowl.

"Hello? Who are you?" I whispered.

But what came back to me was the hoarse, coarse voice I dreaded and had heard countless times.

"Watch your back when you walk to school today," the Rice Krispies said to me. Not that again!

"Shut up!" I yelled back at my cereal bowl. All my brothers were looking at me as if I'd gone insane.

Dan now imposed his brand of discipline by shouting at me. "Stop fooling with your food and get to school!"

I got up, left the cereal on the table, grabbed my books and left the house. I ran as fast as I could to Mark's house. He had a role to play, especially in the light of that warning from Candle Face about walking to school.

Up until now, Candle Face hadn't dared show herself when there had been others around who were active and awake. Hopefully, Mark's presence would keep her away from me. Besides, I always felt safe when Mark was around although I was a bit older. He would be my protector.

I reached Mark's house. As always, I banged on his bedroom window to let him know I had arrived. I then moved quickly to the front door. Ordinarily he would be there when I rang his front doorbell and we would set out together. But this time Mark wasn't there. Had he missed that banging on his window? I went back to his window, banged on it again, and also peeked through a gap in the window shade. There was Mark in bed asleep! I banged on the window again, then rang the front doorbell. When I returned to Mark's bedroom window I banged as hard as I could. Mark stirred slightly and began to move. He

Arthur M. Mills, Jr.

opened his eyes and looked around. He twisted his neck towards the window and realized it was me. I could see something was wrong by the slow way he walked to the window. Mark was just not well.

"Ray, I am not going to school today. I feel sick."

"What? You have to go to school today," I replied. I wasn't thinking. That wasn't a good reply to a boy who was probably running a temperature. Mark looked awful. All that he could say was, "No, I can't."

I knew I was in trouble. How was I going to walk to school on my own, today of all days? With Candle Face telling me to watch my back and without Mark, I was doomed.

Mark closed the window. *Hadn't I done something like this to Candle Face some time ago?* I could swear I heard faint laughter. Then again, it could have been the wind.

I slowly walked away from Mark's house towards the creek a hundred meters or so away. The way past the creek was our only short cut to school. There was a long way, but I had to plan in advance when I wanted to run it. I had suggested the long route to Richard when I wanted him to avoid Carlos, but the long way was easily ten times longer.

I couldn't afford to be late again. Another tardy arrival would definitely get me another pink slip, and I didn't want to get into any more trouble at school, or at home.

I had to take the path past the creek.

I started to run. Going across the bridge, I looked down the worn-down path to see if I could find any evidence of Candle Face. I also looked into the knee-deep water of the creek, up and down the surrounding trees and every possible place where she could be hiding. My heart was thumping, whether from anxiety or exertion I couldn't tell. I could see no signs of Candle Face.

I took a couple of steps down the path, my senses on full alert. The bushes around me could have been a tropical forest, and I was the soldier who had to make it through to the other side under pain of his own life. Nothing happened. I slowed down to a fast walk. Still nothing happened.

By now I was about halfway through the creek and feeling a sense of relief. Maybe the Candle Face voice in the cereal was part of a bad dream. I told myself cereal doesn't talk, never mind the commercials and older brothers. I walked briskly down the path where it ended in a dead end street. *But I was blissfully unaware of the danger that stalked me.*

Yes, I made it. I was safe.

Suddenly I felt something wrap around my right leg and give it a sturdy tug. I fell down—unfortunately head first. My books flew to the front and scattered in the tall grass. My poor back and head hit the ground. I was facing upwards.

I saw her clearly. Candle Face was lying on her stomach in the high grass a foot away. I could see her eyes for the first time, green and wide open. Her mouth was open too. But her face was clearly charred. I could only continue to compare it with melted candle wax. I hadn't noticed this before and could now confirm that Candle Face had no nose, though she did have nostrils. She didn't have cheek bones or a chin. These parts of her face must have completely burned away.

I stared in horror, I couldn't help myself. But she seemed to be enjoying my reaction. She laughed when she said, "What did you expect?" Her right hand still tightly gripped my right ankle. She yanked me towards her, and before I knew it, I was in the tall grass beside her. I couldn't move in her presence, just the way it happened in my bed at home.

She now managed to stand and stride towards the creek, dragging me through the grass. I tried to resist, to hang on to clumps of earth and grass, but as always, nothing helped. She managed to drag me to the very edge, where the grassy verge ended and the water flowed.

Candle Face didn't talk nor did she encourage speech from me. But then, she knew I was mute on such occasions. She jumped into the knee-high water pulling me in with her. Was I going to die? I really didn't know what to expect. The water around her appeared to sizzle and boil. I could feel how hot it had turned. In another second, it was burning my skin. I no longer resisted. I was close to giving up completely. *She* knew I was in pain and she loved it.

Suddenly, I sighted the unlikeliest of help. Some kids were skipping down the path which ran beside the creek. They seemed to be in a hurry, telling each other that they must run or otherwise be late. The specter of the pink slip hung over them as well. They may have been Carlos' sycophants but I didn't care, as long as they could help.

Arthur M. Mills, Jr.

But Candle Face was determined. As the children passed by within a foot of us, she pulled me downwards. Now I was completely immersed, unable to flail my arms or legs. She held my mouth and nose shut with one hand and dug what felt like a claw into my side. Her little bony fingers felt like knives. Worse, I could see children's running legs just above the surface. The underwater reflections in the water rippled, disturbed by Candle Face as she thrashed around trying to keep me down, trying to drown me.

This is it, I thought. I wasn't holding my breath because I had no breath to hold. My lungs would burst because I hadn't got a chance to draw in air before Candle Face dragged me in. The last pair of a child's legs disappeared down the path. No one who could help me now.

Candle Face pulled my head out of the water.

Air! I tried to take that deep breath I should have taken earlier, but she quickly pushed me down again, so I now took in a lot of water. I started to cough and splutter, which meant I was taking in even more water. I was bound to die. I felt myself blacking out. Everything was gone. It felt like forever.

I woke up in my own bed coughing up water from my mouth and nose. My brother was already awake as he usually was.

He yelled at me, "What's wrong with you?"

I looked at him and hoped I could talk soon, given how much water I would have to bring up. But my voice came out normal. We were back to our verbal sparring.

"None of your business," was the only response I could give. What was all that about? What could have happened? It must have just been a dream.

Most people would have been relieved to find out it was only a dream. *But I was to realize that my nightmare had merged with my real life. Had I not thought recently that this was the case with Richard?*

I got dressed for school and sat down to eat breakfast. Dan had come to the breakfast table before I had. He handed me a small bowl and a box of Rice Krispies. I poured in the watered-down milk. The snap-crackle-pop took off instantly. Dan then sat down next to me and asked, "Do you know what they're saying?" He had decided to play the part of the older, responsible adult. He continued, "They're saying, hurry up and eat, or else you'll be late for school."

I didn't need a second cue. I picked up my books, ran out the door and went to Mark's house where I banged on the window. As in my dream, he didn't answer the front door. This was another repeat. I banged again and peeked inside.

Mark was still asleep. I knew he was sick and wouldn't go to school today. I couldn't walk to school today on my own. I wouldn't walk though the creek alone. I couldn't stay at home either. But this time I knew what I had to do. I decided to walk to the nearby H.E.B. Grocery Store where I knew Candle Face wouldn't show her face in such a crowded place. I would spend the day around people.

The minute I entered the H.E.B. Grocery Store, I heard someone call, "Ray!" I turned around and to my horror saw Evan's parents, Lance and Deborah. "What are you doing here, Ray?" Lance asked. "Shouldn't you be in school?"

I wasn't particularly good at talking on my feet so I just blurted out, "I didn't go to school today because I was feeling sick."

"Sick!" Deborah said. "If you are sick, why are you here at H.E.B.?"

Good question but I had a better answer. *Or so I thought!* "I feel better."

She put her hands on her waist. "If you feel better then you should go to school."

This could get ugly real fast. I was desperate to come up with something. "My mother told me to walk to H.E.B. to pick up some medicine and then go back to school after I take some of it. I'll head back to school from here."

That seemed to work because she took her hands off of her waist. "Oh, so you need a ride to school?"

"No!" I answered too quickly. Her hands made their way back onto her waist. "I can run to school faster than you can drive so I will take care of it."

Not giving her a chance to respond, I darted out of H.E.B. and headed to school. I ran all the way to the bridge but remembered the dream about Candle Face tripping me. I thought about running to school by taking the long route but knew I'd get a pink slip for being late. I decided to just run home and play hooky and tell my teacher the next day I was sick. I ran towards my house, hoping I wouldn't get home at the same time as Evan's parents who lived right next door. I also hoped I would get home to an empty house.

I started to open the front door but stopped when I heard Dan and Felix arguing. I let go of the door and instead walked through my own bedroom front door. From my bedroom I could barely hear Dan and Felix's argument which seemed to be about who finished the Rice Krispies. Dan hadn't left any for Felix. He laughed and said, "She asked me to. She couldn't bear to leave any more messages in the snapping and crackling."

There was the "she" again, the one who had spoken to me in her hoarse growl in my cereal. The one who had dictated that I watch my back today. It suddenly struck me that my awful dream and its repetition this morning might be another setup. Candle Face planned for me to be in the secluded spot in the creek alone so she could wrap her arm around my leg and drag me into the creek. But I didn't go to school today. I had outwitted Candle Face again!

I felt as if I had emerged to safety from some war. I knew what I had to do next. I lay down in my bed and tucked my sheet around me the way I liked it. I was going to have a very long snooze. *I was going to watch my back.*

CHAPTER 25

It was a Saturday and both Richard and I had been invited to Nolan's house to spend the day. Richard said he didn't want to go. I tried to persuade him to come with me, tempting him with how much fun we would have and what a good cook Nolan's grandmother was. She had asked the two of us to come early. That way, we could have brunch. I hoped it wouldn't be Rice Krispies, but needn't have worried. Nolan said his grandmother made blueberry pancakes every Saturday, something we never had at home. Nolan even recited her menu for every day of the week, but I didn't listen. It would have made me feel awfully sorry for myself . . . and for Richard. I even tried telling him he would miss the sort of breakfast he might never get anywhere else. *Sadly, that turned out to be true.*

I was so looking forward to the day at Nolan's house. *To be completely honest, I really wanted to go see his cousin Angie. At times she would live with Nolan and their grandparents. She eventually became my first girlfriend and the first person to break my heart.*

Before I left that morning, I again tried to persuade Richard to come with me. I worried our brothers might have nasty plans for this Saturday, but Richard assured me Felix would never go back to being his old mean self, not after he had put Carlos in his place.

In deep thought, I walked onto the front porch to head to Nolan's house. As usual, I noticed the smell from Spencer's sewer truck parked outside his home. Boy, did that truck stink! Worst of all, for several weeks it hadn't moved from its parking spot. I decided to run to Nolan's house in order to escape the sickening odor. Angie was waiting, I kept telling myself.

I seemed to be the only person around. Everyone, like my parents who had to go to work on Saturday, had already left. Only people like Richard and me who normally stayed home on a Saturday were still there.

Spencer was Laurie's father and Laurie was Felix's girlfriend. Her family lived up the street from our house, and Felix was happy to be there most of the time. But Spencer had become seriously ill and bedridden. His family, including Laurie, was busy taking care of him. Felix still spent a lot of his time at Laurie's house, but Spencer's illness was by now getting everyone down.

Felix was sleepwalking practically every night when he was home, looking like he was having bad dreams. Our mother tried everything she could think of to stop him, including locking him into his room. Nothing worked. On one occasion he came into our room. For a second I thought it was Candle Face and was greatly relieved when he passed the light behind him. The orange halo around Felix's head had been distinctively different from Candle Face's.

I fell to musing about what made Felix sleepwalk. Did he have to have bad dreams, or did he have to do something in those dreams? There was Richard who talked and thrashed around in his sleep. And there was me. I wished again that I hadn't run around the empty lot on that fateful night and that I didn't have to see Candle Face when she came.

I got to Nolan's house in record time. Nolan was waiting for me, and we went straight in for brunch. It was the best brunch I ever had, and yes, Nolan's grandmother had cooked a mountain of blueberry pancakes and her specialty: bacon and eggs. Angie wasn't there, but I didn't care because I stuffed my stomach with the best brunch anyone could ever eat.

We had been playing outside when Nolan's grandmother sent us inside because she said it was too hot to play out of doors. She was always overprotecting everyone. Nolan and I were playing in his room when I heard what sounded like a gunshot from somewhere outside. We paused in the middle of our game to discuss what it was. Maybe an old car had backfired? The thought of a real shooting was exciting, but rare in our South Austin area.

A few minutes later we heard sirens. There were lots of them, each with a slightly different tone or intensity or alarm. It sounded like many vehicles were converging somewhere, all with their sirens on, then turning off at the same time. They had stopped nearby.

We decided what we'd heard was a gunshot. Nolan's grandfather thought so too. A fire truck zoomed by. We ran outside and tried to run behind it but it sped off. We noticed it was heading towards my street. In the next few seconds, there was complete silence.

Nolan and I started to walk towards my house, but within a couple of yards I began to worry and started to sprint. After two blocks, I stopped and waited for Nolan to catch up in the complete silence around us. As we got to the bottom of the street and turned into Ben Howell Drive, we saw a couple of police cars, ambulances and the fire truck crowding the other end of the street. I was walking cautiously now.

Richard saw us and ran up. He didn't have the silent, determined look he had sported during the tornado. This morning he plain looked excited, enthusiastic and involved, as though he was part of a drama that was going on. I asked him what was happening.

Richard replied, "Spencer committed suicide. He shot himself."

Now I had an explanation for what we'd heard and seen but couldn't believe Richard's words. In all my eleven years, I had never known anyone who had taken their own life. I was shocked that someone Felix knew—and therefore I knew, had done this, and that it happened so close to us. I also couldn't believe how animated Richard had become by the fact of Spencer's suicide. Lately he had become less outgoing, but now he wanted to rekindle his association with every person who lived on our street or anyone just walking along. He even met some of the men and women at the telephone company at the end of our street during their lunch hour. For the next several hours, Richard ran up and down the street. He would stay on our porch or living room till he saw someone walking by and then would run out to tell them what had happened, making sure the person first heard the gory details of Spencer's suicide from him. He really looked like he thought Spencer's suicide had brought about a new focus to our street and to the neighborhood.

Soon Spencer's body was taken away, and we assumed the forensics people would do whatever was necessary before Spencer's family held the funeral. Our parents and their other friends would spend time consoling Spencer's family, trying to get them to feel less wretched about the way Spencer had chosen to die. I asked Richard why he was still so excited and talking to everyone. Spencer had killed himself, but now it was over.

Richard gave me a you're-too-young-to-know-about-these-things look. But I was still asking, so Richard said he would tell me about a particular suicide and its effects on everyone. He said it was just a story and I shouldn't be afraid. He had read about it at least a year ago but couldn't get it out of his head. I said I'd like to hear it, knowing I couldn't be afraid about a mere story, not after what Candle Face was doing during her frequent visits at night.

Richard began to tell me about this girl who was smart, intelligent and beautiful. She had gone to Saint Edwards University studying to be an astrophysicist. She got herself a job at the best astrological institute in Texas and seemed to love it. Her life was going fine—she hadn't been ill like Spencer and didn't seem to have any reason to kill herself, but that was what she did, by shooting herself with a small Colt as Spencer had. And not just that, she shot herself some four times.

The case had become famous, Richard said, because they couldn't figure out how a person could shoot herself more than once when she had been dead after the first bullet. Richard had followed the investigation because he was keen to know why someone so brilliant and happy with her life should want to kill herself. Well, she may have been an astrophysicist who knew her books and job, but she had been looking around at other stuff in life. She had spent some four months in Africa, working with the people in a village. She had done this for some other bookish society and had written a paper to say that her work, as well as similar work by others, was just not enough. She had also done the same sort of work here in America; feeling discouraged because she thought ill, infirm, and poor people couldn't be helped enough. In short, she had been unhappy for others, not herself.

Richard suspected she had killed herself because she could see how imperfect things were for everybody else. When he had spoken to our friends and neighbors and the people in the telephone company, he had asked them if they remembered the case of the famous astrophysicist. They had, and each offered little snippets which would help Richard understand.

One person used to see her driving to work every morning. Not only was she very beautiful and well qualified, but she looked very young. She had achieved much at a young age. Richard wondered if she had chosen the wrong line of professional work. Perhaps she should have studied religion more closely to see what she could do for others. Perhaps he should do the same.

Felix came home late that night and seemed to be in a daze. He had been trying to console his girlfriend, Laurie. Richard badgered Felix with a lot of questions. He asked about the type of gun that Spencer had used. Felix looked nervous, something I hadn't seen before. He said Spencer had given the pistol he had used to Laurie for safe keeping until about a month ago. Felix had come across it in Laurie's safekeeping place and had handled it briefly till Laurie took it back.

Our father was annoyed and upset about this. He shouted at Felix for having shown interest in someone else's firearms. He lectured Felix about how easy it was for people to leave ammunition behind in a pistol and how easy it was for a .22 caliber to go off by mistake. Felix, of course, said he couldn't care less, and showed it. Richard kept badgering him with questions until our parents put an end to it. Felix stalked off to his room after dinner. He didn't want to go to his friend's garage for the music, not tonight.

All of us felt terrible about the way Spencer had chosen to take his life. None of us hung around after dinner. Richard sat up writing in our room, so at least that was one night when I didn't have to switch off the light. I tossed and turned in my bed with our light on, seeing no signs of Candle Face on this day when death visited our street. But I could see that Richard had his arm around something while he wrote. Just before I fell asleep I thought Richard looked peaceful as he wrote his story. I couldn't see Griffin, but I thought I heard a little chirrupy grunt. I heard nothing else. When our mother came in to wake us up in the morning she told us we had fallen asleep with the light on.

Arthur M. Mills, Jr.

CHAPTER 26

My father loved to watch the TV show *All in the Family* after work. It was a daily ritual with him and I usually kept him company. Instead of staying in our room most of the time, Richard now began to join us on our TV watching couch. Sometimes he brought his scribbling pad and wrote things down. He probably had better ideas about the episodes than the people writing the script.

In several of the episodes, Archie, the main character, pretended to shoot himself in the head with an imaginary revolver. In other episodes, he would use an imaginary rope and pretend to hang himself. This was particularly noticeable when Archie had to enact wanting a way out because his wife wouldn't stop nagging him. When she nagged him on TV, my father would pass a few comments to warn himself and us about what was going to happen. He would then laugh and settle down to watch the gestures which had become predictable on Archie's part.

Richard seemed to want to be with us while we watched TV. He was now following *All in the Family* as closely as we were. I noticed he would become a bit keyed up, make his fists into imaginary pistols and get ready to imitate Archie. He also took up a great interest in guns around this time, even asking Felix if he could see the pistol Spencer used to shoot himself. Felix said the police had taken it away, but when Richard persisted, Felix told him to go look in the school library if he was so interested but discouraged him from real live guns and ammunition.

After Spencer ended his life, Richard often performed a pretend shooting stunt. He carried the details of Spencer's suicide through to his stories and still talked to anyone who hadn't heard. It got to the point where Richard was embellishing the suicide story for all the kids he saw, at school and in the neighborhood. Everyone was fascinated by the way Richard would pretend to shoot himself and slip the noose of the pretend lasso over his head and around his neck.

It didn't matter whether we were at home, school, or church when he copied Archie's antics. Worse, he did the stunt with the imaginary rope as effectively as Archie. I sometimes thought he did it better than Archie, with his head tilted to one side at the end of an imaginary rope and his tongue hanging out after the noose tightened.

Richard's pretend hanging became part of his dramatics on stage. The pretend gun and the noose hanging were now part of his repertoire up in the tree house (Or at least what was left of it). Richard copied Archie so well with the imaginary gun and the imaginary rope that his skills at these antics became legendary. He would invariably be asked to perform one or both of the stunts.

Surprisingly our mother noticed all this and complained to our father, saying his TV watching habits defied her rule about no guns in the house. Besides Spencer, who had shot himself dead for real, and Archie on TV, she knew a lot of play shooting was going on at home and in our neighborhood. It would all come to no good, she said, although she didn't mention Richard or me by name.

At least our father looked embarrassed about Richard's habits learned from TV. He hadn't exactly encouraged Richard to watch TV, but he hadn't discouraged him either, not seeming to care what a bad influence it was. Because Dad had been nothing but a model father to me, I was especially bothered by his little, insensitive gestures toward Richard, like never reading the contents of the notebooks Richard offered to him. Dad had steadily encouraged my running. Why could he not encourage Richard's writing?

Dad didn't forget Mom's comments. He, Richard, and I continued to watch Archie's antics on *All in the Family*, but now, when Richard went into his act of shooting himself with the gun and hanging himself with the rope, we all ignored him. *Looking back, we should have tried to stop him then.* I hadn't seen Richard's invisible friend for a long time, nor had I heard him. I was, as always, worried about Candle Face. She hadn't been around for a while, but one night, after I had tucked myself in but couldn't go to sleep, there she was. As usual,

Richard remained fast asleep and didn't wake up while she tormented me.

She came in quietly and stayed quiet for so long that for a while I didn't realize she was there. At first I could see only her outline in the outside street lamp. My initial hope was that it wasn't Candle Face's outline. Maybe it was Felix sleep walking into our room, as he had before. But soon my spirits sank. Even a quick look indicated that those dreadlocks highlighted by the street lamp could only belong to Candle Face. I could sense her glare but not see her eyes. I could feel her hot breath but couldn't hear the rasp as she drew air in and expelled it. The smell of her still struck me in the face.

Then Candle Face pointed at Richard and began ranting about how he pretended to shoot himself in the head with his handgun, and then died on a noose at the end of a rope. She enacted her little drama by creeping up to Richard with an evil grin on her shifting, unformed face. Using her withered, fibrous arms and deformed hand, she pretended to hold a gun to his head. At this nightmare sight, I thought my heart would stop. What was she up to? Was she showing me she could cause another death? In which case Richard would be in trouble as he lay sleeping.

But he didn't wake up and soon she moved again—over to my bed. As usual, Candle Face saved the worst for me. My mind was still on Richard, so I wasn't prepared when she placed her bony knees between my feet. Once again, I couldn't move. She inched forward on her knees. Finally, she was on my chest, blocking my breathing. To think my heart had quickly gone back to normal when she had decided to turn away from Richard!

I tried to open my mouth for one big gasp, but her awful stench prevented me. It took me back to the time when Candle Face held me under water in the creek. But I couldn't draw in air because I couldn't move, not even to open my mouth to gasp. She leaned forward, brought both hands towards my face. I told myself this was it. I would die and not have to know about anything after this. Her hands stretched across with the thumbs touching and hovered above my neck, as if she was signaling how she could squeeze the breath out of me, whatever was left.

I pleaded for my life now. I tried to look into where her eyes should have been, but she was shaking her head, swinging her dreadlocks around and signaling no. She started laughing her hollow, ghostly and gurgling laugh. Finally she swung her head all the way round so that she was facing Richard. For a minute she stayed this way and brought up what may have been an arm. I thought she was going to strike me, but she stretched the arm back towards Richard and pointed towards him with one of her claw-like digits. Then she brought her face back to me and moved her head up and down in a yes, just as she had the very first night I saw her crawl out of her hole. I was past caring now. I wanted her to either let me go or let me pass out into oblivion. But she still wasn't done with me. She brought her head low and said in her hoarse growly voice, "Watch out for him this time."

I could have laughed. Felix had done away with any enemies Richard might have. Richard was in favor with our neighborhood friends because of his newest antics. It was another matter whether I, or any of us, approved of Richard's shot-in-the-head or hangman's noose play acting. *I was going to be proved wrong in the worst manner possible.*

Candle Face then did something else which left no doubt as to her own feelings. She said that it wasn't easy for anyone to become

Griffin's friend. She said Griffin was the best and that ghosts and people had tried to take advantage of him.

I now knew that Candle Face, ghoul as she was, could feel jealous. Simply put, she wanted Griffin to stay put and be with her alone. She didn't want him to come out, be friends and generally spend time with us. I worried about Richard all over again and felt sad for Griffin. It explained why I hadn't seen him lately. Things were going well for Richard just now, but what if Candle Face put an end to that, as she well could?

Finally she rose slowly, her eye sockets flashing within. I didn't want to look deep inside. I knew what horrors lay there. Candle Face had my head in a jumble. This time I didn't want to know what she had to say. Her warnings were worse than what, so far, had really taken place.

I awoke with a start. It was still early in the morning. From the living room I could hear our favorite program on TV. Archie didn't have many speech inhibitions. Just now I could hear him saying, "Bang bang," and his wife talking in her high pitched voice. Canned laughter filtered through the walls, making me think Archie was doing his amusing stunt. I didn't want to know. I was waiting for my brain to clear from last night's ritual.

I looked across at Richard. His eyes were open. He looked straight at me but didn't say anything. The TV was making the right noises but he didn't do the handgun stunt. The TV was never on this early in the morning, but a new day had dawned and our bedroom was flooded in light. We wondered what the explanation for that could be.

We quietly waited for our mother to come in. She wouldn't have to rouse us from sleep today, but I was aching for my mother after that session with Candle Face.

CHAPTER 27

Mom had already registered her displeasure with Richard's inclination towards miming gun play and hangman's noose. Her reaction seemed to strike a chord with Richard. In one way or another he wanted to hold her attention. I think that in reality, Richard just wanted to be noticed by everyone in our family, especially our parents. There had been the time when he had joined our older brothers when they played drinking games and smoked stuff that wasn't good for them. Since he'd ended up getting very sick, he hadn't tried anything like that again, but I suspected he still hankered for attention.

Richard had been trying to copy some of Dan and Felix's antics, but the truth was, he couldn't pull off these tricks as well as our older brothers could. For example, he would draw our parents' attention to something in a corner of the room during dinner. While they were looking, he would drop something or clap loudly near their ear so that they jumped. Nobody laughed, so he finally had to admit his older brothers were more successful than he was at mean jokes and tricks.

For their part, Dan and Felix told Richard not to worry because he would never be as good as they were.

Then there was me. Richard had always thought our parents favored me because I was the youngest in the family. He had said so more than once, although lately he no longer hit, punched, and threatened me with worse if I told on him. Had he gotten past his resentment? Was this because he'd become introverted and was now mulling over other stuff in his life? Apparently his new-found invisible friend had given him a lot to think about. Of course, therein lay a problem because Candle Face was jealous of the friendship between Griffin and Richard. Up until now she had done what was best for Griffin. I hoped she would realize if she harmed Richard she'd be harming Griffin, too. *So much for my fledgling attempts at psychological analysis.* In the meanwhile, I could only observe and hope.

Richard was seeking something. Now that I am better able to truly analyze what was going on, I think he was looking for his missing friend. I could see that Richard had ultimately decided not to spend a great deal of time in our room on his own. He wandered out absentmindedly at first, but now took to regularly joining our father and me on the couch in front of the TV. I wasn't sure how good it had been for him—that business of miming the shot in the head as Archie did.

During all this, Richard was possibly looking for Griffin. He was also doing other things which we didn't understand then. For instance, he stripped our tree house down to its bare board. All of us were devastated when he did this because it seemed to signal there would be fewer shows, if any at all. *Looking back, I think it was part of his effort to look for Griffin.*

As for the two back lots—our own and the one next door, our friends came around to play only occasionally now. They did, however, hope that Richard would think up an extempore entertainment for all of us like he used to in the old days before the tree house had been dismantled. But Richard seemed to have his mind on other stuff and hadn't obliged except for his Archie Bunker imitation.

By now, our friends were playing fewer childhood type games, and it was a rare occasion when all of us would get together. On one such occasion, all of us except Randy were gathered in our backyard. Randy wasn't there because of his parents, who had made their displeasure known concerning my family, especially us four brothers. We missed him, though, especially Richard, who liked to think of Randy as his best friend. Still, my spirits were high. My friends had been congratulating me about the citywide track meet held recently where I, wearing my famous red Budweiser cap, had done the mile in 5 minutes and 35 seconds, beating the boy who came in second by more than a minute and a half.

That day we played bicycle hop after what seemed like ages. We were exhilarated after performing acrobatics on our bicycles. In fact, I could even ignore the horror that lived in the hole for the time being.

Just like we used to do, we pedaled down Ben Howell Drive, pointed our bicycle wheels in the air, and came down to balance on the ramp before we hopped off the bicycle seat and onto the grass in a practiced sequence. Greatly enjoying myself, I jumped with extra energy, sure my bicycle jump was higher than the others. I guess winning the mile had done wonders for my confidence because that day I felt I was on top of the world.

Afterward, everyone clambered onto the board across the lower branches of our great tree. We made such a huge racket Virgie came out to admonish us. After she went back inside, we turned to Richard and asked him to please put on a show. At first he said he couldn't be bothered but relented when Sean asked. I promised to assist him, just like the old days. Sean also asked to be Richard's assistant. Richard came out of his far-away look and looked at me for a long while. I knew I was going to be the lucky helper.

Everyone clambered down from the board and settled on the wild grass-covered ground, away from fire ants and the round depression in the ground in the far back. I stood next to Richard, who gave me a funny look. I couldn't figure it out, but it made me wonder if I should be feeling as happy as I was. Richard announced I had won first place for the mile run at the track meet. But my friends knew about this. He asked me to show how I had run. I demurred, but he reminded me I was now his helper and would have to do what he asked. So I ran around the perimeter of the empty lot. When I passed the hole in the ground, I looked in, just to make sure I was safe. I thought I heard a jeering laugh.

Richard wasn't through. Next, I had to run up and down our street. By now I was feeling a bit silly. Our friends clapped every time I came back to the starting point below the board, but their cheering was tending to trail off. Now Richard asked me to go fetch my medal. I demurred again, feeling he was making me a spectacle, pushing me through hoops learned from his drinking games with Dan and Felix.

But Richard wouldn't budge. I had chosen myself as his helper so I had to do what he said. Sean looked happy it hadn't been him. I had no option but to go in the house and get my medal which I'd hung by its ribbon on a nail high on my bedroom wall. When I brought it back, Richard reached out, plucked it from my hand, pulled his arm back

Arthur M. Mills, Jr.

and lobbed it high in the air. My medal flew up, followed an arc and landed in the hole in the back of the empty lot next door.

My friends had started cheering when they saw me come out of the house with my prize in my hand. But when Richard threw it in the hole they were speechless, as was I. I think I even cried a bit, eleven-year-old baby that I was. Richard was exultant. He was now daring me to go fetch my prize from where it was hidden. The thought drove me into a frenzy not dissimilar to what I had to face when Candle Face came around at night. I was scared, to say the least, not wanting to go too close. My friends sat around me, Mark on one side and his brother Sean on the other. As with earlier confrontations between Richard and me, they didn't want to take sides and soon left. They would have had to go home in any case. As for the rest of my friends, that accursed hole had always given them a bad feeling, so no one offered to retrieve the medal.

Some of my tears were because Richard had played one of his new-found extempore tricks on me. It was obvious he was now trying his hand at tricks in the same way as Archie on TV, and also Dan and Felix in real life with their unkind jokes. Like before, I figured he wanted attention from the family, our mother in particular. Maybe Archie's antics as played by Richard had got him plenty of attention from our neighborhood boys, but I could have told him he wasn't much good at playing jokes and tricks on others. Both our friends and I could have told him he was best by far at being an entertainer, not a trick player.

I knew I couldn't tell our father. He would probably punish Richard and go get my medal back, thus reinforcing Richard's belief that our father favored me and would do anything to get me to stop crying. So in the end, I couldn't do a thing except worry about what Richard would think up next.

A year-round Halloween and party shop had opened near the H.E.B. grocery store. It had costumes, false moustaches, tricks and masks on display. It also carried "how to" books which Richard thought were ace. Best of all, the party shop wasn't just for Halloween and parties. Some of their tricks, including magic tricks, were a lot more sophisticated than the simpler fare we had known till then.

One day Richard and I visited the shop. Knowing what he wanted, Richard read a bit from one of the books and bought some fake blood.

After dinner that night, he hung around outside on the front porch until it got pretty late. I hung around with him, pretty sure I knew what he was up to. Sure enough, pretty soon he burst a sachet of fake blood and smeared it all over his right arm. Holding that arm, he walked up to the screen door, pushed it open, and staggered in. In a choked voice he told our mother he had just accidentally cut open his arm. Aghast, she immediately jumped up and ran to him.

"Oh my God!" she cried. I could see the terror on her face. She put her arm around him and held him. Her face was pale. She looked terribly shocked. Her knees buckled. I thought she was going to faint. At this point Richard knew he had made a huge mistake. He hadn't thought she would take his word for it without any questions asked, or that she would react in such an extreme fashion. But she had, not remotely imagining it could be just a trick.

"It's not real Ma. It's fake blood. I'm okay." Richard smeared the fake blood on his arm to show there wasn't a cut underneath.

Still in a state of shock, Mom looked at the arm, then Richard's face. By now, Richard was scared too, and sorry, I could tell really sorry for what he had done.

Smack!

Our mother had recovered herself and slapped Richard across his face much harder than I had ever known her to. The sound echoed through the house. Richard's cheeks were aflame. She grabbed both his shoulders and shook him. She told him to never do that or anything close to that stupid trick, ever again. Richard kept apologizing and saying he hadn't meant to scare her that much. Our father didn't say anything but he did give Richard a long hard look.

Mom remained angry. She threatened Richard with everything she could think of. He wasn't going to get any pocket money if he wasted it on such silly things as fake blood. He was going to be grounded for a long, long time. Finally she told him to go clean up, have a bath and go to bed. After he'd gone off, Mom sat down and cried.

Later that night, when Richard had got into bed and covered himself with his sheet, I thought I heard muffled sobs. He was truly sorry. Too late he realized the gravity of his silly trick. He may have also realized that forcing me to make a spectacle of myself in front of our friends wasn't a good thing. It was another one of his jokes that no one found funny. But mainly, I suspected he had realized our mother

Arthur M. Mills, Jr.

would take an awfully long time to forgive him. Possibly it struck him that perhaps she never would.

The next morning when I woke up I saw something hanging high up on the wall. I shut my eyes for a couple of seconds. When I opened them I could see my medal hanging at the end of its ribbon. It was back on its nail. The only problem was, it wasn't as clean and shiny as it had been when Richard took it from me. It was now encrusted in some drippy stuff. I hoped it was only fake blood.

Richard remained subdued the whole week. There were no visits to the party shop, no performances, no more attempted tricks on any of us in the family, nothing.

CHAPTER 28

That week, Richard stayed in his room, hardly talking to anyone in the family, including me. Finally, towards the end of that week on a Friday night, he got up the courage to come and sit with us in the living room. At first he sat there not talking, but looking at our mother in a pleading manner. Finally he got his nerve up and told her that his friends regularly went to the movies over weekends. He, too, would like to go. Could she give him money for a ticket? He would like to go to the movies with Evan, who was going with his family the next day.

My mother pointed out that Evan's family was rolling in money. Other than Randy's, they had one of the best houses on our street. She reminded Richard we were not as well off, despite how hard she worked to put food on the table. She also reminded him that thanks to his silly trick, his pocket money had been cut off and he had been grounded for a month. She then cut to the chase and told Richard we didn't have any money anyway to give to him for the movie.

Now that Richard had got his nerve up, he wasn't going to let go and put his best arguments to use. He would never play a trick like that on her again. He was going to stay away from the party shop. In any case, he would never buy any more fake body stuff. She must know he was truly sorry and had turned over a new leaf. He continued on to tell her that as badly off as we were, she might be able to afford the cash for one tiny movie ticket. He kept pestering her, but this time our mother seemed to have turned a deaf ear. She said no every time Richard asked. She wouldn't budge.

Richard added more to his plea. He told her he was willing to work for the money. He was willing to work hard, whether at home or in a proper job, though he was still not yet thirteen. She said she expected him to help with the housework as always. He asked her for permission to wash neighbors' cars to make the money. She knew he was desperate to go to the movies with his friend, but as far as she was concerned, Richard was still grounded and would have to serve out his punishment.

Richard finally understood Mom would never agree to giving him the money or letting him earn it when he was grounded. But that still wasn't the last word as far as Richard was concerned. He wasn't going to let go. The next day, he and Evan mulled over her arguments and came up with a secret plan. They decided Richard's idea of washing cars was a good one and Richard didn't *have* to ask our mother for permission because paid work was outside the fact of Richard being grounded. *I could only agree with their clever thinking.* I was so taken up with the idea that I hung around. They decided both of them would wash neighbors' cars to make some money. They would keep it a secret from our parents.

The next Saturday morning, after our parents left for work, Richard and Evan walked up and down Ben Howell Drive. They asked all our neighbors if they wanted to have their cars washed for a few bucks. Glad to have this service at their doorstep, almost everyone said yes. That day, Richard made me do his household chores. That meant I did double chores—the ones our mother asked me to do, and the ones she had listed out for him. I happily obliged. Not only did I like being part of Richard's money raising scheme, I was grateful he'd returned my medal. At least, I assumed he was the one who had actually returned it, even though I hadn't actually seen him do it.

So I did what was expected of me, and Richard did what he expected of himself to earn his ticket money. When I finally came out on the front porch, I was convinced the parked cars on Ben Howell somehow looked newer and brighter. A walk convinced me that Evan and Richard had put in their very best effort to wash cars.

Evan and Richard had washed and polished enough cars to cover Richard's ticket money. He could now pay for his way in to watch that movie and have money left over for popcorn. Richard had managed matters, somehow. He could tell himself he was successful.

In the meanwhile, Evan and Richard had thought up the second part of their plan to get Richard into the movie theater. When our mother got home from work, Richard told her that he was, after all, going to the movies. After their last discussion, she was in no mood for another argument, but Richard calmed her, saying Evan was going to pay for the ticket. She questioned him closely about why Evan should do him such a big favor, but Richard managed to convince her, and she finally said he could go.

Thrilled he had got around her, Richard went off to wash and get the best of our shared clothes out of the closet. He took care with how he dressed and how he looked. This was going to be his first outing to the movies with Evan.

The phone rang. I rushed to pick it up, but my father playfully beat me to it. I heard him talking to a neighbor and saw his expression change from laughing to serious. Unfortunately it was one of our neighbors calling to express his appreciation. He told Dad how Richard and Evan had surprised everyone by asking, then washing their cars on a Saturday. What a fine job they'd done washing his car!

As soon as he hung up, Dad informed Mom what Richard had been up to. She looked as shocked as she had when Richard tried to trick her with his bloodied arm. She didn't wait for Richard to get dressed and emerge from our room. She charged right in. Her face aflame, she asked, "So Evan gave you the money for the movie?"

"Yes," he replied. Sensing something was wrong, he launched into a story about how the money for the ticket hadn't come directly from Evan but from his parents. He reminded her she had told him on Friday that Evan's parents were well off and that's why they had decided to fund a trip to the movies for Evan and one friend.

Our mother was stone faced. She'd had enough. "Then how come our neighbor called to tell us you did a good job washing his car?"

Richard's face turned beet red. I knew this because after that phone call from the neighbor I couldn't tear myself away. I was being the sneaky younger brother, seeing Richard's torment through to the bitter end. I heard Mom light into him, saying this latest lie was just a part of his nasty jokes and tricks. She reminded him he had promised never to do such things again. Richard had no defense. I suppose Evan would have vouched for him, but it would have made things worse between him and our mother.

Meantime, Mom's rage wouldn't die down. My father decided to take her out, so later that night they left on one of their rare outings.

Arthur M. Mills, Jr.

Richard and I stayed home. We had no idea where Dan and Felix were till we heard jangly music wafting up the road from the direction of Edwin's garage. When the music stopped, Richard and I tensed, wondering what was going to happen next.

Soon enough we heard our brothers whistling and stomping down the street. They were coming home and would want a meal, but there wasn't anything at home, not tonight. I had managed to make do with cornflakes and watered down milk. Richard said he wasn't hungry. I didn't blame him for losing his appetite after what he had gone through.

We wondered what our brothers would do about dinner and whether we would be involved in any way. I was tempted to run off. Evan's house was closest, but no one would be home because they had all gone to the movies. In any case, Richard said he would stay at home and hope Dan and Felix were not on some kind of a high. He could only hope for the best.

Sure enough, when Dan and Felix got home, they started rummaging through the kitchen looking for something to eat. There wasn't anything and their moods were worsening. They told us they were going to take Felix's girlfriend's car and go to Dunkin Donuts to pick something up. Warning bells went off in our heads. We knew we should stay out of whatever plan they had.

That night Dan and Felix tried to rob a Dunkin' Doughnuts. Out of sheer stupidity, Dan got caught. He had demanded all the money from the till. After he got the money, he asked the cashier for a dozen doughnuts, actually taking his time to choose which ones he wanted. He took so long that he gave the police plenty of time to reach the store and catch him. When Felix heard the sirens approaching, he sped away in the get-away car.

What a good brother! Dan got caught with all the cash and all the doughnuts he had chosen. He was going to spend several years in a juvenile detention facility, but this bit was still in the future, after he had been charged and after his hearing.

Richard and I didn't know what Dan and Felix had been up to on this day. Nor did our parents find out until much later. Our family would have some other grieving to do before Dan's foolishness caught up with him.

I had seen Evan drive off to the movies with his parents. He looked miserable, pressing his face against the back window of their car as they drove by. He looked towards our bedroom off the front porch for as long as he could. Richard must have heard their car drive off as well but didn't say anything.

Richard stayed in a quiet mood, just lying in bed staring at the ceiling. It frightened me to see him like this. I tried drawing him out, asking him to come watch TV with me. I mentioned that his car washing had earned him a fair amount and that at least he had cash of his own, even though he was grounded. I wished Griffin would come and be his friend again. That gave me an idea. Richard had other friends who cared for him, so I rang some of them up and got them to come over. Randy, Mark and another boy named Sam sat in our living room, chatted and watched TV, but unfortunately Richard stayed in our room lying on his back in bed. He hadn't come out to watch TV with me earlier, and he didn't come out to join us now. He wasn't reading anything, nor did he write in his journal.

Arthur M. Mills, Jr.

CHAPTER 29

When Evan returned home from the movie, he joined us in the living room. We were all talking, being noisy, and watching TV when Richard finally came out of the bedroom. We were glad he did, even though he chose to sit in the farthest corner and hardly spoke.

Evan wanted to tell Richard about the movie. His father had chosen a family movie about a war. It had been started against the United States by a country far away. It started with unimaginable flying, diving and bombing by ancient war planes. Everyone in the theater booed because the country under attack was the United States.

Richard sat up and listened. Here was one story not in his repertoire. And Evan was dramatizing details in Richard's manner. It showed the people on the ground who were getting bombed. It showed heroes, ships, and people who died. Evan described the instant deaths. The movie picked up on personal stories of good-looking men and women. Some of them would find happiness by the end of the movie, some would die, some would be treated unfairly.

Richard followed the story closely. He told Evan that life *was* sometimes unfair. Evan agreed. They were both probably thinking of events closer to home, but now Evan was coming to better parts of the story. Heroic pilots from the U. S. Air force offered awesome airborne resistance. Those were scenes worth watching, although Evan said his mother objected to that sort of violence on the screen. Evan said the movie was bound to be shown on TV and asked Richard to keep a watch out and let him know. He would love to watch the movie again, this time with Richard. Unfortunately his kind words only reminded my brother of his disastrous day and how he had been accused, a little unjustly. He lapsed into one of his quiet moods again.

Someone asked Richard to do one of Archie's stunts, hoping to get him more involved, but he didn't seem to care. Meanwhile, Evan felt partly responsible for the trouble Richard got into with our mother. He cared for Richard and would do anything to get him out of his predicament. We left them alone as the two of them sat in quiet companionship, wondering what to say or do next. Again, someone asked Richard to perform one of Archie's stunts. This time Richard got up, walked to the middle of the living room, and stood there, looking around. As on the day I had asked to be Richard's helper, I had a deep sense of foreboding. I wondered if it had been such a good idea to have so many of our friends come over.

Richard started tossing an imaginary lasso. For a while he twirled it above his head, then pretended he had got his head through it. Sitting down with the imaginary end in his hand, he began to pull the noose tight. He made out he was tightening the rope and that his breathing was obstructed. His head fell forward. His eyes were closed and he looked as if he were no longer breathing. Finally Evan got up and gently removed the imaginary rope from Richard's neck. Richard stayed as he was with his head slumped forward.

We didn't know what to think. I went up to Richard, shook him and clapped at the same time. His eyes opened, and I was glad to see the same old Richard had come back to us. I felt like clapping some more. Richard sat there with a knowing expression on his face. We went back to playing our indoor games and commenting on whatever was on TV.

But there was more action that night. We were horsing around, trying out Archie's shooting and rope hanging stunts ourselves. Sam, who is Lori's cousin, was an enthusiastic member, but he hadn't had the opportunity to view Richard's brand of entertainment before today. Sam had heard about Richard's better-than-the-best performance and seen a miniature show today. He asked Richard to do some more of his stunts.

Smiling at all of us, Richard picked up the telephone. He found a spot on the floor, sat down and placed the telephone next to him. Not saying a word, he pulled the telephone cord towards himself until the

Arthur M. Mills, Jr.

slack was completely gone. With bated breath we waited for his next move, all of us wondering what he was going to do with the cord.

My sense of panicky foreboding returned when Richard pulled the telephone cord still tighter to a point above his head. He then began to wrap the cord tightly around his neck, keeping on until the cord was so tightly wound that the cord popped out of the wall. We had been waiting all this time, thinking this was just another of Richard's tricks and all would soon be revealed. But instead, Richard grabbed the end of the telephone cord which had sprung out of the wall and pulled it towards his foot. He wrapped that end around his big toe and actually bent that foot forward as he pulled backwards. The many layers of cord wrapped around Richard's neck tightened. I could see the skin of his neck pucker.

At first, everyone except me thought this was just another one of Richard's impresario acts. I was the only one close to being scared. By now the cord had become so tight it sank into his skin. Blood must have rushed to his head because his face turned redder than the time our mother had smacked him. I could see his blood vessels bulging right out of his skin. His hands had become limp.

After a few frozen seconds, we all jumped up, surrounded him, and unwrapped the cord around his neck. Evan was visibly upset. All of us were shocked, but not as badly as Richard. Richard just lay there with his eyes open. He was motionless. All that I could think about was that he had been in this position on his bed just a little while ago.

All this had taken some 30 seconds. After another half a minute or maybe a minute, Richard's eyes started to blink. We could now afford to be scared. For our friends it was time to go home. They wanted to get as far away from this spectacle as they could. Only Evan wanted to stay on with Richard and me, but he had rules in his house and had to leave as well.

After another couple of minutes there was a commotion outside. Felix had come home, driving rough and in a hurry. The tires of Lori's car screeched to a halt as Felix hurried to put the car back where it belonged. He came in and took a long look at Richard who still lay on the floor, then ran into his room and banged the door shut. Richard didn't react to Felix's noisy entry. I vaguely wondered why Dan hadn't come home with him.

I stayed next to Richard to make sure he didn't try the stunt with the telephone cord again.

In another half an hour our parents came home. They looked at the two of us in the living room—Richard still on the floor and I, hunched next to him, the telephone back in its place. Mom ignored us, probably thinking the two of us were up to another attention-getting scenario. Dad sat down to watch TV before going to bed. I finally helped Richard up, and the two of us went to our room. All Richard managed to do was to flop down in his own bed where he lay, still not moving, still staring at the ceiling.

Knowing Richard was in serious trouble, I decided to talk separately to my parents. I went to my father first, as he watched TV in the living room. I wasn't going to be able to help my stutter, I knew.

"P-pa, d-d-do y-y-you think you could t-t-talk to Ma and she could l-l-let Richard g-g-go to the movie n-n-n-next weekend? Y-y-you know h-h-he d-d-didn't m-m-mean that jazz about his arm. A-a-a-nd there's a special m-m-movie on next weekend."

I waited hopefully, but it was the end of the day and our father was tired. He told me our mother had made up her mind. She had made the rules and Richard would just have to stick to them. It was too bad that

Richard had lied to her about how he had come by the money for the ticket. She was his wife and he respected her rules and regulations for the family, as should we, her sons.

I realize now I should have told my father that Richard didn't deserve such a huge punishment. I should have told him that Richard had tried to hurt himself badly tonight and in front of his friends, and that I knew it could only be a cry for help.

I went to our parents' bedroom to talk to my mother but discovered she had already gone to bed. She worked hard. She was tired. I couldn't disturb her.

If only Richard had put up some sort of signal to let them know all wasn't well with him! But he didn't, so how could they know?

I went to bed with a heavy heart. Richard lay still, encased in his sheet. I didn't know if he had shut his eyes or was still staring at the ceiling.

CHAPTER 30

I got ready for bed with my usual elaborate arrangements. To begin with, I could do without Candle Face, especially tonight. I had still not thought about her warning about Richard's safety last time. Nor did I want to start thinking about the events of tonight. I would have time enough for such contemplation during the long hours after I went to bed.

I remembered the time Candle Face had stolen out of our closet. The thought of a sudden encounter with her now made my flesh crawl. So I checked there first, moving the clothes around a bit, my hands and fingers trembling. Although I made absolutely sure she wasn't in there, I still checked the top of the closet before I closed the door, then propped toys against the outside of the closet door. If she was going to try and get in after I'd gone to bed, the toys should fall and make a noise which would warn me.

I checked under Richard's bed and mine, again, removing dirty clothes from where we had chucked them. Candle Face had hidden under Richard's bed once. I had to be aware of all the places she could think of to hide.

I would have to switch off the light before I got into bed and hoped the dark wouldn't get me before Candle Face did. I mapped my path to the light switch and then to bed. I should have had enough practice by now, but the route was still full of uncertainties and terrors.

Practice meant that just as before, I pretended to turn the light off. In the next instant I had to run towards my bed and jump several feet before I landed on that base. As before, I landed with a crash which might or might not have disturbed Richard and everyone else in the house.

Since I managed the practice landing okay, I decided to go for the real thing. I turned off my light and ran for my bed, the light rays from the street a miniature beacon to light my way. Several feet from the bed, I jumped up in the air, again confident and on top of the world. In mid-air I noticed something under my sheets. Before I could land, the sheets moved to the side exposing what lay underneath. It was Candle Face under the sheets. I landed right next to her but managed to bounce up, ready to run. Quickly she grabbed me. As had happened in the past, I couldn't move and stayed there, terrified, paralyzed and blaming myself. How could she be in my bed after all my elaborate precautions? Should I have checked better?

She was reading my mind and smiling. She patted my head and tried to make a noise which went "Tch, tch." Finding a use for that hated grating voice, she said, "I have something for you."

Didn't want it. Whatever it was could only bode evil. She had even found my hiding place for her offering. She reached under my pillow and pulled something out.

"Here it is," she said.

Her clawed hand reached towards my head. I held my breath. No memory could ever prepare me for the stench that flooded my nose and lungs. But those claws were reaching under my head, ruffling my hair in the gap between my head and my pillow. She was actually lifting my head up. Richard and I were supposed to share our clothes and things, but I had hidden our best belt under my pillow, away from Richard should he look for it in the closet tomorrow morning. Next thing I knew, she was slipping the narrow end of a belt under my head, working it down under my neck and bringing it back in a loop. She had clean lifted my head off the pillow and looped the belt around my neck. Richard, can you help me? I desperately wondered. *Anything, Richard!*

But Richard must have gone to sleep. As before, I tried to yell for help but could not. And, as during such sessions, she took advantage of my paralyzed state. She pulled on the pointy bit of the leather belt, looped it around my neck once more and began to tighten it. I had tried hard not to breathe because of her smell, but now she was doing it for me, trying to get me to stop breathing. I still couldn't understand what she wanted from me, other than the enjoyment of my terrified state. Did I have to die because I hadn't considered that? Some reason lazily stirred in my mind.

Arthur M. Mills, Jr.

Her smokers' voice spat out, "Oh, you like it, too? Richard loves this, it's his favorite." I felt my pulse beating in my temples. I was no longer trying not to draw in a breath and my breathing had begun to make a swizzing sound. Another horrible thought flooded what consciousness I had left. Had Candle Face somehow brought on Richard's actions? I thought back to when Sam had asked Richard to do a stunt, and Richard, though despondent, had smiled back at us. Then he had done that awful thing with the pretend rope. The next "stunt" with the phone cord had been far more extreme. It could have only been a punishment for himself, the worst possible at that. Now that Candle Face was conveying all this to me through her brand of sarcasm, I stopped to think whether it had been Richard punishing himself or someone else. Could Candle Face have . . . ?

Each new thought was even more devastating than the last. And if it had been Candle Face, where had Richard's invisible friend been? I knew that Candle Face cared for Griffin and he for her. But did she control Griffin? Could she turn her brother against mine?

Candle Face found her voice again. She knew by now how deeply her revelations were affecting me. "Oh, you do like it? Let me make it tighter for you."

By now I knew her earlier threats had become stronger with the passage of time. I would have to watch not just my back, but my very existence. She wanted my life. She had killed before and could do it again. Plain torment was now *passé* for her. She wanted more.

My mind raced. How had I been able to evade her clutches earlier? Memories came flooding back. Candle Face had grown bored when I had given up. But she probably read my thoughts and now she was furious. She wouldn't allow me to do what I considered my only way out.

The real leather noose was tight around my neck. I couldn't move, least of all talk, never mind the paralysis her presence brought on. Candle Face was determined not to be cheated out of what she considered her due and right. I had thought too hard, and she was going to put an end to that. She lifted her head, turned her face in my direction and blew that stinky breath of hers straight towards me.

What now? Her ghoulish face hovered over my face. I could see the wretched, rotten horrors that dwelt deep in her eye sockets and in her mouth. I tried to will myself to close my eyes but could not.

A maggot-like tongue began to worm itself in and out of her mouth. The glowing maggots in her sockets squirmed and worked themselves outwards, towards those windows of her soul, that is if she had one.

I was petrified, ready for death, when I heard laughter coming from the next room. I knew Dad had stayed up to watch TV. Mom must have changed her mind about going to bed and joined him because what I was listening to was my parents sharing a good laugh.

Candle Face heard it too and may have thought about how to use this in her cat and mouse game. She was looking at me, that wriggly maggot of a tongue working its way in and out. Her hated voice had found something more to say directly to me.

"They're laughing at you."

I could sense my eyes rolling to the back of my head. The last thing I remember was thinking if she knew so much about Richard's actions with the telephone cord, then what she said might well be true. One of the other thoughts I had as I passed into nothingness was that if she was right then Richard was wrong. My parents were laughing at me, not him. Unlike what Richard thought, being the baby of the family didn't get me any advantages and I wasn't favored at all.

Now my mother's voice was closer still. She was no longer laughing. She was talking sternly in a certain way she had. She wasn't in the next room but in ours. She was telling us to get up and get ready for school. Daylight had broken. I could feel something around my neck, but it wasn't pressing the breath out of my chest. I sat up with a start and felt for whatever it was.

It was our leather belt.

In a flash I remembered all that had happened yesterday. I looked across at Richard. For once, he hadn't gotten up first but was lying wide awake in bed. Around his neck I could see the marks left by the telephone cord. He saw me staring, and I had to look away.

Richard rubbed his neck and remarked, "It still hurts."

I wanted to call our mother back, show her the marks and get her involved. I wanted her to let Richard go to the movies next time with the money he had earned. I wanted to tell her Richard hadn't lied to her. But I did none of those things, maybe because I was just a little kid with a stutter and who would pay attention to me?

　　　　Arthur M. Mills, Jr.

CHAPTER 31

Two days later Richard and I got to sleep in. Cinco de Mayo is not an official holiday in most parts of the country, but it is in Austin so the schools were closed. When we finally got up, the silence was deafening and the house empty. We danced a little dance, wandered around in our pajamas for a while, delighted there was no school today, although Mom had left us a list of chores to do before she got home.

I took a good look at the list of chores. She had two columns down, one for my tasks, one for Richard's. I had to wash dishes. Richard was supposed to clean the back porch. She had specified that he should sweep and swab the wooden floor of the porch. I could see that Richard's household chore was a lot more than mine.

We ate breakfast and switched on the TV, happy no one was around to tell us what to do. We weren't really slacking off, I told myself. Pretty soon we'd get to the chores. For a while we watched TV together. After about an hour, Richard got up and headed towards the back while I continued to watch TV. Hearing the swish of the broom as Richard swept the back porch clean, I felt slightly guilty, knowing I was being lazy. I sensed he was doing a thorough job, still trying to get our mother to appreciate him. I even considered lending him a hand because his chore was a lot harder than mine and was bound to take longer. I alternated between wanting to go out to help him and feeling guilty, but in the end, I stayed put. After all, Mom had given him that chore. I didn't want her thinking my helping Richard was like the car washing stunt or some other kind of cover up.

The rumbling sound soon stopped. I paid no attention because I figured Richard was taking a break, but after another twenty minutes

I heard a high continuous screaming from one of our neighbors. I looked outside but saw nothing amiss. A person screaming wasn't unusual in my neighborhood.

The screaming wouldn't go away but instead became louder and more persistent. It was so bad it was impossible to tell whether it was a man or a woman, but whoever it was, the screaming was coming closer. Finally Violet, the wife of the neighbor that called about the car washing, (She also happens to be my step-fathers daughter from a previous marriage), burst into our home. "Where is your father?" she asked, her eyes wide.

I knew when she asked me that the screaming had something to do with us. I knew I didn't want to know the next bit. I was limp. All I could think of was a direct answer. "He's at work."

Violet spared me for the time being. She said nothing, but ran back out of the house as I followed her. We ran into the empty lot next door. I couldn't put it off any longer and asked her what was going on.

Violet stopped, turned around, and looked straight into my eyes. "Richard hung himself." Letting out a long wail of torment, she turned around and ran back to her house.

It didn't make sense to me. Just twenty minutes ago Richard had been on the back porch doing his chores. So how could he have hung himself? I could hardly breathe. I was looking at spots in front of my eyes.

I then saw Virgie's husband walking away from the big tree. He had a large knife in his hand. I followed all this with my eyes, not letting my mind connect. But slowly I was beginning to understand. I heard what Violet said. I saw our neighbor walking away with a knife in his hand and knew he had used it for something he didn't want to use it for. I knew now it had to involve Richard.

I could do nothing but had to do something, so I started to walk towards our trophy tree, the one where, ages ago, we had propped up the board and built the tree house. Lately we hadn't played there much, and the grass had grown tall.

Once I passed the high grass I saw my brother. He was wearing our favorite shirt, not the one he was wearing while cleaning the back porch. He was lying on the ground, just below the 4 by 4 foot board that was the only sign left of our tree house. It still spanned across the two large branches—the spot where only a few days ago I'd accepted the forfeits Richard demanded.

Arthur M. Mills, Jr.

Now that scene had changed drastically. A rope dangled from the middle of the board. It had been cut clean with the knife that was now probably back in our neighbor's kitchen. The other part of the rope was wrapped in a noose around my brother's neck. His eyes were open. He was looking straight at me.

I had a tiny hope and moved to the side to see if his eyes would follow me. They didn't, and the sickening truth began to sink in. Barely half a day ago Richard had finished his business with the pretend rope and the telephone cord. This morning he must have jumped from the board with the noose of a real rope around his neck. Now he lay on the ground, eyes wide open, looking as if he'd just jumped there during play. He had fallen awkwardly, one of his legs bent beneath his body. The neighbor must have just cut the rope and let his body fall.

Stepping closer, I could still see the faint blue bruise marks. The rope remained around his neck, but I could barely see it because his neck was so badly swollen. I reached for the rope, thinking I should loosen it. That was when I heard car breaks screeching near the curb, then heavy footsteps running towards Richard and me. I looked up and saw John, my step-father's son from a previous marriage running towards us. Violet must have telephoned him. I was glad not only for her presence earlier but glad she was the one who told me and had gotten hold of John.

John was a fireman. He lived a few houses north of Nolan's house on Wilson Street. If anyone could help, he could. John stood next to me and put one arm around my thin shoulders. He told me he had work to do and I had to stay away. He then approached Richard, got the rope off his neck and began Cardio Pulmonary Resuscitation.

Within minutes I heard sirens approaching. I must have been disoriented because suddenly I was transported back to Nolan's house the day Spencer committed suicide. Hearing the sound of sirens again, I felt the same disbelief. Here were the same group of vehicles attending to a response—police cars, ambulances and a fire truck. The paramedics were shouting instructions to each other, running to the three of us, trying to take stock of what had happened. They took over and continued with CPR, telling me not to hang around. I wandered off in a daze and went and sat on the front porch. The image of Candle Face entered my head. The night before last she had shoved her face up to mine. I thought she had been her usual insensitive self when she had poked fun at us, saying Richard liked it, and that I should like it too. Could that have been a warning? That night had I not sensed what she wanted was death? In my confusion and fright I thought it was my life she wanted, but now I saw I could be wrong.

But those were just dreams. I was crazy if I thought my dreams had anything to do with Richard in real life . . . and death.

Sounds pierced my head. Someone else took up screaming. More police cars arrived. Neighbors started to come over, including Evan whose eyes were like saucers as he asked what had happened. I told him and he ran back home to tell his mother. She and his father soon arrived. She couldn't stop crying. No matter what she thought about our family, she must have liked Richard and regretted what she'd said in the past.

I was the only one around who could tell everyone what had happened. Violet had gone home in deep shock, as had our other neighbor who had helped in our time of crisis. Dan and Felix, who had been at Edwin's house, came running from up the street and asked me what was going on. I told them what had happened but could somehow not mention Richard by name. They both ran towards the empty lot. Several policemen had to stop them from getting close to Richard's body. At the same time, a policeman came up to me on the steps of our front porch. He asked if I knew the dead boy and if I knew where he lived. Again, I had the feeling of being the only person around who knew what had happened. *For the first time in my short life, I was the one that knew.* I informed the policeman I was his younger brother. Pointing to Dan and Felix, who by now were acting frantic, I told him they were our older brothers and that my brother who was now dead lived right here.

The policeman next asked if he could come in and look around. I led him inside to Richard's bedroom. Taking his time, the policeman flicked through Richard's notebook of poems and his journal. I found a poem written by Richard which he'd placed on top of his bed. I picked it up and read a few lines before I realized it wasn't really a poem unless I was thinking of one of his compositions about death and destruction.

Richard had left a suicide note.

My head spun again. When had Richard planned to write a suicide note? When had he left it on the bed? Had he decided on the real life

Arthur M. Mills, Jr.

rope when he awoke this morning or had he decided last night or even before? I thought about Archie. When had a TV show jumped into the real world to put the rope in Richard's hands?

The policeman asked to see what I had in my hands. I gave him the note. He read it shaking his head, then placed it carefully in his pocket and walked out to join the other policemen.

I sat down and read some of Richard's poetry. Now, in light of what happened, every line told me how he'd given us some warning. A little later I went back to the front porch. People swarmed everywhere. The number of men in uniform had dramatically increased, and now there were dozens of police cars and other emergency vehicles. Even the people from the telephone company were there, looking grim. I then saw a gurney being pushed to a waiting ambulance. My brother lay on top, his body covered with a white sheet, just like he covered himself before he slept. My older brothers were still trying to get closer, but the police kept wrestling them back.

My mother arrived. Ben Howell Drive not being a very broad street, she had to weave in and out between all the emergency vehicles to get to our house. Dan and Felix saw her and alerted some of the men in uniform. Our older brothers, I could see, were walking towards her car as she slowed down. Several policemen accompanied them.

Mom must have known something was wrong because she jumped out of the car in the middle of the street and started running towards my brothers. Dan held onto her while Felix ran past her to the car and dived into the driver's seat to park it. Holding onto Dan, she looked toward the white sheet-covered gurney. Though Richard was completely covered, she knew who was there.

Mom began to run towards the gurney. The police tried to stop her, but she ploughed through a barrier of several policemen. They were finally able to catch up with her at the ambulance. Dan, who was running behind her, caught her, too, and told her what she had suspected ever since she had shot out of her car. She collapsed to the ground.

The paramedics could do no more. The ambulance drove off. Most of the other emergency vehicles left as well. My mother stayed where she was on the ground, screaming and crying. Dan and Felix sat with her. They tried to console her but weren't much help. She was on her own, with her thoughts and her guilt, convinced she had brought on Richard's suicide.

There was so much I could have told her, like how I tried to talk to her but somehow could never get up the nerve. Like how Richard had taken to writing dark, mysterious poetry long before he tried that trick with fake blood which had so alarmed and angered her. I could have told her, too, about that whole multitude of other warnings, and how I wasn't sure if Candle Face had given me a warning because maybe I'd dreamt the whole thing and there was no Candle Face, not really.

The fact was, Richard had taken his own life. No one person was to blame. I couldn't accept the thoughts running around in my head. I couldn't take my mother's screaming and crying anymore, so I quietly slipped away to Mark's house where I stayed for many hours. His mother and father understood. I will never forget their kindness during that awful time.

When I finally returned home, my first realization was that my mother had stopped crying. My father must have come home in the hours I had been away, but he wasn't around. I learned later he had taken upon himself the responsibility of going to the morgue for Richard's body.

I found my mother sitting in the living room. When she saw me, she opened her arms and I ran to her. She held me for what seemed like an eternity. She had gone back to being my own comforting mother and I knew she loved all of us in her own way. She had misjudged Richard's action and Richard had misjudged her reaction. I also knew she was going to carry a deep sadness and regret for the rest of her life.

Arthur M. Mills, Jr.

CHAPTER 32

Among his creative pursuits, Richard had loved poetry. The teachers and students at Mollie Dawson loved him for his poetry, and our group of friends considered it a special treat when Richard read poetry in the tree house. Our family hadn't always appreciated Richard's poetic efforts, although the fault lay with our own ignorance. He possessed that special gift that enabled him to write the kind of poetry that reflected the anguish dwelling in his soul.

I remember an earlier time, back when he was in his romantic phase and had been at his best writing about love, harmony and peace. He had been in love with Maria then, in a way that was only possible at age twelve. Since he never really got to know her, she remained his mysterious muse, her mystery inspiring his best poetry. Only I knew of all the poems he had written about love and peace with Maria in mind. Only I knew of the poem that Richard cherished more than the others. I knew this because he took the maximum pains to write it and then hide it. It wasn't on a regular page of his notebook of poetic compositions; instead, it was merely a scrawl on one of its margins. He would read it often, probably thinking no one would pay this poem a lot of attention. His notebook was there for anyone to read, anyway.

After he died, our older brothers exhibited their own anguish in a number of ways. Felix was badly affected. Although he never talked about that afternoon when he tortured Richard with the pin, I knew he hadn't forgotten and was glad that at least he'd defended Richard from Carlos that day at the creek. Not that he would ever say so. He wasn't one to express his feelings in words, or to discuss how he felt.

The day after Richard died, Felix visited our room, something he'd not done before. He started examining our dead brother's things, handling every item he came across with sincere tenderness. When he found Richard's notebook, he began not only to read it but he was obviously absorbing it page by page, line by line. Obviously he wanted to know how Richard felt at the time, and Richard's poems gave him what he sought. When he found the gem among Richard's poems, the one Richard had cherished more than the others, he set it aside. The next day, Felix walked the half mile up the street to Wilke Clay Funeral Home and placed the poem into the upper left pocket of Richard's Boy Scout uniform, so it would be close to his stilled heart. Our mother had decided that he should be dressed in his Boy Scout uniform because Richard was an active Boy Scout.

Dan added another little touch. He had remembered that Richard liked to drink at least one can of Dr. Pepper every day. He placed a can of Dr. Pepper into the casket beside Richard's body.

Arthur M. Mills, Jr.

CHAPTER 33

On the day of Richard's funeral, everyone who wanted to attend gathered outside our house. According to the plan, our immediate family and close friends would drive from our house to the Wilke Clay Funeral Home. After a small service, we would accompany Richard's body to the South Austin Baptist Church for his church service. Immediately after, we would go to the Assumption cemetery for burial. Since our mother had decided on the Boy Scout uniform for Richard, I, as well as all the neighborhood kids, wore our Boy Scout uniforms.

We were ready and waiting for my mother who was still in her room. After her complete collapse that first day, she had come to terms with everything. She had made decisions and done whatever she had to do, but now, on the day of Richard's funeral, she couldn't bear to leave her bedroom. Everyone was waiting: people from our street; our friends from the neighborhood; teachers and even our school principal, all of whom had been fond of Richard and would feel his absence. My father kept going back into the house to knock on the door and tell Mom it was time to leave. As I waited on the front porch, I felt everyone was staring at me. I always wanted to be known as "Ray Mills," but today I was "Richard's little brother." I knew they felt for me as well but I didn't want their pity. I walked around to the side of the house that faced Evan's house. His dog was barking. I walked up to the fence and knelt down to pet it. The effect was immediately calming. *But that didn't last.* To the left I heard someone knocking. It seemed to be coming from my parent's bedroom window, only a few feet away. This window was located above the chain-link fence, at the spot where it joined the house. I thought maybe my mother was signaling to me, that maybe she needed me to come give her the courage to emerge from her bedroom. I turned away from the dog and looked up.

It wasn't my mother I was looking at. Instead I saw what appeared to be Richard looking straight at me. I had to shake my head and look away, unsure as to whether I was having a vision or if he was real. My eyes were playing tricks on me, I told myself, but when I looked away, the knocking grew louder and more insistent. I steeled myself and looked again. It was Richard.

This time I didn't force myself to look away or lower my eyes. Instead, I stared steadily at my brother, noticing little details. He was looking angrily at me. His hair was messed up. This wasn't his usual neat self. He was wearing our favorite shirt, the one he'd jumped off the board with. It was the one he and I used to fight over. It was not the Boy Scout uniform in which he was lying in the casket.

I wasn't as frightened as I was during Candle Face's visitations. Instead, I continued to look at Richard, noticing his look of anger was intensifying. He banged on the window, made a cutting motion across his neck, then pointed at me. I just looked steadily back at him. Somehow I was still not afraid.

From Evan's house I heard a screen door creak open and then slam shut. Turning around, I saw Evan walking towards me. He, too, was wearing his Boy Scout uniform. While my head was turned towards Evan, I heard the knocking start up again, intensifying into a banging sound. I looked up. Richard was pointing at me. He was wiggling his index finger towards himself, beckoning me to come inside. I looked back at Evan, wanting to know if he saw what I saw.

Evan had stopped in his tracks, one foot in front of the other, as though he had turned into a statue. So he, too, saw Richard! I hadn't been so wrong after all.

I watched Evan look straight at the window. Behind me the banging continued. Evan remained in the same frozen position.

Unlike my fear factor with Candle Face, I found I not only could move, I could talk as well. "Evan, what do you see?" I asked.

"Richard!" he responded right away.

By this time Richard was banging on the window so hard I thought it might break. But now Evan came out of his initial shock and took

Arthur M. Mills, Jr.

the initiative. "You should go in and see want he wants," he said in a whisper.

Something held me back. I could see Richard was really annoyed. I was wary and said to Evan, "I will go in only if you go with me."

He nodded. Without hesitation, the two of us started walking towards the house. Strange as it seemed, I'd known from the start that Richard's knocking and gesticulation weren't going to frighten me. Evan seemed okay with it too. We entered our house through the front porch door and walked into the kitchen. My parents' bedroom opened onto the kitchen at the back. Their bedroom door was wide open. We could see right in, clear across to the window where we had seen Richard. But now there was no one there.

So what had Richard wanted? I was at a loss and so was Evan. At this point I heard the toilet flush and a door open. My mother walked out of the bathroom and saw Evan and me standing in the doorway to her bedroom. Looking surprised, she asked, "What are you two doing?"

"Ma, s-someone knocked from your b-bedroom w-window while we were waiting outside near Evan's h-house. I wasn't s-sure if it was you. But I t-thought that we were being c-called in. Mom, did you j-just knock on y-your b-bedroom window and call for me to c-come inside?"

I could see my mother was in a daze. She looked around the room and back at me. "No," she said.

Evan and I were sure of what we'd seen. He had even accompanied me in because we had been so sure. Now, of course, we were not, so we didn't have anything else to say to my mother.

"Why?" Mom asked, then shook her head as though she was trying to understand. She gave us a tiny, nervous smile. "Never mind."

Evan and I left the house and sat on the front porch. Shortly later, my mother came out, finally ready to face her child's funeral. I couldn't help but think our awkward presence at the entrance to her bedroom had somehow helped. *I would never know until fifteen years later that we really had been summoned inside to talk to her and bring her back to the present.*

Of course, it wasn't my mother who had asked us in. It was Richard.

The funeral went off smoothly and was conducted without any further incident. My mother went back to being her withdrawn, quiet self. Evan and I never mentioned that event again, but in unguarded moments we knew what each other was thinking when we spent time in companionable silence in our growing up years.

Arthur M. Mills, Jr.

CHAPTER 34

My father always encouraged me in what he thought I was good at. As a result, my love of running and the successes I had on the running track were partly because of him. He made sure I trained well enough on my own. He made it his business to find out when and where the next race was scheduled, and suggest I enter. When I won, Dad would spread the good news, taking pride in my achievements.

In his own way, Richard had tried his hardest to please our father but never received the same encouragement. I remember the time Richard had shyly brought his writings and poems to Dad and asked what he thought. Dad's answer was that he wasn't in the habit of reading. Years later I discovered our father was illiterate. I know this because he eventually told me during one of our few meetings when I was on a visit home. So much became clear when he told me. At last I saw that his inability to read and write explained a great deal about his seemingly indifferent behavior, including his refusal to read Richard's writings and poems.

The beatings I received from Richard still stung. After his death I thought about them a lot but had no desire to discuss them with anyone else in the family. Later I found an ally as I struggled to come to terms with Richard's death.

I remember Richard's attempt at pleasing our father through his Mexican heritage. Richard was the person who said grace in Spanish at mealtime, like our father had taught him. In fact, because Dad's Mexican relatives called often, he taught all of us to answer the phone in Spanish.

Our father now said the prayer that Richard used to say before dinner, but he greatly missed Richard's version in Spanish. The rest of us hadn't taken that much of an interest in Richard's abilities at any kind of oration. My parents and brothers, especially Felix, now wished that they had shown more enthusiasm about his public readings.

My father wanted to build some kind of memorial for Richard, something that would involve his Mexican heritage. He and some of our neighbors recalled the Mexican tradition of placing a cross at the site of someone's death. They also recalled the old rumor about a child who had died in the house fire in what was now the empty lot next door. The belief was that a cross at the site of a death would ensure no one else would die there in the future.

Evan's father volunteered to help. He welded two pieces of metal together to form a cross, then rubbed it down to smooth it out and painted it a glossy black. When the time came, Dan, Felix, Edwin and I conducted a little ceremony to honor Richard as Dan hung the cross from the very board from which Richard had hung himself. The others left after the ceremony, but Edwin and I stayed on. We climbed the tree and sat on the board. I hadn't talked a lot to Edwin before now, but today, after the service and with the cross on that board to remind us of Richard (and the child or children who had died in the house fire), I felt a strong bond with the eighteen-year-old from the small house up the street. Edwin had always expressed an interest in us younger boys. He had taken some responsibility for Andre in life. Dan and Felix spoke about Edwin often, and we were aware he was hosting my brothers' musical ambitions.

As we sat on that 4 by 4 foot board, we talked about Richard for a long time. I never thought I could talk so openly at the site of my brother's death, especially since I considered Edwin a man of the world and myself just a skinny kid not worth his attention. We sat there for nearly an hour. Edwin said everyone loved me. It made me feel better, even though I knew he was making sure I felt loved and appreciated so I wouldn't end up dead like my brother Richard. I, in turn, greatly appreciated his spending his time with me. I respected him for that and never forgot.

Towards the end of our conversation, Edwin pulled out a pocket knife and asked if I would like to become blood brothers. His request meant a lot to me because I knew that being blood brothers meant

Arthur M. Mills, Jr.

a lot where we came from. Edwin made a small deep cut on one of his fingers and handed the knife to me. I, too, made a small deep cut on one of my fingers. We pressed out a pinpoint of blood from our wounds, then pressed the points together. The two drops of blood, one from Edwin and one from me, mingled. Now it was official that we had pledged allegiance to each other and were bonded for the rest of our lives as blood brothers.

Soon after, Dan was sent to a correctional facility because of his role in the attempted theft at Dunkin Donuts. My mother missed him and so did I. Felix began to spend more time over at Edwin's garage, writing lyrics and playing music. Now Felix would show me his compositions. I marveled at his writing, even matching it to Richard's poetry. Edwin and I thought Felix had the same gift for composition that Richard had.

CHAPTER 35

It quickly became clear that our school wasn't going to forget Richard. He had always been asked to play the lead in all school and church plays. He was the solitary theatre personality in the tree house among us in the neighborhood. Among our group of boys Richard could hold his own with a whole act of a play and do all the characters in turn. Every teacher in the school knew Richard.

When I went back to school a week after his death, his teachers made it a point to tell me how sorry they were. Most of them sent notes. I became very conscious of students stopping to stare at me. I would see some of them shaking their heads. The more confident and friendly ones would nod and talk to me about my brother. I tried to ignore those who didn't know what to say. Some students would even come to me and ask why Richard did it. I had no answer for strangers. At times I felt as if I'd been singled out for others to stare and shake their heads at. At times I felt painfully self conscious. Even after his death, I was still known as "Richard's little brother."

At home my room stayed the same. On the day Richard died, when I entered our room with the policeman, I noticed some of Richard's toys and personal effects were missing. No one had been in our room since Richard and I had woke up that morning and went out for our breakfast and our chores. I believed at the time he must have hidden them or thrown them away so no one else could use them. I thought about Griffin. Could Richard have given his toys to his invisible friend to play with?

Felix had found Richard's notebooks but had always put them back where he found them. My parents let everything remain the same and didn't remove his bed. Now I was sole occupant of our room, sole owner of those clothes we used to share and fight over. But the fun was gone. I found no joy in having the better clothes to myself.

In the old days I would never be able to argue with Richard about who should switch off the light. Now, not only did I not want to switch it off, I didn't have to. No longer must I run and leap into my bed in the frightening darkness. After he died, I slept with the lights on, the only defense I had against Candle Face. She knew I wouldn't have to see her against the light from the window. She knew she couldn't hide when my room light was on.

Sleep was still not easy. One particular night it was warm, and my habit of tightly winding the sheet was unraveling. My sheet was loosely covering me. I was lying in bed with my eyes wide open, thinking about how I could have done things differently, regretting anything I may have done or not done to bring about Richard's suicide. I had seen the signs, taken little action and had hung back. I hadn't taken adequate action. I hadn't been a brave enough eleven-year-old old to stand up for his slightly older brother. It was late and I should have been fast asleep. I heard a knock on my outer bedroom door, the one that led to the front porch. I got up unthinkingly to answer. The door started to swing open and in that instant I stepped back. Did I want to open the door for another torture-filled night? Had I been about to make the mistake of letting in Candle Face? Too late. The door opened wide and I saw it wasn't Candle Face but an old man outside my porch door. He introduced himself as a tour guide. Come to think about it, he looked like someone steeped in his own concerns and appeared to be preoccupied. He had white bushy hair under a white cap with a pointy end and wearing a tour guide uniform. He said that he was here for a tour around Richard's room. I was taken off guard again. A tour late at night by someone ready to go to sleep? I knew that Richard was popular, but this was something new.

The old man stepped inside. Without further preamble he turned and spoke over his shoulder. "OK, folks, we're going in." I craned my neck to see whom he was talking to and was amazed at what I saw. About twenty kids stood behind him in a line, single file. They all had cameras slung around their necks. As soon as the tour guide beckoned them, they obediently began to drift into *my* room. The tour guide obviously took his work seriously. He pointed to Richard's bed and said, "This was Richard's bed." The kids clapped and took pictures of the bed. It took them a few minutes and some of them wanted better angles. There was small confusion about which of the beds used to be Richard's. They decided the neatly turned one was his.

The guide spoke again. "Let's move along now. This was Richard's window. He loved to look out the window as he wrote his poems."

The kids clapped louder and took more pictures, some from inside our room, some from outside. I now realized there were many more kids than the twenty I had first estimated. More children filtered in. They took pictures, drew small sketches and took notes incessantly. Everyone looked happy to be crowded inside Richard's bedroom.

No one paid the least bit of attention to me until I coughed and brought myself to the notice of the last person in the tour line. A boy who looked as if he was a year or so older than I turned around, looked at me in amazement and asked loudly, "Who's that?"

I was a little flummoxed when the tour guide answered, "Oh, that's just Richard's little brother. Don't pay any attention to him."

The kids booed me. No one took my picture. I knew Richard would continue to hold center stage among the teachers and kids at school, but who were these children? They adulated Richard as our fellow

Arthur M. Mills, Jr.

students in school did, but I couldn't recognize them or the tour guide. They continued moving around my room, ignoring me. I looked again at the last child, the one who had asked the tour guide who I was. I flushed as I recognized him and realized the boy had Richard's looks. He *was* Richard, wearing the same shirt he died in. For some reason he was taking the tour of his own room, checking on his bed, his window and maybe his books and notebooks.

At first Richard didn't seem to know who I was, but finally he began to point at me, then at his neck to draw attention to it. So Richard was no longer ignoring me. *Maybe he had recognized me after all.* The tour guide had taken over completely. He was now behaving as though he owned the place and owned me. He pushed me aside so the children could have a good look in our small room and so that they could get around me unobstructed. I felt suffocated with so many people in my room. At the same time I didn't know how to hold onto this instant when Richard had come back to tour his room and had drawn my attention.

The tour guide decided it was time to leave. He stepped outside to the porch through the same door he'd entered. They all followed him like the Pied Piper. My eyes were transfixed on Richard as he took one last mournful look at me and departed with the rest.

Like the Pied Piper and his children, I never saw the unknown children again. I would have liked Richard to stay, even if he had forgotten who I was. I would have liked him to go to sleep in his own bed however he wanted. He could have changed out of that shirt and into any of our pajamas. But the next morning, I woke up alone. I looked across to Richard's bed. There was no one there. I remembered that Richard had pointed to me and to his swollen neck. It was a dream. It had to be. But when I sat up in bed and swung my feet down on the floor, I could see muddy shoe prints all over my bedroom floor. Most of them had been made by children's shoes. There was one set of adult footprints in the medley of shoe prints.

CHAPTER 36

About a week after Richard died, I started going to a baby sitter's house. I have never understood why I suddenly needed to go to a baby sitter.

I can truthfully say I started out hating everything at Mrs. Hemenis' house. I hated the drive there with my parents, knowing they were going to dump me off and go their merry way. I hated the block where she and her husband lived, as well as their small, dark apartment that was so unlike my friends' homes, as well as my own, where we had plenty of room to play.

My life may not have been perfect, either at home or school, but I much preferred staying home by myself rather than having to stay with Mr. and Mrs. Hemenis. They were old, and I didn't understand them. Not that there weren't some old people I felt comfortable with, like my friend Nolan's grandparents, but the Hemenis' were completely unlike them.

There wasn't anything in their apartment to play with. I wasn't even allowed to bring toys to their house, except for one small fire truck. The only interesting items in the apartment were Mr. Hemenis' medical gear. Being severely handicapped, he had lots of it. There were tracks on the ceiling to transport him around in slings, and chairs hung from them. That was fascinating, but I was told I couldn't ride on them. There were tubes attached to paraphernalia that helped him breathe. I didn't try that. I had been told by a coach that my lung power helped me run faster and longer, so I didn't need to literally stick my nose into any kind of breathing apparatus.

There were walkers and wheelchairs that enabled Mr. Hemenis to get around. One day I tried his wheelchair when Mrs. Hemenis was in the bathroom. That was loads of fun, but there wasn't a lot of space for me to maneuver around in. Mr. Hemenis caught me and watched with a twinkle in his eye. He didn't tell on me. In fact, I suspect after a few weeks he became sort of an ally.

I felt sorry for him because he had nothing to do except sit or sleep on the couch all day. He didn't even watch TV. A couple of times I tried to get him interested in my favorite programs. I like to think he was beginning to show some interest, but unfortunately that was around the time my baby-sitting came to an end.

Sometimes Mrs. Hemenis would let me play outside, but even that wasn't much better. The apartments were old and rundown. I don't recall seeing a single blade of grass or anything green except for the weeds that grew through the cracks in the walls and asphalt. But I managed to keep myself occupied. Mrs. Hemenis allowed me to play with my fire truck in front of her door. At those times she would leave the door to her apartment open so she could keep an eye on me.

One day when I was playing outside, a school bus stopped and a group of boys and one girl got out. They were older than I and seemed they could be closer to Felix in age. As they walked past me, one of the boys purposefully kicked my fire truck out of my hands. The truck flew off a couple of feet. I ran to pick it up, at a loss as to how I should react to such behavior. The boys and the girl thought it was funny, all of them laughing at my predicament.

The next time I was at Mrs. Hemenis' apartment and she sent me outside to play, I was on guard when the school bus arrived. I was clutching my fire truck when another boy walked up and tried to kick it away as he walked past me. I was moving my fire truck to my other hand for safekeeping when I saw his kick coming and moved aside just in time. The boy told me to stand up. When I did, he punched me in the face, then pried the toy out of my sweaty palms and threw it some distance away. I ran to my fire truck, picked it up and ran back into Mrs. Hemenis' apartment. Dented or not, that fire truck was my most cherished possession just now. I thought of the bully, Carlos, who used to beat up Richard until Felix stepped in. I hoped for the same kind of protection from my baby sitter.

When I went inside, Mrs. Hemenis was busy tidying her dining area. She was, after all, supposed to take care of me, so I wondered how she could protect me in the future. As she stood there wiping her dining room table, I told her what happened. I complained loudly, but she didn't even look at me while I explained the ordeal I had just gone through. She said nothing.

The incident outside may have bruised my ego, but at least I was hopeful that in the future Mrs. Hemenis wouldn't want to baby-sit me. However, when my parents came to pick me up, she said nothing. During the drive home, I told them about the bullies at Mrs. Hemenis' apartment. I complained about Mrs. Hemenis not protecting me enough and begged my parents not to send me there anymore. They didn't comment on my complaints either.

A few days later I was again dropped off at Mrs. Hemenis' apartment. This time I didn't want to be sent outside to play. Instead, I tried to be extra good and left Mr. Hemenis' medical stuff, especially his wheel chair, strictly alone. I dreaded it when Mrs. Hemenis told me to go play outside at the usual time. I didn't want to go, but not wanting to show how scared I was, I went outside just as the school bus arrived. Seeing it, I lost my nerve and ran back to Mrs. Hemenis' door. I couldn't get in. She'd locked it!

I cried and banged on her door, but it didn't open. By now the group of bullies had got off their bus and seen me. Laughing and joking, they approached. I briefly considered running to a different apartment to ask for help, but what if the people who lived there were even worse? I'd had enough terror coming my way from Candle Face and had often been warned about not talking to, or asking for favors from, strangers. There was no hope for me. The same boy who had thrown my toy last time sauntered up and punched me in the stomach without saying a word. I dropped my fire truck and fell to the ground, watching helplessly as another boy grabbed my toy and walked towards the small, dirty swimming pool close by. Those nasty kids cheered as the boy tossed it into the pool. He did this despite my tearful state and my cries to him to stop. One of the older kids turned to me and gave me one last vengeful push. Then they all left, leaving me a sobbing heap on the ground and my fire truck somewhere in that soupy swimming pool.

I was still frightened, wondering what if they came back and did worse? But I knew I still had to save myself and crawled to Mrs.

Arthur M. Mills, Jr.

Hemenis' door. I managed to get my fingers around her door handle and haul myself up only to find the door still locked. Surely Mrs. Hemenis would have heard my earlier banging on her door. Surely she would have heard the commotion outside. Why, then, was she determined to keep the door locked now?

The thought occurred to me that Mrs. Hemenis had deliberately set me up. She sent me outside just before it was time for the school bus. She knew, because I had told her, what had happened before. The answer was fairly obvious, so when she ultimately opened the door, I didn't even bother telling her what happened. My stomach hurt, my pride had taken a knock, and I had a feeling she already knew.

When my parents picked me up, I begged them again never to send me back to Mrs. Hemenis. They paid no attention, and I found myself back at her apartment the following week.

Already suspecting Mrs. Hemenis had set me up the week before, I had a nasty suspicion she was planning to do it again, especially because she kept looking at the clock. When she decided it was the right time for my lesson, she told me to go outside. As with Candle Face, I could only take punishment to a certain extent, so I refused point blank.

Mr. and Mrs. Hemenis were not going to stand for this. "Boy, get your butt outside," Mr. Hemenis commanded.

Mrs. Hemenis decided action was better than words. She grabbed my hand, trying to force me up from where I was seated. I must have thought she was an old weak woman forcing me to do something because I capitulated and allowed her to pull me up. With Mr. Hemenis watching from the couch and chuckling, she grabbed me by both arms and declared, "Son, you can't let people walk all over you. Sometimes you have to fight and defend yourself. Now get outside and stick up for yourself."

What happened next was to have a profound change in my life.

She opened the door and shoved me out. There wasn't a thing I could do. I had just confirmed that she *had* locked me out and set me up. Mrs. Hemenis may have planted a basic idea about defending myself, but she hadn't elaborated on how I should do this. I had older brothers, one of whom had helped teach a bully a lesson when he beat up my brother Richard. That was a decision Felix had made. I was being told that I, too, had to make my own decisions in life. I would have to make decisions about myself—what to do now and what to do next.

I didn't have a lot of time to dwell on the matter because at the instant when Mrs. Hemenis shoved me outside, the school bus came rolling to a stop. The same group hopped off and came up to me. They all looked delighted to see me standing there, knowing I was going to be a sitting target again. As expected, the older boy punched me in the chest. My thin body flew backwards and hit Mrs. Hemenis' apartment door.

Arthur M. Mills, Jr.

The Empty Lot Next Door

Had Mrs. Hemenis heard me shoved against her door? Was she going to impose her brand of truths about self-protection? Yes she was, I realized, when the door stayed closed and probably locked from inside, just like last time.

The only girl in the group walked up to me, clenched her fist and made punching movements an inch away from the tip of my nose. The boys stepped back to watch, smiling as though they were going to enjoy the outcome. The girl took her time looking me up and down. She was smiling, too, as she looked back at the boys. They were going to play this game to the hilt.

The oldest boy said to me, "If you hit her, we will kick your ass."

I knew I couldn't hit her even before he told me this. I had grown up playing with the boys in our neighborhood. Since girls were banned from our group, I never had cause to be angry with a girl until now *(Except for Candle Face)*. The girl who faced me couldn't have known this, but she stepped closer and began to lift her right arm, which I figured was her hitting arm.

I had been humiliated by this group last week and was now scared that I was going to get my butt kicked by a girl. I looked around wildly for some help. What I saw from the corner of my eye was Mrs. Hemenis looking steadily at me from her kitchen window. She lifted her hand, made a fist, and punched the air.

The girl was getting ready to pulverize me. When the boys yelled, "Now!" she got the incentive she needed and began to throw her punch.

She didn't know I had something up my sleeve. Knowing I didn't want to hit a girl. I made punching motions as Mrs. Hemenis had, a few seconds ago, in the air. I pretended that if she hit me, I would punch her back. Even as my fist got close, she withdrew hers. She also withdrew herself, squealed and ran behind the boys. Now the oldest informed me he was going to see his threat through. He was going to kick my ass. But I thought quickly on my feet. I no longer had to be concerned about having to hit a girl, even if she was at least five years older. Before he could hit me, I threw two quick punches and hit him in the stomach. I should have been scared again because my thin eleven-year-old arms didn't faze him a bit, nor did my small fists. But his return punch to my face fazed me a lot. I got beaten up bad that day.

Arthur M. Mills, Jr.

I staggered back and found the door to Mrs. Hemenis' apartment unlocked. Mrs. Hemenis dressed my wounds. She had a smile on her face like my teachers sometimes had when I finally understood something complicated. *She* thought I had done all right by scaring the girl and hitting the boy before he could get a chance to hit me. That I had lost didn't really matter to her. I gradually got the feeling she was actually proud of me. With this realization, I felt I could be proud of myself.

I didn't mind going back to her apartment after that. In fact, I actually began to enjoy it. Now I would wait for the school bus outside, but the group of kids never messed with me again. Better still, Mr. Hemenis was my friend now, even if Mrs. Hemenis no longer gave me friendly advice for the future.

Unfortunately, my parents either took notice of my bruised face or finally took my earlier pleas seriously. After a few days, they stopped sending me to Mrs. Hemenis' house.

CHAPTER 37

One of my favorite pastimes as a child, and even later, was to join in a race or run on my own. I ran everywhere for the sheer joy of running. My father made sure I caught up with my running practice when I fell behind, but that seldom happened. Occasionally I ran the long road to school. Most evenings I did a lap of our neighborhood. My childhood friends later told me I was the Forrest Gump of my time.

A week after Richard's death, I decided to run the four miles to the Assumption Cemetery to visit Richard's grave. I started from our house and passed all the houses on Ben Howell Drive, some of the neighbors giving me the pity-look that I'd now grown accustomed to. It was a long run, but I eventually made it to the gate of the cemetery. I remembered Andre was buried there as well. It had been just a few months ago that Andre had irritated Richard and me, and maybe Candle Face in her hole in the empty lot next door. When I entered the burial ground, I slowed down and started to walk. Wanting to pay my respects, I first stopped by Andre's grave. He hadn't deserved an early death by accident, nor had Richard deserved his death at his own hand. My mind was in a whirl as I walked on to my brother's grave, about a hundred meters away.

Richard's was the newest grave among the many around me. It was the grave where the earth had been turned just about two weeks ago. It was tidy and clean and surrounded by cut flowers, making me suspect our mother had been coming here every day since Richard was buried. There were brand new tiny saplings, too. For a long time, I stood at his grave, looking at the headstone, trying to come to grips with the circumstances that lead to Richard's death, as well as Andre's. I suppose I succeeded. At first I envisioned Richard performing on stage in the tree house. I then gradually focused on Richard as I knew him. Being so very aware of his talents, I wondered what he would have been like had he lived.

Richard would have been the successful one, possibly a professor of some sort, or a famous actor, writer, or poet. I sat on the soft grass in front of his grave, my thoughts growing muddled. I couldn't fight the guilt that surfaced again. If I wasn't as talented as Richard, maybe I should have been the one who died, not him. Richard should have been given a chance to live his life. It should have been me in the casket below my feet.

And then a strange, faint sound broke the tranquility of this green and peaceful cemetery. I didn't know where it was coming from, but whatever it was sounded urgent. I quietly stood up. Listening more carefully, I couldn't figure out the words but could tell the yelling came from below my feet. I stood there, feeling, and undoubtedly looking, foolish. The sound couldn't be coming from Richard's grave, or could it?

But yes, the shouting had to be coming from under the ground. I told myself I must do something. What if I hadn't come here today? Our mother had visited as often as she could. Had she not heard what I heard because of her all-enveloping grief?

I lay down and placed my ear on the still fresh dirt over his grave. Within the next few seconds, I heard Richard's voice. He knew I was there and was addressing me directly.

"Ray, help me. I am not dead. Help. They buried me by mistake."

My thoughts shot all over the place. Under my breath, I muttered, "Oh my God. We buried him alive. I can't believe we did that. I must get him out." I got down on my knees and started to claw frantically at the soft dirt. It seemed like I dug for hours but couldn't slow down because I so badly wanted to talk to Richard. As I dug, I talked to my brother continuously, apologizing for not seeing the desperate signs he sent asking for help. I told him I knew he intended me to be the messenger of his distress signals and that I should have been more diligent. Obviously in one of his introspective moods, Richard replied, apologizing for not being a better, bigger brother. We talked and talked as I continued to dig what seemed to be fistfuls of mud of the smallest measure. At long last, I touched wood. Although I'd run out of breath I couldn't hesitate now. Using all my strength, I pulled the lid of his casket open.

Richard sat up, and I quickly realized he had changed from his introspective bigger brother mode to attack mode. He lunged straight towards my neck yelling, "It should have been you. You should be in here!"

How could he have known this was my exact thought just minutes before? He continued to choke me but ultimately released my neck with one hand. I managed to get my breathing back, but I was still under attack because Richard had other punishments in mind. He began to scratch my face with his fingers and whatever nails he had. I could not withdraw. It was back to my paralyzed self for me. I couldn't and didn't want to fight back. I couldn't have done anything anyway because now I couldn't move. In this state I fell into his casket, unable to fend for myself. Then Richard closed the casket lid over me. I hadn't expected that, particularly after that long conversation in which he apologized for the wrongs he had done to me.

My soul and body were in pain. "Don't, Richard," I said wordlessly. "I'm still alive, as you were."

Arthur M. Mills, Jr.

I don't know if I slipped into unconsciousness, or did what I had to do. Could I have recovered myself and opened the lid of Richard's casket? Could I have emerged from that now-dreaded spot underground and run the four miles home again? The next thing I knew, I was waking up on my front porch, still in the t-shirt and shorts I wore to the cemetery. Confused and bewildered, I jumped up and ran to my bedroom before my mother came home. I slowed as I passed my bedroom mirror and saw several scratches up and down my face. So it was true. I had run the four miles, had a discussion with Richard and heard him apologize before he turned on me as usual.

Or was it true? Just to be sure, I checked my hands to see if I could find any signs of all that digging. I saw the dirt under my fingernails. It was fresh, soft earth.

CHAPTER 38

The next day I decided to go to Mark's house where I knew I'd be safe. I didn't know where Richard went after he shut me in his casket. What I did know was that I didn't want to be anywhere near my house.

Mark's mother noticed I was really wound up and asked if everything was okay. I told her I had a lot on my mind but everything was fine. She was a kind person who relied on her religion to help her when she had a problem. She departed Mark's bedroom and came back with her Bible. Sitting next to me, she told me the Bible has all the answers. All I had to do to find the right one was skim through it, randomly stop at a page, and point to a verse. That verse would give me the answer to my problem. She got up and left me there alone.

I skimmed through the Bible asking if Candle Face was real, then quickly opened it and pointed to the first verse I saw,

Luke 24:39: Look at my hands and my feet, because it's really me. Touch me and look at me, because a ghost doesn't have flesh and bones as you see that I have."

Reading the verse over and over again, I felt it truly held a message for me. Jesus had said to his disciples that he wasn't a ghost. Was this an admission by Jesus that ghosts do exist? Why would Jesus say he wasn't a ghost if ghosts didn't exist? I had my answer: Candle Face was real!

Just then I heard my father whistle. I placed the Bible on the desk and left Mark's house without another word. A couple of hours there had helped me feel vastly better. Mark's mother had helped me pinpoint the answer to my most urgent query.

But now that I knew Candle Face was real, how should I deal with her?

I went home as I was expected to do. My father and I sat on the couch and watched TV. I had dinner with my family. I wished my parents good night and went to my room to do a little homework and go to bed. I still felt awful and disturbed and knew that tonight was one night I would want to sleep with the lights on, as I had for the past many nights. I wanted to keep watch, especially tonight. I was jumpy and didn't want to be disturbed by Candle Face. I didn't want to see Richard either, especially after what had happened at the cemetery.

I must have eventually fallen asleep. About an hour or so later, I heard faint sounds, as I had at the cemetery before I uncovered Richard's casket. I surfaced from sleep feeling tense and anxious. What I heard were faint, mumbling sounds like Richard would make when he moved and talked restlessly in his sleep.

At first, I didn't want to look, especially after my last experience in Richard's presence, but I knew ultimately I would have to check out the scene. I was still on my right side, reminding myself why I had slept on my right side . . . . to be able to see the room at a glance. I had to be brave now. My eyelids opened cautiously. When I looked towards Richard's bed, I wanted to pinch myself.

He was there!

It was as though he hadn't died, had a funeral, been buried. Richard was wrapped tightly in the sheets, just as he used to be before his body was put on that gantry under a sheet and into the ambulance more than two weeks ago.

I had to will myself out of this sight. "Here we go again," I told myself sternly. I couldn't afford to stay in my dream-like state. Why could I not stop seeing and dreaming about Richard and Candle Face?

Arthur M. Mills, Jr.

But this Richard did something different from the old Richard who always slept with the sheet covering his face and head. I realized he wasn't asleep. He lifted his arm from where he lay and curled his fingers up towards his head. He pulled the sheet off his head and turned his face so that he was looking directly at me.

I then did something I had never been able to do before. I shut my eyes and turned my head away. I heard Richard's voice. He wasn't mumbling in his sleep any longer but clearly said to me, "Ray, look at me. Look at the rope burns on my neck. I tried to show them to you the day of my funeral and again when I came in for that silly tour around our room. Don't you want to see my rope burns? Don't you want to feel how real they are? They're just the same as the day everyone thought I died."

Horrors were being forced upon me. I didn't want to face them no matter how much Richard pleaded with me. Hadn't he done the same thing once before? I tried to ignore him but my other senses were on full alert. I could hear his sheet rustle and his bed squeak. He was either turning in bed or else getting up.

He had done both. Within seconds, I felt chilled air on my left side. Richard's cold breath struck me on my left ear. My dead brother was talking to me. As before, he had forced his presence upon me. The whispered voice that could only belong to Richard was saying, "Ray, I'm here whether you like it or not. I don't suppose you like it because in any case it was all your fault. You're going to get what's coming to you."

This time I didn't move, not because I couldn't but because I didn't want to. I wanted him to know I could ignore him. It was the only defense left to me. I heard Richard's soft footfalls as he walked away from my bed, laughing at my pretend play. I think he got back into his bed and under the sheets.

I wondered if I was dreaming but already knew the answer. I couldn't be dreaming because I was able to move, not like before when I could never move in my dreams, especially if the dream was about Candle Face. *If they were dreams!*

I sat up on bed, still reasoning things out with myself. See, I can't be dreaming. Richard is dead so it must be his ghost here in my room. Doubts flooded my mind again as I asked myself, am I dreaming or not?

I felt so confused, not knowing when I was awake and when I was asleep, but I must have fallen asleep again on that dreadful night Richard came back. When I woke up the next morning, the first thing I did was look across at Richard's bed. His sheets were a twisted mess. If he had lain in his bed, he must have moved a lot. I had to accept that he had slept in his own bed. He had called out to me, as I could remember clearly.

I went to school that day as I always did, but couldn't focus on schoolwork, which in a way wasn't new because I never paid attention in class anyway. But this time I couldn't stop thinking about seeing Richard and hearing what he had to say from his spot at the cemetery and again last night. The message I kept getting was that he wanted my attention. He had called out to me twice, yet both times his words and actions made me feel worse and more threatened. Was I dreaming or not? Why was I able to move? Why had he just left?

Arthur M. Mills, Jr.

CHAPTER 39

For the next few days I alternated between a state of dreamy suspension and a state of clarity of mind where I could clearly think things through. In all previous dreams with Candle Face I had been paralyzed with fear, so if my experience with Richard had been a dream, why had I been able to move? In the future, how would I know I was dreaming? Even if I'd been dreaming on the night I saw Richard in his bed, why were his sheets twisted the next morning when I woke up?

Was I in a suspended dream-like state or was I awake every time I had seen Candle Face and then Richard after he died? If I wasn't really dreaming, then I should be able to control myself. On the other hand, was it a state of dreaming or was it my huge imagination that was taking over? In which case I wouldn't be in control. How had I managed to stay in control in my last dream of Richard?

An idea slowly formed in my head. I decided that the next time I saw Richard or Candle Face, I would try to keep my thoughts and feelings under control. I would fight back. Mrs. Hemenis had tutored me about the correctness of this, and in the long run it had worked. There was no harm in that. I would have to live to adulthood in the same way I had lived to be eleven years old. I would be in control. I would fight back and defend myself as only I knew how. I recalled the Bible verse, Luke 24:39 that I found that day at Mark's house. It had worked for me, and now my mind was somewhat at peace. I didn't have to be afraid of going to sleep.

That decided, the next couple of nights I actually looked forward to going to sleep. Things stayed quiet. I would drift off to sleep even though a part of my mind told me I would like to see Richard and

Candle Face. I began to sleep well for the first time in weeks, if not months.

For the next few nights I challenged Richard and Candle face to show themselves. I had made a great mistake when I jumped in the hole in the empty lot next door and disturbed Candle Face. I could not undo that action, but if I wanted, I could walk into the empty lot next door and jump into the hole again. I was waiting for Candle Face to be disturbed.

I started going to bed early. I would need all the hours of the night if either Richard, Candle Face, or both came to visit me in my room. There would be a lot to do besides getting enough sleep before I headed off to school the next morning.

Late one night sleep eluded me. I got up, walked out and sat in the empty living room. I was prepared with my plans and wasn't afraid. Soon enough I heard someone knocking on the outside door of my bedroom. My heart started to pound, but I told myself I shouldn't worry, it was just someone knocking on my door. I walked into my room and saw the door knob was being turned from the outside. Again, I steadied myself, telling myself not to worry. After all, the door was locked. I was safe and didn't have to go to Mark's house.

I heard a hoarse, rough voice say, "Come out, come out, wherever you are." I knew that voice: Candle Face.

I willed myself to return to the living room, telling myself I was having yet another new experience. Back in the living room, I could see that I was actually looking at myself lying on the couch. It was like an out-of-body experience! It knew I was dreaming. In a way, knowing I had to be dreaming set my mind at rest. It was the answer to my unanswerable queries to myself, and it gave me the best feeling in the world at that moment. For the first time I felt as if I was in complete control of my life. I felt my body lift off the floor and found I could go in any direction I wanted. I was flying!

"Go right. Go left. Go up," I directed my newly flying self. I could slowly fly in any direction and willed myself to go farther into the living room, finding I could control my dream state. I heard Candle Face again. She was scratching at the living room window screens as she had done long ago without success. Remembering that time, I felt confident she wouldn't be able to enter this time either. I had stayed out of her reach then because I was able to act quickly. I could do it again. I could see her nails and palms leaving smears on the screens. I looked carefully, and we suddenly make eye contact. That is, I could see into the sockets of her cloudy face. It unnerved me. I could feel my control slipping as my body quickly dropped to the floor.

Her lips moved into a sort-of smile. "There you are!" she said.

My feel-good spell disappeared as my doubts came flooding back. It had taken just that one hypnotic look. Once I saw her, I was scared all over again. *I can't fight her. I can't*, was the thought that flooded my consciousness. Holding on to what little courage I had left, I got up and rushed to the window to shut it, but by the time I got there, she had already ripped the screen off.

She headed to the next window. I beat her to that one and managed to close that window. We carried on like this along the entire row of outside windows. But now I could hear her at the back porch screen door. That was the one she had started with the last time. I rushed to slide the back door chain lock, but she opened the door an instant before I could lock it. I pushed against it with whatever strength I had, but before I knew it, her entire right arm and right leg had snaked around the door and inside the house. She began to scratch and flail at me whichever way she could. Her scratches burnt. They felt like fire.

At my wits end, I wasn't sure I could withstand her onslaught. At this instant I heard the front door slam shut. If Richard was going to join her in fighting me, I knew no matter what Mrs. Hemenis had taught me, I would be sandwiched in the middle between two ghouls and this would be the end. At the same time, I had no option but to fight. But how was I going to manage that? I had never been in a real fight where I fought back. My friends and I may have grappled in mock wrestling matches but never the real thing. I had punched the teen-aged boy outside Mrs. Hemenis' apartment, but he had reacted as though those were minor stings, not real punches. How did real people throw their punches?

I got a feeling someone was close behind me. Looking back, I saw Richard standing within inches of my face. He had a rope in his hand. Out of the corner of my eye I could see my body still sleeping on the couch, in deep sleep and content. That's it! I am dreaming. I know this and by knowing this, I can control this dream! It was as though my mind was on two levels. On one I was my dreaming, sleeping self; on the other, I was in a desperate struggle with Richard and Candle Face.

Arthur M. Mills, Jr.

I looked back at Richard who was now preparing a noose with the rope. When he was alive, he didn't speak when he was busy, and he didn't speak now. Candle Face was still trying to claw her way in. Mrs. Hemenis' teachings came to me without any effort on my part. I must keep defending myself. I would not be like Richard, I thought, remembering the time Felix had fought Carlos when Richard refused to defend himself. "I wish Felix was here to fight for me," I muttered to myself as I felt the noose being placed around my neck.

In an instant, Richard disappeared and Felix appeared, but I knew better than to blindly think it was a miracle. "That's it. I'm in control again," I said aloud. I let go of the door and stepped back because I knew what was going to happen next. After all, I was in charge! The door flung open. Candle Face rushed in but came to an abrupt halt. She looked straight at me and then at Felix. She actually looked confused, and I wondered, not for the first time, whether I had all my facts at my fingertips. Did she expect to see Richard instead? And since it was now Felix whom she saw, how *did* she relate to Dan and Felix?

I was wary all over again. My best option would be to plunge in. Whatever Felix thought of her, I must do my best to get him on my side. I must show him just how I felt. I looked at Felix and said, "Felix, this bitch is trying to kill me."

He turned to face her. Candle Face dropped her arms to her side as if *she* was now paralyzed. "I'll take care of it," Felix said, just as he had said he would with Carlos. Felix raised his right arm, cocked it back, and proceeded to punch Candle Face in the face. She flew straight out of the kitchen, through that door which had seen so much struggle, and onto the back porch. She attempted to get up and run, making me remember the times when I wished I could have done the same in her presence.

Arthur M. Mills, Jr.

Felix approached her and said, "If you ever come back, I'll do it again. You will have to face the same humiliation."

Candle Face should have known better, but she began to screech and squeal. As she had that first time, Evan's dog plus all the other dogs in the neighborhood began to bark. The barking sounds seemed to be mocking her. I couldn't believe it, but *she* was now scared. It was actually funny as I watched her claw her way back out of the back porch screen door with nearly as much vigor as she had clawed her way in. She slithered down the steps, ran to the fence between our house and the empty lot and jumped over it. Felix and I watched her flight back as she dived into the hole in the empty lot next door. Whether it was my dream-self or me, I smiled and turned to face Felix, wanting to thank him for being my protective elder brother. He wasn't there. I pinched myself. I wanted to wake up but couldn't. I tried to stomp on one foot with the other but stayed put where I was.

Remembering I had been flying around at some point, I looked at the couch but could no longer see my sleeping body. Again the front door opened and slammed shut. What now? I took a few steps to the side and stood against the wall, ready to fight again if I had to.

It was Felix. He looked at me and asked what I was up to. I just shrugged my shoulders. I had been through a long battle, was truly exhausted and in any case, didn't know what kind of an explanation I could give.

Felix and I sat down on the couch and talked, mainly about the time Felix fought for Richard in the creek. He said he felt good that he had done that and would do it again if he had to. *Little did he know he just had, only for me this time.*

I slept well that night. When my mother woke me up the next morning, she gave me a little cuddle. She said I was growing up fast and would no longer remain the baby of the family.

CHAPTER 40

I never saw Richard and Candle Face again. When I reflect upon this, I know I hadn't only managed to get on top of what was happening around me, but I also managed to stay in control of my life. In fact, I never had a dream about Richard again. I visited his grave every week or so but never again heard his voice. I saw no signs of him anywhere, except for the black metal cross that hung in the tree to commemorate him and any other children who might have died.

Richard's bed remained in my room. His books in which he scribbled his compositions stayed where they were, undisturbed. I never found the toys that had disappeared the day he died.

Sure enough, our friends missed him. People in school talked about Richard long after he was gone. I missed him, or at least I missed the twelve-year-old brother I would have liked to have had. Sometimes I let myself dream about what he would have been like as an adult. I talked to Edwin about this. He and I had a great many concerns to share and confidences to sort out. I started talking to my mother about Richard, too, but could see she easily became distressed on such occasions. When this happened, she would dab her eyes, pat my shoulder, and declare she couldn't wait for me to grow up.

Even in the days and weeks after that last bitter battle with Candle Face, I somehow knew I would never see her again. The dream-like state in which I had watched her disappear over the fence and scramble back to her hole in the empty lot next door, continued in real life. She wasn't going to emerge from there ever again . . . *or maybe on just one more occasion.*

I was no longer afraid to go to sleep. Since that day when I willed Felix to come to my rescue, I looked forward to sleep and my rightful rest. I would never know to what extent Andre's death, then Spencer's, then Richard's, were tied to Candle Face's emergence. There was much about Richard's death that would remain forever unexplained.

Griffin seemed to have had enough even before Richard died. I don't know if Richard saw him in those last few weeks. I didn't see him in the last month before Richard's death, and never again afterwards. I took to paying attention in class and was rather surprised when I began to appreciate what I was being taught. I can honestly say that at last I was taking a genuine interest in school. No one was forcing me to do anything.

My mother informed me she'd heard from my teachers that I was doing better class work and even doing my homework. She was proud of me and started to take more of an interest in my life. At last we were able to talk freely. Even my stutter began to dissipate.

I finally felt that Felix was there for me, no longer had to sleep with the light on and even looked forward to my dream-filled sleep. I felt I had nothing to be afraid of. The fact of my being in control of my life was true for my dreams. I had no more monsters to contend with.

Unfortunately my mother and step-father divorced soon after Richard's suicide. For a while, Felix, Mom, and I remained in our little house on Ben Howell Drive. I didn't tell my mother this, but I missed my father a great deal. I missed his company when I watched TV. I gradually watched TV less and less, and then not at all.

My father remained supportive of my interest in running. It was going to be a lifelong interest. I continued running, and winning. I would always love to run. For many years I kept my trophies and held on to my records. I like to think that one or two of my best records have still not been beaten.

Twisters continued to visit Austin. They were frequent and occasionally worse during hot summers. Neighbors close to us lost a roof, but I would never forget the excitement of running down to Stacey Lane the day the tornado hit. No one stayed outside during these storms as Richard had in the summer of my eleventh year. However, people had heard about how Richard had prayed through the hailstorm that summer and they did occasionally pray for the storm to pass.

Along with all my friends, I graduated from high school. I knew I wanted to be in the Army and joined soon after graduation.

Dan, Felix, and Edwin grew to excel in music. Felix wrote the lyrics and played the base guitar. I gave my brothers the respect due to wiser, older brothers. When I was writing this chapter, I finally got my courage up and asked Dan and Felix why they had done what they had done to Richard on the day they sniffed paint under our house. Dan said he couldn't remember the occasion at all. Felix, who I thought was more under the influence on that day, said that it would remain the most regrettable action of his life. I suppose we all have our regrets, even now.

After Dan and Felix married and moved out, my mother and I moved to another part of town. I decided to go back to my birth name "Arthur" instead of my nickname, "Ray," given by Raymond, my step-father. "Arthur" is what my wife, family, friends and colleagues call me now.

After the first couple of years of missing him dreadfully, I initiated contact with my father, and we continued on with our great relationship. I still consider him my father instead of my stepfather, even though my mother has remarried. He discussed his own regrets and failures with me, revealing the fact that he couldn't read or write. I was surprised because I would never have guessed had he not told me. It did tie in with other facts when I thought it through.

I will always remember how he had refused to read Richard's poems and his stories, but now I understood.

Arthur M. Mills, Jr.

CHAPTER 41

When I was serving in Germany, I got a Red Cross message stating that my birth father has passed away. He had been married to my mother during the years when she had Richard and me. I was now his only kin.

I was permitted leave from the Army because of a death in the family. My wife, kids, and I flew from Germany to San Antonio, Texas, to prepare my father for burial. By that time, my mother had moved from Austin and was living in Temple, Texas. We arranged for my kids to stay with her while my wife and I traveled to Pleasanton where my father had lived and died.

We stayed on in Temple for a day or two with my mother to settle the children with her. I was glad for the extra time because I hadn't seen my mother for a few years. We took up where we left off, talking about our lives when I was a child and even later. She was now able to talk at length about Richard.

I knew I was broaching a new topic, but I had always known that someday I would reveal to her my ordeal with Richard and Candle Face. This was the first time I ever mentioned Candle Face to my mother. I expected I'd need to explain a lot, but she easily remembered the discussion we had about the house fire next door that occurred before we moved to Ben Howell Drive. I also spoke to her about the ordeal I had about Richard soon after he died. My mother seemed to understand about that, too.

My wife listened quietly as Mom and I chatted for half the day. She knew what was being said and that it would take time for me to let it all out. It had taken me all these years to bring up the topic and how it had affected me directly. I was telling my mother about my nightmares and about the real events for the first time.

I was surprised that my mother took all my revelations in stride. She wasn't surprised and had her own story to tell. Recalling the day of Richard's funeral, she asked if I remembered how she had stayed in her room while everyone was waiting for her to go to the funeral home. She explained that she couldn't leave her room because she sensed Richard's presence. She could hear his voice, although it was faint. She felt he was calling out to her to save him, that he had made a mistake and didn't want to be buried.

I reverted to my eleven-year-old self when she told me this. I remembered clearly how, on that very day, I had gone around to the side of my house, the side we shared with Evan's house. I remembered seeing Richard clearly at my mother's bedroom window, the gestures he made, and how Evan had seen him, too. I had gone to her bedroom to see if Richard wanted me there. I told my mother about my excuse when she saw Evan and me hanging around, looking scared and unsure. She now told me that she, too, had been scared and that she didn't want to bury her son if he didn't want it for himself. She told me how relieved she'd been when she saw Evan and me standing by her door. It was then she realized she must proceed with Richard's funeral. The sight of Evan and me caused her doubts to vanish.

I knew we should have talked years ago but was glad we were talking now. It fitted in with my visit to the cemetery and what I felt Richard had said to me, first from his casket, and then directly, when I had released him. Richard's presence had returned. My mother and I could confirm this. Evan could, too, but this wasn't the only time my experience coincided with my mother's. There was more to her story. She told me Richard had also visited her a few weeks after his funeral. Being an adult, she now knew it was his ghost she was seeing. Richard had walked up to her while she was sitting in the living room and sat on her lap. He looked sad, but told her she must not take the responsibility for his death onto herself. He'd had time to dwell on it and knew it was his decision. He said to her, "Ma, everything is going to be okay."

My mother's story was a revelation to me. Because Richard *had* been right. Things were okay after this. I told my mother that this must have been on the day of my last nightmare—the day Felix

Arthur M. Mills, Jr.

fought Candle Face for me. I told her I was sure of it. Now that I had verbalized what I had always considered a secret, I discovered my mother and I could account for events that had taken place at the same time. We could also talk about how correct our experiences and observations had been.

Arthur M. Mills, Jr.

Both of us now found some peace. We recognized what we had really seen and what we might have imagined. This new-found knowledge gave me the courage to think about my birth father and his life. I was going to give him a good funeral.

CHAPTER 42

It's been a long time since 1984 when I was eleven. I've thought a lot about Richard and Candle Face since those last sightings. What I have not revealed is that I talked to my childhood friends about those events and still talk about them whenever I visit Austin.

I told my wife all about it in 1999, just before I left for Kosovo. Whomever I have talked to always listens closely and at the end of the story wonders aloud whether Candle Face was real. I did, too. The Bible seems to suggest ghosts exist, but was Candle Face real?

Everyone I've talked to says they cannot get the story and its details out of their head. My wife says she was annoyed in 1999 when I told her, especially since it all came out when I was about to go off to war-torn Kosovo. She claims my strange story occupied much of her consciousness, something she could have done without just then. She kept thinking about it, she said, and some years later suggested I write a book about my ordeal. She advised me to account for all events as accurately as possible. Doing so, she said, might turn out to be therapeutic for me, considering I had buried the story twice. The first time I had 'forgotten" for some seven years. A small sign had triggered my memory and I had been able to relate it in full, but had lost a friend because it was so real. The second time, I was nearly thirty years old but still felt compelled to get to the truth.

I finally decided to put my ordeal on paper when I was stationed in Korea again. This time my wife and children came with me. Twenty-five years had passed, and I found I needed help. In fact, the help I needed would fill a research dossier. I decided to call Randy.

Oddly enough, during our childhood Randy wanted to be the one to leave home; yet, as it turns out, he was the only one to stay. When I called, I discovered he now lives in his parents' house on Ben Howell Drive. Randy remembered the empty lot and the hole in the back that all of us took pains to avoid. He remembered what had been said about one or more children perishing in a house fire there. When I told him a little about my experiences in 1984, he assured me he would go to the local library and research the local microfiche for any evidence reported in the local papers when that fire took place.

We reminisced about how we considered the lot belonged to us because we played there so much. I asked Randy if the lot was still a playground for children who now lived in the area. After a long pause, Randy said, "Hey, Ray (my childhood friends still call me Ray), the empty lot is no longer empty. A house was built there about three years ago."

I asked, "Do the people who live there know the history of the place?" After a slight hesitation, he responded, "I don't think so."

I was back to thinking and wondering. If there had been a cover up, why had it been made? The most reasonable answer, of course, was that the realtors wouldn't want the local rumors to affect the price of that one lot. An irritating thought kept popping up in my head. Could they have not wanted to scare the new buyers? And what were the buyers likely to be worried about? Randy informed me he was going to research what really happened to the house that once stood on the empty lot.

CHAPTER 43

You may think this section is a stream of incomplete and unorganized thoughts. I do too. I suppose I just got a bit impatient while I was waiting for Randy to complete his research. He has been going over things quite meticulously and has already sent me a great deal of relevant information. I am impatient for the rest of it.

Randy called me back and let me know about my initial queries. He confirmed there was indeed a fire that destroyed the house next door. He also confirmed that only one child was killed in the fire. It wasn't a girl as we all thought. Instead, it was an eight-year-old boy. I had heard this mentioned by the ghoul who terrorized me. Candle Face had brought it up, claiming the little boy had been her brother in real life.

I thought, this can't be true because only one child died in the fire and it wasn't Candle Face.

Randy had more to tell me about the house fire. The family had managed to escape as the house burned down. They had initially run out with their little boy, but sadly, neither the parents nor neighbors noticed the boy had somehow made it back into the house. When he realized his child was missing and may have gone back in to retrieve his toys, the father ran into the house after him but couldn't find him. The father had to retreat in the face of the inferno. The next day, a firefighter found the little boy's body behind the water heater.

There was no little girl; therefore, Candle Face could not have existed. Yet I had more or less known how the boy had died. I had known because Candle Face, who claimed to have also died in the house fire and claimed to be the boy's older sister, had told me.

Randy had just confirmed it was a little boy who had died. On another level, Candle Face, who couldn't have existed, and Richard, who had, had both been attached to kind, good-hearted, knowledgeable Griffin, the boy who had died in the house fire on the empty lot next door.

Richard and I had heard Andre's garbled version about the toy cars in his possession. Andre had also died twenty-five years ago. If he had those same toys in his possession years after the inferno, how *had* they come to him? Could they be Griffin's toys? According to Randy's inquiries, Candle Face wasn't real, yet it was Candle Face who had given me information about events in the future which came horribly true. How could she not be real when the events really happened?

I reminded myself how Mark's mother had found a way to answer problems. I had tried her methods, and the answer I received from the Bible seemed to suggest that ghosts were real.

Candle Face had revealed her inadequate form to me, while Griffin had revealed himself to Richard and not always to others. I will have to bury my memory of tiny handprints on windows and on the window screens. I don't know how I will manage my reaction to tiny handprints if I ever see them.

About a week later, Randy called me back with even more shocking news: the house I grew up in wasn't there when the house next door burned down; it was moved there after the fire. Our lot had actually been part of the lot on which the house had burned down. I called my mother and she confirmed the story. She and my father had bought the house and lot separately. The house was located several miles away, and they had it moved. My mother said the house had recently been remodeled and the price was a bargain. In essence, this all meant that back before the house burnt down, our lot was the empty lot next door!

Several days passed before Randy called me back with even more shocking news. He told me my old house used to be a duplex before it was sold to my parents and moved to Ben Howell Drive. I told Randy about the teenage girl who came to my house and said she used to live in the house when it was a duplex located in east Austin.

After a long pause, Randy replied, "Ray, according to newspaper articles on microfiche, your house used to be a duplex and most of one half of the duplex burnt down about six months before it moved to Ben Howell. Ray, an eleven year old girl died in the fire."

I could not believe my ears. This girl must have been Candle Face, and Candle Face didn't die in the fire next door but died in the house I grew up in before it was moved to Ben Howell. The teenage girl who visited me that day lived in the part that didn't burn down. That would explain the two front doors and the girl's description of the house. She had asked me if I had ever seen anything weird in the house. Had she also seen Candle Face? Is that why they sold the house to my parents? My mother told me she was unaware of the house ever being part of a duplex and a fire.

Arthur M. Mills, Jr.

CHAPTER 44

My last vision of Richard and Candle Face took place years before my graduation from high school. I had been a puny eleven-year-old at the time. Once I settled down to life without Richard and Candle Face, I buried those memories in some deep place. They only came back to me years later when I was forced to acknowledge what had happened. You can say I received one small sign some seven years later. When the memory came back to me I told myself I had not forgotten. I had only suppressed the memory of that whole ordeal for several years.

I was forced to acknowledge all this in 1992 when I thought I had finished with all matters connected with my childhood. I was still in Austin, and it was the night of my high school prom. The prom was over. It was the end of an evening of dancing, fun, and wanting to remember high school. We were eighteen or so and on the threshold of adulthood. We couldn't wait for life to begin. I was going to work and study some more, then sign up with the Army. I was on top of the world.

It happened out of the blue as I was driving my prom date back home in my ancient 1979 Toyota Corolla hatchback. I was proud of my car and had earned it through a job working the night shift at Hut's Hamburgers. My date lived far out in the country. It was late and dark, but I knew my way around and was enjoying the drive. There were few street lights along the long country road. When I drove under one of the lights, I looked in the rearview mirror to see if I could observe any traffic behind me. It was just a glance, but the tiny hairs all over my body alerted me before my brain did. I was looking through the mirror at a small handprint on the hatchback window of the car. My next thought was that I was going to veer off the road, despite my pride in my driving capabilities.

Arthur M. Mills, Jr.

When I swerved, my date must have thought I had fallen asleep at the wheel because of the hours of merriment. I quickly assured her I was very much there. I kept going. I wanted to get to the next street light quickly so I could check on what I had just seen, so I put my foot down on the accelerator and sped up. When I drove under the next light, I realized there was no escape. I saw the hand print again, even more clearly than the first time.

The memory of that summer of 1984 was still taking its time to register. She's back, I recall thinking. I pulled over to the side of the road underneath the next street light, hopped out of the car and walked to the back. I had given no explanation to my date but felt compelled to check what my eyes were telling me. Night had fallen a long time ago, but light flooded us in a large circle and I saw the hand print clear as day. I tried to smear it with my hand, but it didn't appear affected in the least. Was it on the inside?

By now I was more than a little alarmed, but I had to get the handprint off that glass, had to know where it came from. I bent down and opened the hatchback, aware my date was staring at me, no doubt wondering what I was doing. I reached for that accursed handprint with my bare palm and swiped at it from the inside. The handprint smeared.

How could it have been made from the inside of my car? Who had made it? Again, I had a sense of not being able to believe what I was looking at. But my eyes couldn't lie. It had to be true. My heart began to beat just as hard as it used to when I was a kid and had landed myself in some disaster.

My date looked scared as well. She could obviously not figure out why I had to keep wiping a smudge on the car window way past midnight. She kept asking what I was doing, but my mind was still racing and I was too preoccupied to answer.

There was so much information pouring into my head that at the moment I couldn't sort it all out. And of course I wondered what if *she* was around here? It was late and I had no cover. My first instinct was to get out of there, so I got back in the car and sped away. Meanwhile my date started asking what all that had been about. Although she was persistent, I remained silent until finally I realized I must explain my shock and bizarre behavior. I pulled over to the side of that country road and told her the whole story. When I finished, she didn't ask one single question. In fact, the story must have deeply frightened her because after that night she never spoke to me again.

I will never know how that handprint got there. When I thought about it the next morning with a clear head, I didn't think it was Candle Face leaving a little sign again, as she used to. But when I went out to investigate that hand print, now smudged on the back window of my cherished car, I wasn't sure.

Maybe she was just letting me knew that she is still around—dormant—and waiting.

Arthur M. Mills, Jr.

Edwards Brothers,Inc!
Thorofare, NJ 08086
04 June, 2010
BA2010155